No Justice
in Hell

ALSO BY CHARLES G. WEST

Hell Hath No Fury

No Justice in Hell

A JOHN HAWK WESTERN

Charles G. West

PINNACLE BOOKS
Kensington Publishing Corp.

www.kensingtonbooks.com

PINNACLE BOOKS are published by

Kensington Publishing Corp.
119 West 40th Street
New York, NY 10018

All Kensington titles, imprints, and distributed lines are available at special quantity discounts for bulk purchases for sales promotions, premiums, fund-raising, educational, or institutional use. Special book excerpts or customized printings can also be created to fit specific needs. For details, write or phone the office of the Kensington sales manager: Kensington Publishing Corp., 119 West 40th Street, New York, NY 10018, attn: Sales Department; phone 1-800-221-2647.

ISBN-13: 978-0-7860-4202-9
ISBN-10: 0-7860-4202-8

First printing: May 2018

10 9 8 7 6 5 4 3 2 1

Printed in the United States of America

First electronic edition: May 2018

ISBN-13: 978-0-7860-4203-6
ISBN-10: 0-7860-4203-6

FOR RONDA

CHAPTER 1

I've done a lot of damn fool things in my life, he thought as he turned the big buckskin's head toward the mouth of the canyon. *But this one might be the dumbest.* He had been tracking the Blackfoot hunting party for the better part of the morning, hoping they would lead him to Walking Owl's village. A party of eight, the Blackfoot hunters knew he was tracking them and had known for at least three miles. He was sure of this because he had come upon a spot at the foot of a mesa where their hoofprints told him they had stopped. A single set of tracks led up the mesa, telling him that one of them climbed up to look over their back trail. From that point on, there was no effort on their part to hide their trail. It was his guess that they must have sighted him, and since he was alone, they decided to purposefully lead him into an ambush. And looking at this canyon now, it looked like the perfect place.

Five days ago, he had left Fort Ellis on a special

assignment for Major Brisbin. The major charged him with the responsibility for persuading old Walking Owl to bring his people to the reservation. He had been picked for this unusual task for an army scout because Brisbin knew of his close relation with the Blackfoot village, even though it had been three years since he had lived with them. He had returned to the village only once to hunt with his friend Bloody Hand, and that was almost a year ago. At that time, the Blackfeet were at peace with the government and the government was content to let them live as they had always lived, free to move about the northern Montana Territory. The army had enough trouble on their hands trying to protect the settlers along the Yellowstone River from raids by the Sioux and Cheyenne without adding responsibility for the various Blackfoot bands. Since the battle at Wounded Knee, the threat had been greatly reduced, although there were still renegade bands of Sioux and Cheyenne refusing to go to the reservation. So now, more of the government's attention was turning toward the other tribes, the Blackfeet among them. Aware of this change in attitude, the Blackfoot bands had pushed farther into the Rocky Mountains with an eye toward avoiding army patrols.

The sharp cry of a hawk brought his mind back to the business at hand and the narrow canyon before him. Steep slopes on either side, thick with fir trees, gave it a dark sense of warning. And although he paused to consider the wisdom of following the trail, he knew that his chances of picking it up on the far side of the two mountains were not very good if he circled around them. *What the hell . . .* he decided and gave Rascal a gentle nudge with his heels.

Passing the mouth of the canyon, he found himself following an old game trail that led between the two mountains. Ahead of him, some twenty-five yards, the trail took a sharp turn around an outcropping of rock. *That would be my guess*, he thought, *right past that rock*. For, if the Indians were thinking like he figured, they would take the first opportune place they came to. By now, they were certain to be curious enough to learn why they were being followed by a single white man. He reached down and drew the Winchester 73 from his saddle sling and proceeded toward the turn in the trail. Just before reaching the rocks, he took his rifle in both hands and held it straight up over his head. It was a gesture that held no meaning that he knew of. He hoped only that the Blackfoot warriors he suspected were already watching his every move would take it as a sign of peace. At least it should tell them that he knew they were waiting in ambush and maybe they might be curious enough to hear him out. *And maybe I ain't as smart as I think I am, and they're way up ahead, still following this game trail.* The thought had no sooner occurred when he heard the sound of horses' hooves coming down from the trees behind him. Rascal whinnied a greeting to the horses. He could only assume his peaceful-like approach had at least bought him some time and maybe a chance to talk.

Without looking behind him, and still with his rifle held over his head, he continued on to the rocky outcropping, aware of the horses pacing steadily at his back. As he expected, the rest of the hunting party was waiting for him when he rode around the rocks. Astride a spotted gray pony, a lean warrior with hair black as night, tied in two long braids, sat facing him in the middle of the trail. Like his fellow hunters on either side of the narrow trail, he held a rifle leveled at the white intruder. Saying nothing, he waited for the white scout to speak.

"I come in peace to talk to Chief Walking Owl. I am a friend of the Blackfoot."

The Blackfoot warrior, obviously the leader of the hunting party, said nothing for a few moments while he studied the white man wearing a deerskin shirt and a hat with one feather stuck in the hatband. "You are the one called Hawk," he finally declared. "You ride with the soldiers."

"That's true," Hawk replied. "But there are no soldiers with me now. I came alone to talk with my friend Walkin' Owl. I came alone so that the Blackfeet would know I didn't come to fight. The Blackfoot are my friends."

"I think you are a fool," the warrior said. "The white man is no longer a friend of the Blackfoot. You want us to ride to your reservation and give up our way of life, the life of our fathers and their fathers before them, to sit around and wait for the white man to feed us. Why should we listen to what you have to say? These mountains, these streams, the grass, and the buffalo, they were all here long before the first white man set foot on this land. Now the white man comes and says, 'This all belongs to me.' The land belongs to no man, and Na'pi brought the Blackfoot here to live in peace. You were a fool to come here. Look around you. You can see that Walking Owl is not here."

Hawk didn't have to look around him to know there were two warriors behind him with weapons aimed at his back, just as there were three rifles and three bows leveled at him in front. He lowered his rifle very slowly until it was aimed directly at the warrior facing him. "I think you can tell me where to find Walking Owl's village and then I will leave you."

"I think we can just shoot you and there will be one less white man in our territory," the warrior said, drawing grunts of approval from the other hunters.

"That's true," Hawk replied. "But there would also be one less Blackfoot in the territory."

The warrior's stern countenance was betrayed by the beginnings of a sly smile, aware as he was of the Winchester aimed straight at his gut. Even the slightest reflex of his finger would send a bullet to kill him. He had heard of this man, Hawk, from friends who followed old Walking Owl, so he did not doubt his word. "You are a scout for the soldiers. Why should I tell you where Walking Owl is camped? You will lead the soldiers against his people."

"If you have heard of me, then you know there is iron in my words and that I have never fought against my friends the Blackfoot. I give you my word that I will not lead the soldiers against Walking Owl's camp. I only come to talk with him and visit some friends that I have not seen for a long time. My fight is with the Sioux and the Cheyenne, the same as you." He paused and waited while the Indian thought it over. "What are you called?" Hawk asked after a long moment.

"I am Black Bear," he answered, then turned to talk with the warrior closest to him. "What he says is true. He is a friend of Bloody Hand." After a few words with the other Indian that were too quiet for Hawk to hear, Black Bear turned back to him and said, "We think you do not lie. You may go in peace. I do not know if Walking Owl is still there, but when we last saw him, he was camped on Sun River, north of the big river."

"I thank you for your help in finding my old friends," Hawk said, and turned away, his rifle back in the saddle sling now. "Good huntin'," he called back as he headed toward the mouth of the canyon, aware of a slight twitching between his shoulder blades. It took only one of the eight hunters to disagree with Black Bear's decision.

Clear of the canyon, he turned the buckskin gelding toward the northeast, intent upon striking the Sun River, a smaller river that emptied into the Missouri, the big river Black Bear referred to, near a place called Great Falls. Had he not lived in Walking Owl's village, he might have been at a loss as to where on Sun River the old chief might be. But since he knew of several campsites that had been used before, he concentrated his search on that section of the river. It would be two days, however, before he came upon the tipis of Walking Owl's camp, settled on a wide, grassy expanse where the river doubled back to form the shape of a horseshoe.

River Song, Walking Owl's wife, stood upright to ease the stiffness in her back after filling her water skin at the edge of the river. A lone rider approaching along the western bank of the river caught her eye, and she squinted in an effort to identify him. He was not close enough yet for her aging eyes to tell for sure, but there was something familiar about the way he sat his horse. A few minutes more and her face broke out in a delighted smile. "Hawk," she murmured to herself. It had been almost a year since she had seen that imposing figure on the big buckskin horse. She turned at once to alert the others in the village. Within a few minutes' time, a small gathering of people came down to the water's edge to greet one who had once lived with them. Following right behind them, old Walking Owl hurried to see his young friend, a wide smile parting his wrinkled face.

Hawk waved to the reception waiting for him when still fifty yards away, pleased to see he was still welcomed as a friend. As he approached them, he scanned the faces, hoping to see Bloody Hand, but his friend was not among them. He crossed the river and dismounted to greet the gathering of smiling faces, obviously delighted to see him. "Hawk," Walking Owl exclaimed as he made his way through the pocket of mostly women and older men. "It has been a long time."

"Yes, it has," Hawk said. "I have been scoutin' for

the army—against the Lakotas," he hastened to add. He looked around him. "I was hopin' to see Bloody Hand. Where is he?"

"Bloody Hand has gone to the north with the rest of the young men," Walking Owl answered. "They have heard that the white father in Washington wants to send all of the Blackfoot people to live on the reservation and they are not willing to go." The smile faded from his face for a moment and he said, "When I saw you, I thought you had come to tell us we must go. Is that why you have come?"

Seeing the concern in the old man's face, Hawk could not help a feeling of guilt for the mission he had been given by Major Brisbin. He had been sent specifically to persuade Walking Owl to bring his people onto the reservation. He could not, in good conscience, however, tell the old chief that his people would be well taken care of by the government. The few times he had been to a reservation, he had seen no sign of prosperity for the Indian. He had accepted the assignment because he wanted Walking Owl to receive an accurate picture of reservation life. Answering Walking Owl's question, he confessed, "I was sent here to persuade you that life would be much better for your people if you will lead them to the reservation. But I feel in my heart that your young men were right in leaving this territory and I wish the rest of your village had gone with them."

"We talked about it," Walking Owl said. "But we decided that the older people would slow the young ones down, so we did not go with them. We decided we would not go to the reservation, either. There are still some of us who can hunt, so we will do the best we can."

"The farther north you go, the better off you'll be," Hawk advised. "The army has all it can do to fight the Sioux and, right now, they don't have enough troops to mount a large-scale campaign against the Blackfoot. I think you're doin' the right thing."

"My heart is glad to hear you say that," Walking Owl said. "Come now and we will smoke a pipe while the women cook something for us to eat."

"I brought some things with me, gifts from the army," Hawk replied, and nodded toward his pack-horse. "They sent you some flour, some coffee, sugar, and some salt pork. I was also lucky enough to run up on half a dozen deer waterin' at the river this mornin'. I managed to get a shot at one, so the women can cook that if you want." His proposal was met with eager smiles from those close enough to have heard. It told him what he had already suspected—the village was short of food. They were sorely missing the young men who had done most of the hunting, and it appeared that the older hunters had not had much luck. He thought about what he had told Major Brisbin before he left, that he would most likely spend some days in the village. When he said it, he was thinking that he would spend the extra days with his friend Bloody Hand, maybe riding up into the mountains to hunt again. Finding the village without the young men, however, he decided he should take the time to hunt on his own to help a little.

The deer Hawk had killed provided enough meat for the whole camp to enjoy one big feast, since their size had been so severely reduced. While they ate, Hawk proposed a hunting party to the mountains to the west, recalling a valley where he and Bloody Hand had almost always found game. Two Toes, one of the ablest of the men still in camp, volunteered to go with him, so they planned to leave the next morning.

When morning came, Hawk left River Song's tipi at sunup to find Two Toes already waiting, his pony ready and two extra packhorses standing by. *He may be old,* Hawk thought, *but he ain't lazy.* He felt a little guilty that Two Toes had to wait for him. He responded to Two Toes's smile of greeting with a guilty grin and declared, "Looks like you're rarin' to go!" He whistled for Rascal, and the buckskin came immediately to be saddled. By the time he was ready to go, they were sent off with the well wishes of the women already tending their breakfast fires.

A good part of the first day was spent making the thirty-five-mile ride to reach the mountains. Once they gained the foothills, it was another five or six miles to the valley Hawk remembered. He found Two Toes an easy companion to ride with, very seldom speaking, and then only when absolutely necessary. The thing that was disconcerting about the Indian, and caused Hawk to wonder, was the almost constant smile on his face. But he was always a step ahead on any chore, eager to do his part before Hawk might have to tell him to. He was armed with a Spencer cavalry carbine, but his supply of cartridges was limited. Consequently, he was reluctant to shoot if he didn't have a sure target. Hawk thought that was a sensible policy, even if cartridges were plentiful.

Hawk had deer in mind when they had started out, but there was no sign of deer on their way to the mountains, and none when they reached the narrow valley he had counted on. The valley had not lost its promise of luck for the hunter, though. For after making camp, they awoke the following morning to discover a small herd of approximately two hundred buffalo passing through the valley on their way to the grassy plains beyond. It was one hell of a stroke of luck, as far as Hawk was concerned, but a sign from Na'pi in Two Toes's eyes. He was convinced from that point on that the man with the feather in his hatband had big medicine.

Having had no thoughts that they would be killing buffalo, the two hunters had not brought any hides to disguise themselves while approaching the slowly moving herd. But disguises proved to be unnecessary. After tying the horses in the trees at the foot of the mountain, they advanced on hands and knees upon the moving mass of meat. When within range, Hawk brought the first cow down with one shot behind the animal's left front leg. They crawled closer to the herd then and used the carcass of the cow as a shooting platform. From that position, they methodically brought one beast after another down until satisfied they had as many as their horses could carry. There was no need to hurry their shots because they knew the buffalo were accustomed to hearing thunder, so the sound of the rifles did not cause them to stampede. The animals were also accustomed to seeing other buffalo collapse from sickness or accident, so again there was no inclination to panic when one dropped.

After the buffalo passed on through, Hawk and Two Toes prepared to go to work butchering the meat. It was at this point that the usually smiling and silent Blackfoot made a statement that Hawk agreed with. "Make mistake not bringing women."

"Reckon so," Hawk concurred. There was a great deal of butchering to be done, as well as smoking the meat. The weather was too warm to pack the fresh meat all the way back to the village, where the women could help, so the two of them were going to have to do the curing themselves. They set in to the task with a vengeance. It was not long before they were joined by a pack of wolves that had been following the buffalo. So they fought them off with a few more shots until conceding one of the buffalo to the pack. The rest of the task consisted of butchering the six other carcasses to get the cuts they needed before the wolves challenged for them. By working steadily, they arrived at a compromise with the scavengers, leaving them the remains of the carcasses they had butchered. This consisted of mostly intestines and organs, which Hawk had no use for. Short of starvation, he never ate the insides of anything. However, Two Toes helped himself to the raw livers and hearts.

When the work was all done, the two weary hunters cleaned their knives and hand axes, then retired to their blankets to catch a little sleep in what was left of the night. The sun found them early the next morning, heading back to the village, two riders with three packhorses following behind, two with meat piled high and one with buffalo hides. Hawk couldn't help noticing that Two Toes appeared to be riding tall and proud, certainly more so than on the days before. He suspected that the old warrior might be feeling confident again in his ability to provide as he had done when he was a younger man.

It was late in the afternoon when the hunters crossed a small stream about a mile short of the Blackfoot village. Hawk reined his horse to a halt and dismounted. When Two Toes pulled up beside him, Hawk said, "I ain't sure, but Rascal might be favorin' his left front hoof. I'm gonna take a look. You go on ahead and I'll be right behind you." Two Toes nodded, his perpetual smile still in place, and proceeded on. Hawk lifted Rascal's hoof and pretended to inspect it. He let Two Toes get about fifty yards ahead before he dropped Rascal's hoof and stepped up into the saddle again.

He heard the cries of welcome ahead of him before he cleared the trees by the river and knew that the people had spotted Two Toes. When he reached the bank of the river, he could see Two Toes riding straight and tall, like a triumphant war chief returning to his village. Another cry of welcome arose when the people saw Hawk emerge from the trees. It was a good day for Walking Owl's village, and Hawk hoped that it might help the people in their resolve to move farther north to escape the reservation. That thought caused him to pause a moment to examine his conscience. As he usually did, he looked at the problem in the simplest way possible to determine what was best for the most people. He had agreed to find Walking Owl and get him to bring his people into the reservation. He felt that he could truthfully tell Major Brisbin that he had done that. Although the major wanted him to persuade Walking Owl that to do so was in the best interest of his people, Hawk had not promised he would do that. His job was done to the extent he had agreed. The rest was up to Walking Owl. Feeling satisfied with his sense of conscience, he put it from his mind and joined in the celebration of the hunt.

He stayed for another day before saying farewell to his Blackfoot friends. He had already been gone longer than he expected when he left Fort Ellis. The major would no doubt wonder if he had run into trouble, or he might have stayed even longer, so he climbed aboard his horse and rode out one morning. Behind him, a determined Walking Owl prepared his people to move, aided by a newly confident Two Toes as his hunter. Leaving the Sun River, Hawk planned to drop down to cross the Missouri and ride east of the Big Belt Mountains to Bozeman.

CHAPTER 2

As near as he could estimate, it was about twenty miles to the Missouri River, so that's where he planned to rest his horses. It was around noon when he approached the trees along the bluffs of the river and began looking for a good place to swim the horses across. Once across, he dismounted and let the horses drink and graze along the bank while he built a small fire and filled his coffeepot. He couldn't help noticing a great deal of deer sign around the place he had picked to cross the river. Being a natural-born hunter, he was tempted to wait there till evening, when he might get a shot at a nice doe coming down to drink water. *Best get on back to Fort Ellis*, he silently reminded himself. A couple of cups of coffee and a biscuit that River Song had given him, followed by a short period of shut-eye, and he deemed the horses rested enough. Back in the saddle, he headed south, planning to stop for the night somewhere around Hound

Creek. Barring any unforeseen trouble, he figured
to make Fort Ellis in two days from there.

He hadn't ridden two miles before he saw the
smoke drifting lazily over the fir trees lining a
creek, just as he crossed over a low hill. He pulled
up to give it a longer look and decided it was
someone who had pulled off the Mullan Road, the
east-to-west road the army had built from Fort
Benton to Walla Walla in Washington Territory. It
was either that or another Sioux raiding party
intent upon attacking freight wagons on the road.
That made sense to him because, if that was a party
of Sioux, they would likely camp a good distance
from the road. And he guessed they were half a
mile from it in that spot. It was mighty damn early
to be making camp, though. It made him wonder
enough to have a look for himself, so he turned
Rascal's head in that direction and rode down the
slope toward the creek.

The trees along the bank were too thick to
permit him a really close look, so he tied his horses
and went forward on foot. Close enough to see
then, he knelt beside a tree to watch. Mildly surprised, he discovered a wagon pulled up under the
trees. *They sure picked a long way from the road to make
camp,* he thought. The party appeared to be a man
and two women. All three were gathered around
the fire and they appeared to be roasting some
meat. *What in the hell are they doing in this country all
alone?* Surely the soldiers at Fort Benton told them
about the danger of Sioux war parties. If not, then
the folks at the little settlement of Great Falls
would have warned them, if that was the direction

they had traveled from. He scanned the area, thinking to discover at least one other man. He looked back at the wagon again and could see only one horse standing by the creek. It was a far too curious situation for him to ignore, so he went back to get his horses.

"Mama," Blossom Dubose pronounced softly.

When Bertie Brown looked up to see the sudden look of alarm in her daughter's eyes, she turned at once to see what had caused it. She glanced quickly at JoJo, who was also staring at the rider approaching from the edge of the trees. There was no time to run for cover, so she warned them. "Just set right there," she said. "Don't make no move to run." She reached down to touch the Henry rifle near her feet to make sure it was readily available in the event it became necessary.

"Is it him?" JoJo whispered anxiously.

"No," Blossom replied, after a moment to make sure. "That's not Zach."

"Hello, the camp," Hawk called out when within about thirty yards of the fire. "Mind if I ride in?"

"You're welcome to come on in, if you're of a peaceful mind," Bertie answered. "You're welcome to share some of this meat with us if you are. If you ain't, then I'll be happy to introduce you to this Henry rifle." She got to her feet, bringing the rifle up with her, so he could see that she wasn't bluffing.

"Thank you kindly," Hawk said, realizing then that the person he had mistaken for a man was, in fact, a woman. It was an easy mistake considering the bulk of the woman, with her hair drawn back and tied in a ponytail down her back. Adding to it were the men's clothes she wore, including boots. *So,* he thought, *it's three women alone, at least so far.* "Won't be any need to meet Mr. Henry," he said. "I'll stop for a spell, or I'll just ride on, whatever you say."

"Come on in, stranger. Least we can do is offer you a cup of coffee and something to eat. We've got plenty."

He could almost feel their eyes upon him as all three women stared at him, and he was pretty sure they needed help. So he rode on in and climbed down. Glancing from one of the still-wary women to the next, he saw a generous amount of anxiety in each face. "My name's Hawk," he volunteered. "How'd you ladies get yourselves in this fix?"

"What fix?" Bertie responded. "Who said we was in a fix?"

"I don't know which way you're headin'," he replied, "but my guess is you were travelin' on the Mullan Road about a half mile yonder way. You're all by yourselves, no men with you. Your wagon is double rigged, but I don't see but one horse." He paused, but she didn't respond at once, so he continued. "Where's your other horse?"

Bertie continued to pause, then, as if making a decision, she smiled and replied, "That's him on the fire there."

"Run him to death?" Hawk asked as he fixed his gaze on who he figured was the youngest of the three, and she immediately dropped a piece of meat she had been chewing, and it fell to the ground. She looked at the young woman beside her, as if they had been caught eating forbidden flesh.

Bertie answered him. "I reckon that's what happened to him. He was a good bit older than the other horse, and I reckon he just gave out. We was just in too big a hurry, I reckon." She grinned at him again. "Anyway, he does better as supper than he did pullin' that wagon. You want some?"

"I reckon not," Hawk said. "I just had a little something to eat before I came across you ladies. Besides, I ain't especially fond of horse meat unless that's all there is."

"Well, Mr. Hawk," Bertie replied, "that's all there is on the menu."

Hawk considered that for a few moments before continuing. "I figured that." He paused again, reluctant to go forward with what his conscience was telling him. "And I expect you need help. But if I'm gonna help you, I need to know what's goin' on. Who are you runnin' from, the law?"

"Hell, no," Bertie replied. "We ain't broke no laws, though, unless you call tryin' to save your life breakin' the law."

In all of Montana Territory, I had to pick this trail to follow, he thought, already anticipating trouble ahead. *Better me than a Sioux war party*, he told himself. "Where are you tryin' to get to?" he asked.

"Helena," Bertie answered.

"So you're headin' west," he said, and paused to think about that. "Where the hell did you start out from?" There wasn't a town of any size that he'd

ever heard of east of where they stood unless you
went a hell of a long way.

"Great Falls," Bertie said. Then thinking it a
good idea to introduce themselves, since he had
the look of a chivalrous man, in spite of the buckskin shirt and the feather in his hat. "JoJo, pour the
man a cup of coffee." She turned back to Hawk.
"That young girl is JoJo. My name's Bertie Brown
and the pretty one there is my daughter, Blossom."

He nodded to each one in turn, noticing that
there was no sign of offense taken from the
younger girl when the other one was referred to as
"the pretty one." To the contrary, she offered a
broad smile that almost eclipsed a doglike face. He
couldn't help thinking that JoJo was an appropriate name for the girl. On the other hand, Blossom
was a fairly handsome woman, her only obvious
flaw a scar across the side of her face. Hawk estimated her to be about twenty years old. He turned
to Bertie again and made an attempt to show some
manners. "Pleased to meet you, Birdie," he said,
mispronouncing her name.

"It's Bertie," she quickly corrected him, empha-
sizing the *t*, long accustomed to doing so. "I mighta
got by with Birdie when I was a little younger, but
it'd be more like Buzzard now, I reckon." She
laughed with him. "What's your line of work,
Mr. Hawk? You don't look like a cowhand, or a
lawman."

"One thing and another," he replied as he accepted the cup of coffee JoJo handed him. "Mostly
I ride scout for the army out of Fort Ellis." More interested in why three women were on their way to

Helena with no escort, he quickly shifted the conversation back to them. Putting two and two together, he asked, "Who's chasin' you?"

Bertie grinned. "Why, nobody, I hope. But you can't never tell in this country, can you? We're just in a hurry to get to Helena."

"You know somebody in Helena?" he asked.

"Matter of fact, I do. Sam Ingram, owns the Last Chance Saloon. He's wantin' me to help him build up a better hostess business. He's got one hostess that's been with him since he opened the place. You ever been in the Last Chance?" When he said that he had, she continued. "Gladys Welch, she worked for me in Cheyenne, but that was a long time ago. Blossom wasn't much more'n a young'un then. I expect Gladys is lookin' to go out to pasture about now."

That confirmed suspicions he had already entertained, that the three of them were prostitutes, although he doubted that Bertie was still a working girl. Looking at Blossom, he could see the vast improvement she would make over Gladys. He was a bit surprised, though, when he considered she was Bertie's daughter, thinking she might have hoped to prevent her daughter from following in her footsteps. All that aside, now that he knew the situation he had stumbled upon, what was he going to do about it? *Climb on my horse and ride,* was his immediate thought, already knowing that he wouldn't. First off, he felt pretty certain that somebody was chasing the three women. He didn't buy Bertie's story that they were just in a hurry to get to Helena. "All right," he said. "I'm gonna help you get back on your way to Helena. We'll hitch my packhorse up with your horse to pull that wagon. He ain't gonna like it, but he's been hitched to a wagon before. Now, suppose you tell me who the hell you hope ain't chasin' you."

"I reckon you've got a right to know, since you're gonna help us out," Bertie said. "Feller name of Zach Dubose, Blossom's husband. That's who's chasin' us."

"Blossom's husband? I thought you said Blossom was a . . ."

"She was," Bertie went on, "and she will be again." Seeing his confusion, she decided to tell him the whole story. "Blossom was doin' just fine in Great Falls until Zach Dubose came to town with that sorry bunch he runs with. From the first time he set eyes on my Blossom, he was sure he had to have her. Well, he sweet-talked her into marryin' him, tellin' her how easy her life was gonna be since he was such a successful businessman. Course, she had to give up whorin', he couldn't be sharin' his wife with half the drunks in Great Falls, even as small as it was. I couldn't blame him for that, could you?" Hawk shook his head. Bertie went on. "Well, Blossom came to find out two things about her husband. One, the business he was so successful in was holdin' up stagecoaches in Dakota Territory and stealin' cattle in Wyomin'. It was that other thing that Blossom couldn't live with, though. Zach is a low-down mean drunk, and when he ain't ridin' with those gunmen friends he hangs out with, he's lookin' for a reason to beat her up. He was accusin' her of entertainin' gentlemen while he was out of town on one of his jobs."

"That scar on the side of her face?" Hawk asked.

"That's right," Bertie answered. "He done that with a whiskey bottle."

When her mother said it, Blossom looked away, as if ashamed. "Mama, he don't wanna know all that."

Bertie ignored her and continued. "He damn near killed her, so I figured it was time for her to leave the son of a bitch. He always claimed he'd kill her if she ever tried to run away from him, so I decided we'd best leave Great Falls. It wasn't much more'n a wide spot in the trail, anyway. I got talked into goin' there in the first place because folks were sayin' it was gonna be a real town. Anyway, JoJo said she'd go with us to help out, so we bought that wagon and them two horses when Zach took off to do some business up near Fort Benton. So now you've got the whole story." She stepped back then to judge his reaction.

"What about the wagon?" Hawk asked. "What kinda shape is it in?"

"Ain't nothin' wrong with it, as far as I know," Bertie said. "It got us this far without no trouble."

He walked over to take a look at the wagon, checking the axles and wheels. They had hauled it over some pretty rough terrain when they drove it back this far from the road. But she was right—he could see no real damage. He took a moment to look up at the sky then. "All right," he announced. "We've already used up a good piece of this day, and by the time we get the horses hitched up and my packs off my horse, we'll use up another big chunk of it. So we might as well just stay right here and start out in the mornin'. Is that all right with you ladies?"

"I reckon so," Bertie replied with a good bit of enthusiasm. She felt sure now that he wasn't going to back off his offer. "We're fixed pretty good for supplies. Oughta be plenty to take us all to Helena. We've got some salt pork, but there's a lot of that horse left."

"Like I said," Hawk replied, "I ain't particularly fond of horse meat if there's something else available. And I saw a lot of deer sign back by the river. It ain't but a couple of miles from here, so I think I'll go back this evenin' and see if I can get a shot at one." There was no need to ask the women. He could read the approval in the faces of all three.

"That bein' the case," Bertie said, "I reckon I've got time to see about makin' some biscuits. I've already got a pot of beans soakin' in the wagon, so how's that sound to go with some venison?"

"That sure suits my taste," he allowed. So he busied himself with the transfer of his ammunition and supplies from his packhorse to the wagon, filling what little space was left. It looked to him like they had brought half of Great Falls with them. When he was satisfied they had enough wood for the fire, he stepped up into the saddle, preparing to go hunting.

He wheeled Rascal around to discover JoJo standing before him. "You are comin' back, ain'tcha?" It was a plaintive and sincere question, that much was obvious, and the first hint of the fear they had of Zach Dubose. Perhaps the fact that he was taking his packhorse with him caused her to wonder.

"Yes, miss," he assured her, then reminded her, "Hell, you've got all my possibles and half of my ammunition in your wagon."

She favored him with a grin. "That's right, we do, don't we?"

"Sure do," he replied, gave Rascal his heels, and headed back toward the river, leading his pack-horse behind him.

He found that he had read the sign right when he had stopped there before, for after tying his horses in the trees, he waited for only thirty or forty minutes before they showed up. Descending the bluffs on a commonly used trail, a large buck led four younger bucks down to the river. Hawk counted ten points on the old buck's antlers. "I'll be doin' you a favor if I take one of your bucks off your hands," he murmured as he sighted his Winchester on the rearmost deer. "And you won't have to fight him when mating season comes around this winter." His intent was to drop the deer before he got to the water, so he wouldn't have to drag him out of the river. One steady pull on the trigger accomplished that and sent the other bucks bolting back into the bluffs. Hawk put the dying animal out of its misery with his knife, then loaded the carcass on his packhorse.

Back at the wagon, the women heard the shot some two miles away. They all paused to see if there were more shots fired, unsure if the sound had come from their new friend or from another source. "I reckon that was Hawk," Bertie decided. "Leastways, it came from that direction."

"It wasn't but one shot," JoJo said. "I bet he got him a deer." She grinned as she formed the picture of him in her mind. "He looks like he could hit anything with that rifle."

"I reckon we'll just have to wait and see," Bertie told her.

"I hope he got one," Blossom said. "I know I don't want any more of that damn tough old horse." They all laughed at that, the feeling unanimous.

"He got one. I guarantee it," JoJo insisted.

"You'd be awful disappointed if he shows up without one, wouldn't you?" Bertie asked. She gazed at the homely young girl with her boyish figure. Barely past her fourteenth birthday when her no-account husband ran off and left her stranded in Great Falls, the only luck she had was that he had not gotten her pregnant. "Don't go gettin' yourself used to havin' him around," Bertie said. "As soon as we get to Helena, that'll be the last you'll see of him."

"Wonder why he wears that feather in his hat?" JoJo questioned. "You reckon he's part Injun?" No one answered her, so she posed another question. "You think you oughta charge him if he wants a ride?" This she directed at Blossom, assuming she would be his choice. "I mean, since he's kinda comin' to our rescue, so to speak," she added.

"Hell, JoJo, I don't know. You ask too many questions." This came from Blossom.

They both looked at Bertie in astonishment when she threw her head back and laughed. "I reckon we'll find out soon enough what kinda deal he's got in mind. So far, he ain't asked for nothin'." The fact that he hadn't was enough to make her suspicious, but she still had a feeling that he would cause them no harm.

Their speculation was wasted effort because Hawk returned to the wagon with a four-point buck loaded on his packhorse and his thoughts focused on skinning and butchering it. Bertie worked on her biscuits while Blossom and JoJo roasted fresh venison over the fire and kept an eye on the pot of beans sitting in the coals. When Bertie told Hawk he had cut more than enough for them to eat that night, he concentrated on cutting strips to cure by smoke. In weather this warm, the meat wouldn't keep long before it turned, and he wanted enough to last them till they reached Helena. If he was lucky enough to find fresh game to kill, that would be a bonus. From where they were camped, he could only guess at the distance, but he figured it to be around sixty miles. That would not be two full days on horseback, but he had to figure at least three days for the wagon.

It was late in the evening by the time Hawk had prepared enough of the deer to satisfy their needs. The ladies had spread their bedding under the wagon and were prepared to turn in for the night when Bertie came to the edge of the stream, where Hawk was cleaning his hands and arms of the remaining deer blood. "You all set for the night?"

Bertie asked. "Anything you need before we turn in?"

"Reckon not," he replied, getting to his feet.

"What time in the mornin' are you thinkin' about gettin' up?"

"Sunup, I reckon," he answered. "Then, if you ladies can get started, we'll start out right away and stop for breakfast when we rest the horses. Is that all right with you?"

"Whatever you say," Bertie answered, then paused for a long moment. "Nothin' else you need?"

"Nope. See you in the mornin'."

"Did he say he needed somebody to keep him warm?" JoJo asked anxiously as soon as Bertie crawled back under the wagon.

Bertie chuckled. "No, he didn't need nothin', and he said to tell that young'un to get to sleep. He didn't wanna have to drag you out from under this wagon, come sunup." It was too dark to see the smug smile of contentment on the young girl's homely face.

The big buckskin horse was saddled, the fire rekindled, and the coffeepot on the fire by the time Bertie stirred from sleep. Surprised that she had slept so long, she could attribute it only to a feeling of security since Hawk had joined them. She roused Blossom and JoJo, who evidently had enjoyed a good night's sleep for the same reason she had. "Roll up your bedrolls," she told them. "I don't wanna keep him waitin' for us women."

"I swear, I think I smell coffee," JoJo said. "He said last night we weren't gonna get no breakfast till the horses got tired."

"I gotta pee before I do anything," Blossom informed them.

"Me, too," JoJo said, and followed Blossom toward a clump of bushes upstream. Bertie dropped her bedroll in the back of the wagon and went to meet Hawk as he was leading her horse to the wagon.

"You change your mind about breakfast?" Bertie asked.

"Nope, but I thought you might like to have a cup of coffee before we start out." He glanced at the two younger women heading upstream to do whatever business was necessary and told himself he was glad he filled the coffeepot before that. "Gee or haw?" he asked then, looking at the wagon tongue.

Confused by his question at first, she then understood. "The left side," she answered. "He was on the left."

"Might as well hitch him up on the side he's used to," Hawk said. "My horse ain't gonna like either side." His packhorse was reluctant to be hitched up, but he didn't balk as much as Hawk expected. "You drive?" She said that she was driving the wagon, so he advised her that the horse might show a bit of orneriness at first. She assured him she could handle him.

When everybody had gotten a cup of coffee, Hawk poured what was left on the fire. "I reckon that means we're ready to go," Blossom remarked.

Ignoring the hint of sarcasm in her voice, he replied, "Reckon so, as soon as you finish that cup." He went to the stream to rinse out the coffeepot. A short time later, they were on their way back to the Mullan Road, where they turned west, headed toward Helena. Hawk rode along beside the wagon, but every once in a while, he would ride up ahead just to see what might be awaiting them. Whenever he rode far enough ahead to put him out of their sight for a short while, Blossom would begin to fret. "It ain't what's ahead that I'm worried about," she complained. "I wish he'd be more concerned about who might be catchin' up behind us."

"He's just makin' sure we don't run up on an Injun war party," Bertie said. "He ain't ever outta sight that long, anyway. We're most likely worryin' too much about Zach. You said he told you he was goin' to Fort Benton and wouldn't likely be back before Sunday. Hell, that's two days from now. By the time he gets back to Great Falls, we'll be set up in Helena, and Helena ain't like Great Falls. They're a regular town, got a sheriff and everything."

"Besides," JoJo chimed in, "Zach won't have no idea where you went."

"Maybe so," Blossom allowed. "But Helena's probably the first place he'd look." Further discussion on the subject was interrupted by the reappearance of their broad-shouldered scout at a sharp curve about a quarter of a mile ahead.

Hawk sat there waiting for them to catch up to

him. Rascal sidestepped gracefully as Bertie pulled the wagon up beside him. "I'm thinkin' those horses oughta be about ready to take a rest," he said. "There's a fair-sized creek on the other side of that next hill—be a good place to stop and have a little breakfast. Course, you ladies might not be hungry yet." He had a slight grin on his face as he waited for their response. He was not disappointed.

"I thought you were never gonna stop," Blossom complained. "I thought I was gonna faint I'm so hungry. I've already sneaked a handful outta that barrel of dried apples."

"Why, Blossom Dubose!" Bertie yelped. "You stay outta those apples. I'm savin' those to bake a big ol' pie to celebrate you gettin' away from that son of a bitch you married—against your mother's advice, I might add."

"Oh, I didn't take that many," Blossom said. "I gotta watch my figure, now that I'm gonna be a workin' girl again." She reached over and gave JoJo a playful bump on the shoulder. "JoJo's the one who oughta be eatin' the apple pie. We need to fatten her up some if she's gonna be in our business. The customers wanna see a little more padding on your bones, the more, the better."

"I already eat like a hog," JoJo said, "and I can't ever put on any weight. I think there's something wrong with me."

Hawk didn't say anything for a long time, listening with amusement to the senseless bantering between the women. He couldn't help noticing the lighter mood displayed at present, a vast difference from the tense beginning of their partnership. "Let's go get some breakfast goin'," he said, and started off toward the hill. "There ain't nothin' wrong with you," he said to JoJo, leaving the young girl with a wide smile on her face.

The first clue he saw that something was wrong was the door of the shack standing ajar. "What the hell?" Zach Dubose demanded when he reined his horse up before the shabby dwelling of rough boards on Hound Creek. "Blossom!" he called out, but there was no answer from inside the shack. He had returned two days earlier than he had told her he would and his immediate thought was that she had slipped out to Trotter's, where she worked when he had first met her. *Well, that's gonna get you a good whipping,* he told himself. *You'd better be asleep in there.* He dismounted and stormed through the door, causing it to bang loudly against the wall. A quick look around told him that she was gone and so were the few little personal things she brought with her to their marriage, as well as all her clothes. The corner of the shack that served as the kitchen was stripped of her pots and pans. Standing in the center of the small dwelling, he looked all around him, his anger building into a burning rage. "Bitch!" he thundered. "I told you what I'd do to you, if you ever tried to leave me!"

He stormed out of the shack, just then noticing the tracks left by a wagon. "The bitch ran off with somebody," he growled. "He's a dead man when I find him." He stood staring at the tracks for a long moment as if hoping they would reveal the man's identity, his rage steadily increasing. Finally, he broke from his trance and tried to think where to look before he realized the tracks led back toward the settlement. At least that much was obvious, even in the fading light of dusk, so he climbed back on his already exhausted horse and started for Trotter's. The trading post and saloon was where his partners were heading when he left them. Somebody there should know something about Blossom's whereabouts, her mother in particular, or that little dog-faced girl that hung around the saloon.

He found his partners' horses tied at the rail at Trotter's front door and when he walked inside, he saw them sitting at one of the saloon's three tables, sharing a bottle. "Damn," Red Whitley exclaimed. "Lookee here, Hog. I thought he'd be home doin' some plowin'."

"The little woman might notta been in season." Horace "Hog" Thacker laughed. "What are you doin' here, Zach?"

"I'm fixin' to kill a cheatin' bitch," Zach fumed as he looked around the near-empty saloon. "Where's Bertie?"

Aware then of the serious wrath brewing in Zach's brain, both men realized this was not a joking matter. "Hell, I don't know," Red answered. "She ain't been in since we got here. Ain't been nobody but Juanita over there." He nodded toward a tired-looking woman sitting in a chair near the end of the bar.

"And we ain't got drunk enough to where she looks good," Hog commented.

Having no patience for humor at the moment, Zach turned and walked over to the bar to confront Luther Trotter. "You seen Blossom here tonight?" Zach demanded.

"No, I ain't," Trotter replied. "I ain't seen Blossom since she took up with you."

"Where's Bertie?"

"Bertie ain't here no more," Trotter said. "Said she was movin' on. JoJo went with her. I couldn't blame her. There wasn't much business here for them to make a living. Juanita can handle the little bit of business we get ever since you married Blossom."

The picture became very clear to Zach then. It was obvious. "Where'd Bertie say she was headed?"

"She didn't say," Trotter replied, suddenly realizing that Bertie might be in for some trouble from the hotheaded drifter. He knew that she had been in touch with a fellow she knew in Helena and if he had to guess, he'd bet that was where she went. "I didn't much care, so I didn't think to ask her," he said.

"How long ago was it she left?" Zach asked.

"Day before yesterday," Trotter answered. When Zach just stood there, biting his lip, trying to decide his next move, Trotter asked, "Want me to pour you a drink?"

"No, I don't want no drink," Zach blurted, then

changed his mind. "Yeah, pour me a drink." He downed it, hardly noticing the burn. Then he turned to confront Hog and Red when they got up from the table, having realized the deadly mood he was in. It was easy to guess the cause of his anger.

"She run off?" Hog asked.

"Yeah, she took off, and she's gonna pay for it." He glared at Hog. "I told her what was gonna happen to her if she ever did."

"That's right," Hog said. "You warned her. She's got it coming. Where'd she go? Did Trotter say?"

"He don't know, but he said Bertie and that homely little gal are gone, too. So it looks to me like they all went together. Helena is what I think. Where else could they be goin'? That's the closest town. They wouldn't likely head north 'cause we were up that way."

"Yeah," Hog mused. "That didn't turn out worth a shit, did it?" He was thinking about the reason they had come back to Great Falls before they had planned to. "That was poor luck to find a cavalry patrol ridin' with that payroll."

Ignoring Hog's musing, Zach said, "I'm goin' after that bitch, and the other two with her. We oughta be able to catch 'em before they get to Helena." He automatically assumed they would go with him. Neither spoke up at once, so he said, "You ain't got nothin' better to do."

Red glanced at Hog and shrugged. "I reckon you're right about that," he said. "Might as well, but we need to let those horses rest before we go anywhere. We damn near wore 'em out coming back."

Zach grimaced when he remembered that, but he realized they had little choice but to let the horses recover. It was not to his liking, but he was still confident that they could overtake the wagon, probably before it reached Helena.

CHAPTER 3

The night passed peacefully enough for the three women and their guide. As a precaution, Hawk had backed the wagon into a narrow ravine where it was hidden from view of anyone passing on the road. He built the fire in the back of the ravine, where the smoke was largely dispersed by the foliage on the slope above it. Although he made no show of being overly concerned with the possibility of Blossom's husband coming after them, he saw no sense in being careless about the camp. A jealous man was a dangerous man, and from hearing them talk about Zach Dubose, he sounded like the kind of man who would not take her leaving without seeking some measure of revenge. As before, he had spent the night bedded down close to his horse while the women slept under the wagon again. He had positioned his bed in the mouth of the ravine, so if a visit from Dubose did occur, he would have to pass by him to get to the wagon. He was a naturally light sleeper, plus he counted on the big buckskin to alert him if other horses approached.

With the early rays of the sun filtering through the thick foliage on the sides of the ravine, Hawk rolled out of his blanket and took a quick look around the camp to make sure everything was in order. When he walked back in the ravine to get the women up, he was met halfway by JoJo, carrying a cup of coffee for him. "I thought you might want some coffee before we hitch up," she said, outwardly pleased by his look of surprise.

He laughed. "I sure do," he said, taking the cup from her. "Thank you. What about the other two?"

"I woke 'em up," she said. "They can get their own coffee."

"Well, thank you again." He took a sip of the hot liquid. "That's mighty good. You sure make a good cup of coffee, lady." She blushed sweetly as he smacked his lips after another sip. "Yes, ma'am, some lucky young fellow is gonna get a winner when he picks you." While she puffed up proudly, he told her to tell Blossom and her mother they could walk up the creek a ways to perform whatever they had to do before starting out again. "And tell 'em they don't need to wander off too far. I'll be saddlin' Rascal and hitching up the wagon." She waited until he gulped the last of his coffee down, then she took his cup back to the wagon. *Poor little homely girl*, he thought as he hesitated a moment to watch her walk away. *She ain't got much chance of getting married, or making it as a whore, if that's what she's hoping to do. But I don't know. I reckon there's a mate for everybody somewhere.* He had to admit, she was starting to get into his mind. He couldn't help feeling sorry for her. "Ain't my problem," he mumbled, turned around, and went to get his saddle. He said good morning to Blossom and Bertie when they passed him, on their way downstream to take care of business. They were soon under way again.

This day passed as the day before had, with no sign of anyone: freighters, Indians, soldiers, or anyone else. It was as if the road were for their private use only. Occasionally, upon passing a hill or mesa that offered a good view of the road before and behind, Hawk would climb up to look over their back trail. He finally decided the women were right, Zach Dubose was still somewhere near Fort Benton, unaware that his wife had left him. The end of the day found them less than twenty miles from Helena. A lighthearted spirit prevailed among the women as they went about the business of making camp. "This time tomorrow we'll be in Helena," Bertie cheerfully announced when she dropped an armload of dried branches for the fire JoJo was in the process of building. Blossom paused to smile in response. She, who had actually suffered abuse at the hands of Zach Dubose, was feeling free of the evil man's influence at last. She and her mother seemed to feel they would be safe in Helena, for, according to Bertie, they would have rooms in the saloon as Sam Ingram had promised. And as far as trouble outside the saloon, Helena had a sheriff to take care of that. Hawk hoped everything worked out for them, but he figured he didn't know Dubose well enough to predict his actions. If he was like the typical drifter turned outlaw, he'd probably get over the loss of Blossom and soon turn his attentions to some other whore. But you never can tell, he told himself. At any rate, he knew he would be glad to see them safely to their destination. He was long overdue at Fort Ellis. Major Brisbin was most likely wondering what had happened to him and what kind of luck he'd had talking Walking Owl into bringing his people to the reservation.

The only member of the party who was not eager to see the journey end was JoJo Feeley. Having been treated as a cull by boys and men since she was a small child, she was at last feeling the respect that other women received from most men. And she feared that it would end when they reached Helena. Her infatuation with the rugged-looking cavalry scout was hardly concealed, giving both Bertie and Blossom cause for concern for the immature girl. Childlike in her adoration of Hawk, JoJo would be hard to convince that a man like him was not a man for her. Bertie knew that once they reached Helena, Hawk would disappear just as suddenly as he had appeared. She wished that he had not given JoJo as much attention as he had, but it would be difficult to complain to him about his kindness. *Well, I reckon she'll get over it*, she thought. *Lord knows, she oughta be used to rejection.*

Once the camp was set up, Hawk left them to take his customary scout around the perimeter, just to check out the neighborhood, as he called it. They were a considerable distance from the road, as far as they could get with the wagon, in a forest of fir trees, divided by a busy stream. To the northwest, the rugged peaks of the Rocky Mountains stood, a constant challenge to a man of Hawk's nature. And had it not been for his feeling of obligation to Major Brisbin, no doubt he would have accepted the call. He reminded himself of the job he had taken on in the meantime and continued his circle around the camp.

"I was wonderin' if you'd left us," Bertie joked when he came back into camp. "What'cha got there?"

He held up the rabbit he was carrying. "I found this one back down the stream a ways," he replied. "Thought maybe you might wanna throw him in a pot, or roast him over the fire, to add a little something to smoked deer meat. I was expectin' to find some porcupines. Wasn't expectin' a rabbit."

"Porcupines?" Bertie responded. "Why'd you want one of them?"

"I didn't. I just thought there were some around." He pointed to several fir trees with bark eaten away. "They like to chew on the bark."

Still puzzled, she stared at the trees for a moment before pointing out the obvious. "You sure it was porcupines that did that? Those rings are six or eight feet off the ground, and last I heard, porcupines ain't near that tall."

"You're right, they ain't," he said. "They eat the

bark in the winter when food's scarce and the snow was that high on the tree then."

"Hadn't thought of that," Bertie said. "I didn't hear no gunshot. How'd you get him?" He reached in his saddlebag and pulled out a sling made with rawhide cords. He had made it when still a boy, living in a Crow village. "Well, I'll be . . ." she started. "If that ain't somethin'." She grinned wide. "You must be one helluva shot with that thing to hit a rabbit. Ain't that right, JoJo?"

"I reckon so," JoJo answered, not surprised by anything Hawk could do.

"I don't know about that," Hawk was quick to disagree. "It took me four shots before I hit him. And the damn fool rabbit just sat there when the first three missed. I think he thought he was safe as long as he didn't move. Either that or he figured he was supposed to go in a cook pot, so he didn't run. He mighta committed suicide if the fourth shot hadn't accidentally hit him."

"Posh," JoJo exclaimed, certain he was making it up. "I don't believe you."

"You can believe it," he said. "I'll skin it and we'll stick him over the fire. I need to take care of Rascal first."

"I can skin a rabbit," JoJo immediately volunteered. "I'll help you."

"All right," Hawk said, and started toward the stream with JoJo walking along beside him.

"Maybe I oughta have a little talk with him about her," Bertie said to Blossom, who had come up in time to hear the conversation.

"Maybe so," Blossom agreed. "It might break her heart for sure, if he was to take advantage of her damn innocence."

"Oh, I ain't worried about that," Bertie was quick to reply. "I don't read any mischief in Hawk a-tall. I'm sure he ain't got nothin' like that on his mind. He's just too damn dumb to see she's got a crush on him. Hell, he oughta know he can have a ride with any one of us whenever he feels like it. He just don't realize she ain't the child she acts like."

Blossom nodded thoughtfully. "I guess you're right, and that kinda bothers me a little. Maybe there's something wrong with us." She paused, then added, "Maybe there's something wrong with him."

"We're wastin' our time tryin' to figure him out," Bertie said. "I'm just glad he came along when he did." She gave a little chuckle. "We were down to one horse and eatin' the other one. Whaddaya reckon woulda happened if we tried to pull that wagon with one horse?"

"I don't know. It mighta pulled the wagon round and round in a circle and we wouldn't have gone anywhere." They both laughed at that picture.

The man they puzzled over was not immune to feminine charms, and he had given some thought to one woman in particular, now that they were so close to Helena. He remembered the dining room next to the Davis Hotel and the little lady who owned it. Sophie Hicks was her name, and she had told him to be sure to call on her again whenever he was back in Helena. And he had gotten the impression it was not because she just wanted to sell him more food. *I expect that's one call I'll make*, he thought. *Right after I deliver these ladies to the Last Chance Saloon.*

He figured to make Helena in the afternoon the next day, reclaim his packhorse and all his possibles, then leave the horses in Bowen's Stable that night. As he usually did, he'd probably sleep in the stable with his horses. *I'll stop by to visit Miss Sophie Hicks for supper tomorrow, then I'd best head out early the next mornin' for Fort Ellis, or I'm liable not to have a job.* His thoughts were interrupted when JoJo came to get him for supper. She greeted him by blurting, "Why do you have that feather in your hat?"

He was accustomed to being confronted with that question on occasion, usually from a child or a woman. This time it was from a woman who looked like a child. His usual practice was to create a story that might entertain the inquirer, instead of admitting that he just found it by the trail and decided to stick it in his hat. He thought for only a minute before creating one he thought she might like to believe. "I lived with a Blackfoot village a few years back and they had a custom none of the other tribes had. A young warrior would stick a hawk feather in his headband, or his hat, if he wore one. Then all the young girls would know he was lookin' for a wife. And if one of the girls fancied him, she would pluck his feather. None of the girls ever fancied me, so I'm still wearin' a feather in my hat."

She looked him in the eye for a long moment before responding, "Posh, I don't believe a word of it. I never heard of anything like that."

He laughed. "Like I said, it was a custom only practiced by that village."

"We can't be that far behind 'em," Zach Dubose claimed. "Those tracks ain't that old." He pointed at some deep ridges left by a wagon wheel at a stream crossing.

"Maybe, maybe not," Hog Thacker said. "It's damn hard to tell in all that loose rock. But the fact is, if we don't rest these horses, we're gonna be on foot."

"Hell," Dubose retorted, "my horse ain't even worked up a sweat yet. We can't stop now. We've almost caught 'em."

"Is that a fact?" Hog replied. "Well, my horse needs to rest, so I reckon you'll be goin' on by yourself. I ain't aimin' to kill my horse just so you can catch that woman."

"Hog's right," Red Whitley said. "My horse is about done for the day and so's yourn. It don't make no sense to kill the horses and walk into Helena."

"I thought you boys were tougher'n that," Dubose mocked. "I reckon I shoulda just come on alone." He knew they were right—his horse was exhausted, too. He just couldn't stand the thought of quitting when he felt they were so close to overtaking them.

"Suit yourself," Hog said. "This stream right here looks like a good place to camp, so I'm throwin' my bedroll down right under them trees yonder."

"Looks good to me," Red said. "Let's get us a fire goin'." They both turned their weary horses toward the bank Hog had pointed to and left Dubose to steam over it for a while. Long accustomed to riding with Dubose, neither man feared him and they knew he would not go on without them, no matter how much he threatened. One big reason was that horse he was so proud of, a spotted horse with unusual markings. Dubose had shot the previous owner after a fight broke out over a card game. The horse was called a Palouse, named for the Palouse River, where it was supposedly bred by the Nez Perce Indians, and Dubose was not likely to run that horse till it foundered. As they expected, in a few minutes' time, he came along after them, still mumbling insults under his breath.

"How far do you think it is to Helena?" Dubose asked when he dismounted.

"Hell, I don't know," Hog answered. "About fifteen miles or so," he said, and looked at Red for confirmation.

Red shrugged indifferently, already wishing he had stayed in Great Falls and let Dubose go chasing after his wife by himself. Blossom was a fine-looking woman, but she was still just another whore as far as he was concerned. He was tired after a long, full day of hard riding and he wished he had a drink. "Helena ain't even a full day's ride from here," he offered. "What we need to know is how far ahead of us that wife of yours is."

"That's right," Hog agreed. "And we don't know for sure that's where she's headin'."

"Where else would she be goin'?" Dubose blurted, unwilling to accept the possibility that Blossom had tricked him into thinking she was heading to Helena. He couldn't help thinking that it might be the case, however. "Damn it," he fumed, "we shoulda caught up with 'em by now."

"Maybe we did," Hog said, more as a way to aggravate Dubose. He winked at Red. "Maybe they pulled off somewhere to make camp and we passed on by 'em."

"Damn, you could be right," Red said as he pulled the saddle off his horse. "I bet they're behind us. They're chasin' us now. That was a fair-sized stream we passed about three miles back. They mighta pulled off there and hid up in them trees for the night. It was too dark to see any tracks, if that's where they went. Maybe we oughta go back there and find out."

"Go to hell, both of you," Dubose blurted, finally catching on to the japing he was a victim of. It was no secret that he had trouble controlling his temper, and they were obviously intending to amuse themselves at his expense. "We ain't caught 'em yet, but we'll catch 'em tomorrow. If we don't, I'll just find 'em in Helena. One way or the other, she's gonna pay. You just be ready to ride early in the mornin'."

* * *

As he had warned, Dubose roused Red and Hog out of their blankets at the first sign of daylight. Amid a minor protest of grumbling, he threatened to shoot both of them if they delayed his quest for vengeance another minute. Well aware of the crazy streak that ran through Dubose's brain, they decided it unwise to push him any further. So they saddled up and started out for Helena, knowing that if they didn't catch the runaway wife before reaching town, at least it was a short ride to breakfast.

Approximately three miles behind them, the woman Dubose pursued brought Hawk a cup of coffee as he was hitching the horses up to the wagon. "I know it's a little too far to drive the horses on in to Helena without stopping to rest them," she said. "So we'll make breakfast then. All right?"

"That would be best," Hawk agreed.

She started to leave, then hesitated. "I don't know if I've told you enough how much I appreciate what you've done for us. You're one of the most decent men I've ever met. I know you were on your way to Fort Ellis, and I hope we haven't messed up any plans you had before you were unlucky enough to run up on us. But you've made this trip a whole lot easier for the three of us."

Her words of gratitude left him a little uncomfortable, since his thought upon first meeting them had been to regret his bad luck. "Well, I'm right glad I was here to help," he fumbled. "But we ain't got to Helena yet."

"But we're not that far, are we?"

"No, ma'am," he said. She smiled, confident that she had gotten away from Zach Dubose. "I expect I'd best get your wagon hitched up," he said.

She hesitated again when she saw JoJo hurrying toward them. "And I guess I should thank you for not taking advantage of JoJo," she said quickly, in an effort to say it before the young girl was close enough to overhear. His puzzled expression caused her to say, "I reckon you know she's pretty much taken by you."

"Ah no, ma'am, I didn't," he replied honestly. "I just thought she was bein' friendly." There was no time to say more before JoJo walked briskly up to them.

"I was fixin' to bring you a cup of coffee," JoJo announced, "but I couldn't find your cup. I see why now." She forced a smile in Blossom's direction.

"You three women are gonna spoil me for good," Hawk said, unable to think of anything better. "I'd best get you on up the road to Helena."

"You need any help?" JoJo asked. "Want me to go get Rascal for you?"

"Ah no, ma'am," he said. "He'll come when I call him." She almost looked disappointed and it struck him that maybe Blossom was right. "Thanks anyway, I appreciate it."

She shrugged and turned to go back to the

wagon, then stopped and turned around again. "How old do you think I am?" she asked.

Thinking it best to make light of the situation, he answered, "Oh, I don't know—about seventy-five."

She glared at him for a long moment, obviously not amused. "My mama wasn't but thirteen when she got married," she informed him, and turned again to go to the wagon.

He could not recall if he had ever met any woman or girl who was "taken" with him before, even one that looked as young as JoJo. He wondered if Sophie Hicks had been "taken" with him when she invited him back. He shook his head to clear it of nonsense and went back to work hitching the team.

It was still early when the three outlaws rode along Last Chance Gulch, looking for the saloon by the same name. "Yonder it is," Dubose declared, and pointed toward a weathered sign hanging on a building next to a dry goods store. "That's gotta be the place where Bertie Brown knows the owner. Last Chance Saloon—Blossom said somethin' about it one time, said Bertie always had a job there, if she needed one." Dubose turned toward it immediately, certain this was the place the women were running to. Hog and Red followed his lead and pulled up to the hitching rail beside him. Dubose was already at the door before Hog and Red had tied their horses. "I hope they got somethin' in there to eat," Hog said as they stepped up on the narrow porch.

Inside, they found Dubose talking to the bartender and it didn't appear that he was getting answers to his questions. At least none that seemed to please their hotheaded partner. "I told you, mister," they heard the bartender say, "Mr. Ingram ain't here right now. He don't usually come in till later in the morning." It was obvious that Dubose was heating up pretty rapidly and that was usually a source of entertainment to Hog. He grinned at Red as they walked over to the bar.

"Has Bertie Brown or Blossom Dubose been in here?" Dubose demanded.

The bartender, a normally mild-mannered little man named Dewey Smith, was beginning to lose his patience with the overbearing stranger. "Like I've been trying to tell you, I ain't been working here but a few months. If the two women you're looking for have been in, I wouldn't know it." Already near the end of his tolerance, he couldn't resist a little sarcasm. "The kind of women who wander in here ain't likely the kind that introduce themselves."

That was enough to light Dubose's fuse. He drew his .44 and stuck it in Dewey's face. "Whoa, there, partner!" Hog blurted, and he and Red quickly grabbed Dubose and pulled his arm back. "Simmer down. Hell, he said he's new. He don't know Blossom and Bertie from anybody else." Turning to Dewey, whose face was suddenly drained of any color, he said, "He don't mean nothin' by it. He just ain't had his breakfast this mornin'. Take him over and set down," he said to Red. When Dewey appeared to have recovered from his fright, Hog questioned him. "My friend is lookin' to meet his wife here in Helena and she's a friend of your boss. She's travelin' with her mama and a young girl. You see anybody like that? Mighta come in lookin' for your boss? It woulda been in the last day or two."

"I ain't seen anybody like that," Dewey said. "This ain't the only saloon in town. Maybe they went to one of the others."

Hog doubted that, and he believed the bartender was telling the truth, so he concluded that they had been chasing a bad idea. The three women went somewhere else. He paused and thought about it—*or maybe we got here before they did.* He remembered joking about it the night before. Maybe they did pass them on the road, when the women had pulled off to camp. That was a possibility and something to consider, although it would surprise him if the three women were careful enough to hide their exit from the trail. "Anyway," he said to Dewey, "my friend don't normally act like that. He don't mean you no harm. The three of us need some breakfast. You got any coffee, anythin' to eat with it?"

"I can fix you up with something to put in your belly," Dewey said. "We've got coffee, and Daisy, she's my wife, bakes up biscuits every morning. So if that'll do, I'll tell her to bring you out some. If you want a full breakfast, you can get that at the diner next to the hotel."

"Fine," Hog said. "That'll do just fine." He was

already thinking they would be in town for a while until they decided for sure that the women weren't coming to Helena. And there was no use in causing trouble in this saloon and end up getting the sheriff involved. "All right, then, I'll go over there and sit down with my friends. If you'd tell your wife to bring us out some coffee and biscuits, we'd surely appreciate it."

"What was all that jawin' about?" Dubose asked when Hog came to the table.

"I was tryin' to make sure that bartender didn't send somebody to get the sheriff," Hog said. "You damn fool, there ain't nothin' like makin' an announcement to the whole damn town that we're here, and we're lookin' to shoot a woman."

"That's what I'm tryin' to tell him," Red insisted. "He still thinks they're hidin' 'em somewhere."

"Hell, they ain't hidin' nobody," Hog said to Dubose. "That bartender don't know Bertie Brown." He glanced over at Red. "I got him to bring out some coffee and biscuits. Maybe that'll settle ol' Dubose down a little while we decide what we're gonna do. After we get somethin' in our bellies, we can look over the whole town, if you want." He was looking straight at Dubose now. "But I'll tell you what I think. I think we got here before they did in that wagon."

Red shrugged and considered the possibility. "We might have, at that," he finally decided. "We made that trip pretty fast, almost cost me a good horse." He paused to reflect. "One of the best horses I ever stole," he said, thinking about that particular day. Back to the present, he nudged

Dubose. "Whaddaya think, Zach? That makes sense, don't it?"

Recovered somewhat from his need to shoot someone, Dubose raised his dark, brooding eyes from the table to meet Red's gaze. After a long moment, he finally allowed, "Maybe you're right." After another moment, he decided, "That's what happened. We just damn sure outran 'em." He convinced himself that that was what happened, primarily because, if it were not the case, then he had no idea where else to look for Blossom.

Further discussion was interrupted at that moment by the arrival of Daisy Smith, who brought coffee and biscuits from the kitchen. "Pay Dewey," she said when she placed everything on the table.

Hog grabbed a biscuit as soon as the plate hit the table. "Dewey? Is that his name?" He took a huge bite out of his biscuit. She nodded. "And your name's Daisy. Ain't that right?" She nodded again, not really interested in making conversation. He chuckled, spraying bits of biscuit out of his mouth. "Damn, that's the driest biscuit I ever et," he said, and took a gulp of coffee to wash it down.

"If you'd been in here this morning when they were baked, they wouldn't have been dried out," she said, obviously offended.

"I was just japin' you a little, ma'am," Hog quickly apologized. "The biscuits are fine, Daisy." He laughed then, unable to resist teasing her more. "Dewey and Daisy, that's a pair to draw to, ain't it, Red? Better'n a pair of aces."

Not amused, Daisy repeated, "Pay Dewey," turned, and returned to the kitchen.

"Damned if you ain't still got a way of charmin' women," Red said with a laugh, as he eyeballed Daisy's ample bottom all the way until she disappeared through the kitchen door. "I wonder if she's for sale. She don't look half-bad."

"You never can tell," Hog remarked. "Maybe she might be ol' Dewey's money crop. Why don't you ask him?"

"I'll let you do that," Red came back, "since you're already in so good with him and his wife. Then if she'll give you a ride, I reckon she'll give anybody one."

"Why don't you two shut the hell up?" Dubose interrupted, his anger beginning to flare again as his impatience wore thin. "Let's finish up here and go have a look around town. They might already be here."

"All right," Hog said. "But I need a little drink of whiskey to get rid of the taste of that coffee. How 'bout you, Red?"

"Couldn't hurt, at that," Red replied. He signaled Dewey to bring a bottle over, ignoring Dubose's scowls.

CHAPTER 4

At approximately the same time Zach Dubose and his two friends were finishing off their breakfast with a couple of drinks, Bertie's wagon was parked beside a creek five miles short of town. Breakfast, considerably better than the dry biscuits enjoyed by their pursuers, was finished as well, and Hawk walked to the edge of the creek to get the horses. "Well, looks like you'll soon be rid of me," he said when he looked up to see JoJo coming to help. "It ain't but about five miles from here to Helena."

"That's what I came to tell you," she said. "I wish it was a hundred miles to Helena. I don't wanna get rid of you."

Her statement startled him, leaving him unsure how to respond. "Is that right?" He stumbled for appropriate words. "I didn't know you were enjoyin' the trip so much—thought you'd be anxious to get to Helena, like Bertie and Blossom."

"It ain't about gettin' to Helena, or gettin' away

from Zach Dubose," she said. Having made up her mind to do it, she was determined to lay her heart bare for him, for she knew he would be leaving soon. "I wanna go with you." When she saw the surprise in his eyes, she said, "I don't care. I said it and I mean it. I won't be no trouble. I'll help you and do for you."

Shocked as never before, he searched for words that wouldn't come to mind. "I swear, JoJo . . . I mean, you can't go with me. That wouldn't be a decent life for you. I've got nothin' to offer a woman. Hell, I'm gone most of the time, scoutin' for an army patrol, or off on some job, like the one that caused me to be up in this part of the territory, never knowin' when I'd be back." He could see the rejection in her face, but he didn't want to tell her that she was no more than a child in his eyes. It was possibly the worst situation he had ever been in, for she was plainly hurt. And that was the last thing he wanted to do, for she had been hurt so many times in her life.

"I know I ain't very pretty," she started, but he cut her off.

"There ain't nothin' wrong with the way you look," he insisted. "You oughta be glad you're a little late comin' along, 'cause when you do start to bloom, you'll be head and shoulders above the rest of the ladies your age. I guarantee it. And you'll be mighty glad you didn't throw your life away following an old saddle tramp like me around."

"You ain't a saddle tramp," she said, now with a definite resolve in her tone. "And you ain't old. You're the finest man I've ever met. I just want you to know that." With that, she ended the proposal and returned to her usual air of cheerfulness, although it did nothing to ease the pain he felt for her. She had been rejected before, many times, and she was accustomed to picking herself up again. He was now more anxious than ever to complete this task he had taken upon himself and get back to Fort Ellis. "I'll let you get away this time," she said, teasing him now. "But when I start to bloom, like you said, I just might pluck that feather outta your hat one day."

"You might at that," he responded.

With Helena now only a few miles away, Bertie and Blossom were eager to get started, so they had the wagon packed up when he returned with the horses. So impatient were they, they started rolling before he had saddled Rascal. "Go ahead," he said when Bertie stopped momentarily. "I'll catch up."

Sam Ingram was tending bar, having relieved Dewey Smith while his bartender was sitting in the kitchen having dinner with his wife. He glanced up when someone came in the front door. "Well, I'll be go to hell!" Sam blurted. "I don't believe it!" He came out from behind the bar to greet them. "Bertie Brown!" he exclaimed. "I didn't think you'd really show up here. Come here!" She stepped forward to receive a great bear hug from the overjoyed man."

"Hell, I told you I was comin'," Bertie said when he released her.

"Who's this?" Sam asked then, looking at

Blossom. "Is this your daughter?" Bertie nodded vigorously. "I swear, I wouldn't have known her. She wasn't much older than this other little girl last time I saw her." He turned to Blossom. "Welcome." Then, glancing at JoJo, he added, "You, too, honey."

Blossom gave him a smile and said, "Thank you, we're mighty glad to be here." Her relief when they finally rolled into town had been spoiled somewhat when they passed a saloon next to the post office and an unusual horse tied at the rail happened to catch her eye. It was a spotted horse like the one Zach was so proud of, and the sight of it gave her a start. She had to remind herself that Zach was up near Fort Benton somewhere and nowhere near Helena. Now she was safely in the Last Chance Saloon, she could forget about her husband.

One who was not especially glad to see them hesitated for a few moments, but decided she might as well make a show of welcome. "Meet Gladys Welch," Sam said when she walked up. "She'll be glad to have you helping out around here."

"I know Gladys," Bertie said. "How are you, honey? It's been a long time since Cheyenne, ain't it?"

"I reckon it has," Gladys said. "But I can still kick pretty high."

"Well, that's all that counts," Bertie said, and gave her a wide smile, while thinking to herself that Gladys's days were running short now that she was here. Turning her attention back to Sam, she said, "This young lady is JoJo Feeley. She's a willing worker at just about any job and she's interested in maybe joining us in our profession."

Like most people meeting JoJo, Sam was surprised to hear that. "Well, looks like we'll have to fatten her up a little." He returned his attention to Bertie. "I've got a couple of rooms upstairs that you can move in." He paused, then asked, "You three women come down from Great Falls all by yourselves?"

"No, we had a fellow, name of Hawk, who came with us to make sure we got here all right," Blossom answered.

"Hawk?" Sam reacted at once. "John Hawk—big fellow, wears a feather in his hat?"

"Yep, that's the man," Bertie replied. "You know him?"

"Sure do. Rides scout for the army. He's been in here a time or two." He laughed then. "Did you pay him, or did he take it out in trade?"

"No," Bertie started, but was interrupted by JoJo.

"Hawk didn't touch anybody," she declared. "And he didn't ask for no money, either. He done it because he's a gentleman."

"That's a fact," Bertie said. "He didn't ask for anything."

"Well, I declare," Sam said, "this has sure turned out to be a good day. Where's all your things?"

"We pulled our wagon around behind the building," Bertie said. "There's a few pieces of furniture I brought with me. Hawk offered to come back to help us carry our stuff in, but I told him he'd done enough just gettin' us here."

"Let's go have a look," Sam said. "I'll see if my bartender has finished eating his dinner." He started toward the kitchen door just as Dewey walked out. "Come meet some friends of mine," Sam said. He had not told Dewey about his efforts to persuade Bertie to come help him in Helena because he really wasn't sure Bertie would come.

Dewey immediately thought of the other three strangers who had been in the saloon earlier that day. He stared at the three women for a moment before commenting. "You must be the folks those fellers were asking about this morning," he said.

"What fellers?" Bertie asked, at once alarmed. Blossom grabbed JoJo's shoulder for support.

"Three fellers," Dewey said. "They stayed here awhile eating biscuits and drinking coffee. One of 'em stuck a gun in my face when I told 'em you weren't here. The two fellers with that hothead pulled him back. They said he was looking for his wife. I think she was supposed to meet him here. Acted like they were friends of yours, Sam." Dewey was suddenly aware that he had set off a bomb. Bertie was obviously distressed and JoJo had to help Blossom to a chair when her knees threatened to fail her. Confused and dismayed when he began to fear that Bertie had somehow brought some trouble to his doorstep, Sam just looked from her to Blossom, searching for an explanation. Dewey tried to remember anything that might further explain the incident. "They didn't give their names," he said. "But I heard them call one of 'em Hog. He's the one who did most of the talking."

Blossom gave a whimper at the mention of that

name. "Hog Thacker," she said. "He rides with Zach. They've found us. I'm as good as dead."

"Not yet, you ain't," Bertie exclaimed, regaining some of her fight. "They're gonna have to go through me to get my daughter!"

"And me, too!" JoJo cried with equal defiance.

Not at all comfortable with the way his morning had turned, Sam said, "I think you'd best tell me what the hell's going on, Bertie. Do I need to send somebody to get the sheriff?"

"You might at that," Bertie confessed. "Believe me, Sam, I didn't mean to bring our troubles to your door. I don't know how they knew we were comin' here. I guess I'd best tell you the whole story."

After hearing the reasons Bertie felt compelled to help her daughter escape from a man as brutally insane as Zach Dubose, Sam could readily understand her motive for coming there. And while he could have wished she had gone somewhere else, he could not in good conscience turn her away. "All right," he decided. "Dewey, go on over and get Porter Willis. It sounds like we're gonna need the sheriff. We can unload your wagon later. Just get anything you need right now. I think it would be best if you ladies go to my room behind the kitchen. We'll move you upstairs after we're through dealing with those men." Dewey left at once to fetch the sheriff. Sam looked at Blossom then. "We won't take any chances, but maybe those men moved on when they didn't find you here. Dewey said they were here this morning. That's been a while and they ain't been back. Anyway, we'll get Sheriff Willis over here and let him know what's going on."

"You don't know how much I appreciate your help, Sam," Bertie said to him. "I wouldn't have blamed you one bit if you had thrown us out. I'll get my rifle out of the wagon, then I'll be right behind you."

"Make it quick," Sam said, and led Blossom and JoJo toward the kitchen and his quarters behind.

With no notion that the three women he had accompanied to town were in desperate need of the protection he had provided on their journey, Hawk sat at a table in Sophie's Diner. As he had hoped, the attractive owner of the dining room did, indeed, remember him and welcomed him back graciously. "Are you gonna be in town awhile this time?" Sophie asked him.

"Well, that depends, I reckon," he replied. "I ought not. I oughta been on my way back to Fort Ellis three days ago, but I couldn't pass up a chance to sample some more of your cookin'—see if it's as good as it was last time."

"Is that right?" she asked coyly. "Well, how is it?"

"Every bit as good," he said.

"Well, I'll have to tell Martha," Sophie confessed. "She really does most of the cooking."

Their conversation was interrupted by a request for more coffee at a table on the opposite wall where some men were eating. Sophie went to get the coffeepot, and Hawk found himself admiring the way she carried herself. When she disappeared into the kitchen, his gaze shifted to the men at the table. There were three of them. They had come in the diner at the same time he had and he noticed then that they were a rough-looking trio. They weren't cowhands. Of that, he felt certain. Two of them were loud and seemed to find a lot to laugh about. The other one was a dark, brooding man, seemingly oblivious to the conversation between his two companions. Hawk couldn't help thinking about Blossom and her mother, running from Blossom's abusive husband. *Someone about like any of those three*, he thought, recalling the description JoJo had given him. The thought of JoJo naturally brought to mind his uncomfortable parting with the childlike young woman. He sincerely hoped she would somehow find a happy path to travel, something better than being a common whore. His thoughts were brought back to the present when one of the three men got up from his chair and announced that he had to go to the outhouse, loud enough to inform everyone in the dining room.

Sophie was filling their coffee cups when the man came back to the table, but did not take his seat. Instead, he talked excitedly to his two friends, not so loud as before. Whatever he told them served to excite them as well. They got up immediately and hurried out of the room. Sophie walked the coffeepot over to Hawk's table. "I wonder what got into them," she remarked. "They sent me to the kitchen for more coffee, but didn't wait to even take a sip of it."

"Looks like it's a good thing you make everybody pay in advance," he said. "Just so you don't make a trip for nothin', you can fill my cup. On second thought, don't fill it. I've got to check on something right now." He pushed his chair back and stood up.

"You, too?" she protested.

"'Fraid so," he said, and headed for the door. "I told Grover Bramble I'd pay him for my horse an hour ago. He said he was leaving early to go home and I forgot all about it while I was talkin' to you, so it's your fault. I'll be back. You're still the prettiest woman I've ever seen." He left her standing there, shaking her head.

Sheriff Porter Willis followed Dewey back to the saloon and met Daisy standing there waiting. "They're out behind the building," she exclaimed. "You better hurry!" When they hurried to the back door, Daisy grabbed Dewey by the arm. "You stay here. Somebody's gonna get killed out there."

When the sheriff went out the door, he found himself in the middle of a standoff. The three outlaws were standing in the yard, facing two terrified women and Sam Ingram, who were huddled together on the back stoop behind Bertie. Standing defiantly, her Henry rifle in hand, she was determined to protect her daughter. "What's goin' on here?" Willis demanded.

"This ain't none of your business," Dubose

snarled. "I just come to get my wife and this crazy bitch won't let her go."

"She don't wanna go," Bertie said. "So you can climb back on your horse and you and your no-account friends can ride on outta here.

Willis looked at Blossom. "Is this your husband, ma'am?"

"It was," Blossom answered.

"See," Dubose snapped. "I told you this is somethin' between me and my wife. Ain't nobody else's business."

Willis returned his gaze to Blossom. "Do you wanna go with him?"

"No, sir, I don't," she replied.

"Well, mister, you heard her. She don't wanna go, so she don't have to go. I expect you and your friends best ride on outta town, unless you wanna spend the night in my jail for disturbin' the peace."

"How about that crazy old bitch standin' there holdin' that rifle on me?" Dubose demanded. "You gonna put her in jail?"

"She's got a right to protect her family," Willis said. "Now, get on outta here before I have to lock you up." He stepped between the two parties to face Dubose, his shotgun up before him. Concentrating his gaze on Dubose, he didn't even see Red draw his weapon. Moments later, he was doubled over with a .44 slug in his gut. The sound of the gunshot caught everyone off guard, but Hog was quickest to react. He lunged at Bertie, knocking her down before she could raise her rifle to fire. When she tried to retrieve her weapon, he knocked her down again with the butt of his pistol and she lay there, unmoving. He picked up the rifle and with a leering grin on his face turned to face Blossom and JoJo, who were cringing against the back door of the saloon. He shifted his gaze to Sam Ingram, his eyes seeming to invite some reaction from the saloon owner, but none came. Sam was frozen in shock by the sight of the sheriff lying on the ground at the gunman's feet.

Dubose stepped forward and grabbed Blossom by the wrist. "Now, you worthless whore, I told you what I'd do to you if you ever tried to run out on me." He shouted over his shoulder, "Get ready to ride, boys!" Back to the frightened woman, he said, "I'm takin' you for one last go-around. Then I'm gonna let Red and Hog have a go with you till they get tired of it. Then I'm gonna blow your brains out." He proceeded toward his horse, dragging Blossom, who was helplessly trying to resist, while crying and pleading for mercy.

Devastated by the sight of Blossom being dragged across the yard, JoJo ran after her, screaming at Dubose to let her go. He was almost to his horse, but JoJo caught hold of Blossom's skirt and fought him to a standstill. "Damn you," he snarled when she wouldn't let go. In a fit of rage, he drew his pistol and shot her, the bullet slamming into her chest. When she dropped to the ground, he stepped up in the stirrup, determined to drag Blossom all the way out of town if she refused to step up behind him. Suddenly, he released her with the simultaneous sound of a Winchester rifle and his own cry of pain as the bullet ripped into the back of his shoulder. Almost immediately, a second shot was fired, the bullet snapping between the horses.

"Get outta here!" Hog shouted when Dubose fell forward on his horse's neck. Not waiting to see if his companions heard him, Hog whipped his horse into a gallop. With no time to do anything else, Red and Dubose followed him, charging down the alley behind the buildings at a full gallop.

Behind them, Hawk ran from the street in front of the saloon, trying to get to the back alley in time to get off another shot. But he was too late, getting only a glimpse of the rump of the spotted Palouse that Dubose rode, as the outlaws rounded the stables. He had no option to give chase, since his horse was still at the blacksmith's. His concern was elsewhere, anyway, having witnessed the brutal execution of the young woman.

He ran back to gather JoJo's limp body up in his arms and he knew at once that she was fading rapidly. Her white bodice was already soaked with the red stain of her blood and her eyelids fluttered momentarily before remaining open for a brief moment. "Hawk," she whispered so softly that he could just barely hear her. "I knew you'd come."

"I woulda come for you, JoJo. I woulda always come for you." He paused and listened for her to speak again. After a moment, when there was not another word, he realized she was gone. He felt sick inside, filled with rage that anyone could be heartless enough to shoot an innocent soul barely more than a child. He looked up when Blossom knelt beside him. She told him that her mother was all right, but still groggy from the blow to her head. Hawk nodded, still holding the poor homely little girl in his arms. "What was her name, her real name?" he asked.

"Joanna," Blossom answered, tears streaming down her face. "She died trying to save me."

"It's my fault," Hawk said. "I shoulda stayed with you till I was sure you were all safe." He looked down at Joanna and made a pledge to himself that the three who did this horrible deed would answer to him and God. He looked up to find Sam standing next to him, his face still drained of color.

"I didn't have a gun," Sam said, apologizing for his lack of action. "I'll go get Fred Carver." It was not necessary, for the undertaker was already on his way, one of a small crowd running to the sound of the gunshots.

"We need to send for Dr. Taylor, too," Bertie said when she knelt beside the sheriff and found him to be alive. "Sheriff's hurt bad, but he ain't dead." One of the spectators volunteered and was off to fetch the doctor.

One who was badly hurt, although it was not a wound a doctor could heal, was the man called Hawk. He still held the lifeless body of the young girl known to the saloon crowd as JoJo. So small in the arms of the powerful scout, she looked even more like the child she resembled in life. He could not forgive himself for not having been there when she needed someone the most. Whether or not he might have been able to prevent her death was beside the point. He should have been there.

"I'll take her from you," a man behind him said.

"I'm Fred Carver. I'm the undertaker. I'll take good care of her."

Hawk handed the body over to Carver, who, with the assistance of a young boy, laid JoJo carefully on the bed of a hand-drawn cart. "I want her to have a first-class funeral," Hawk said, "with a decent coffin and a permanent headstone."

"I'll see to it," Sam Ingram volunteered. "I'll take care of the cost. Bertie can help with what to write on the headstone." He was not sure what the relationship was between the young woman and the rugged rifleman who had escorted the women from Great Falls, but he was obviously greatly concerned.

"I appreciate it," Hawk said to him. He started to leave, then hesitated to look at the body on the cart for a moment. He reached up, pulled the hawk feather from his hat, and placed it in her hand. He glanced up at the undertaker and said, "This belongs to her. Make sure she's holdin' it in her hand when you bury her." He waited for Carver to nod his understanding, then turned and walked away.

He did not get to the front of the saloon before running into Grover Bramble. "I heard the shootin'," Grover said. "I was at Sophie's, lookin' for you. I figured you'd forgot I needed to leave early today."

"I'm sorry, Grover," Hawk said. "I was on my way when I heard the shots, and things got busy after that."

"No matter," Grover said. "I saddled your horse and left him tied in front of my place with your packhorse." Hawk paid him for the shoeing and went to get his horses. He had one thing on his mind and that was to get on Dubose's trail. And then he remembered Sophie and the fact that he had left her very abruptly, promising to come back right away. It caused him to pause to decide. He cared enough to let her know that he had something very important that had to be taken care of, so he led his horses back up the street to the diner.

"Well, I was wondering if you were coming back," Sophie greeted him at the door. "I heard the shots and I thought somebody might have shot you," she joked. "I don't go running out every time some drunken cowhands start shooting at each other." It was then that she noticed the grave expression on his face. "Did those shots have anything to do with you?" she asked in all seriousness now.

"Yes, ma'am, they did," he answered. "And I have to go now, but I didn't wanna leave without comin' back to tell you I'm sorry I have to. I was lookin' forward to visitin' with you a little longer. But I ain't got no choice."

She hesitated, not sure how she should respond. "Well, maybe next time you're in town, you can stay longer," she finally managed.

"I hope so," he said, and left.

Strange man, she thought, *and just when I was thinking I wanted to know him better. I guess it's lucky I didn't get too involved with him.*

CHAPTER 5

Making no attempt to hide their trail, the three outlaws urged their weary horses on, their hooves pounding on the rocky stream bank, throwing small pebbles and sand flying in their wake. Finally, Hog threw up his hand, signaling a halt. When his two partners pulled up beside him, he warned, "We've got to rest these horses, else we're gonna be walkin'."

Red dismounted and started leading his horse along the bank. "Let's walk 'em for a little way, then let 'em rest."

"Good idea," Hog said, and stepped down. "How 'bout it, Dubose, can you walk? How bad are you hurt?"

"I can't walk," Dubose replied, angered by the suggestion. "I'm shot, damn it! I've got a damn bullet in my back."

Hog walked over and looked at the wound. "It's more in your shoulder than your back," he pronounced. "You oughta be able to walk."

"Well, I ain't," he said defiantly. "I need a damn doctor."

Hog had little patience for him. "Well, we ain't got one real handy right now." He paused, waiting for a response. When there was none, he shrugged and said, "Suit yourself. Maybe that fancy Palouse of yours don't need no rest." He and Red walked, leaving Dubose to follow, still on his horse.

"You reckon they'll come after us?" Red wondered aloud.

"Maybe . . . I don't know," Hog replied. "They wouldn't have had time to get up a posse, especially with the sheriff dead." He assumed Red's shot was fatal. "Maybe you shouldn'ta shot that sheriff. That'll get all over the territory. There'll be wanted posters out on that."

"Hell, he was fixin' to bring that shotgun to the party," Red replied. "If I hadn't shot him, he'd most likely be raisin' a posse right now." He paused a moment to relive the scene. "He was sure one surprised-lookin' son of a bitch when that .44 slug doubled him up," he said with a satisfied grin raising the tips of his mustache. "With him dead, it'll take a little more doin' to get enough men to ride after us."

"I hope you're right." Hog pushed on. "This stream oughta meet the river pretty soon and when we strike it, we better start thinkin' 'bout hidin' our trail. If they do get up a posse, that son of a bitch with the rifle will most likely ride with 'em. We're damn lucky he wasn't close enough to get a better shot."

A couple hundred yards farther and they came

to the Missouri River, still with no sounds of anyone chasing them, and they decided they'd best not push the horses any farther. Red and Hog helped Dubose off his horse and the three of them sat down to decide what they should do. "One thing for sure," Dubose said, grunting with pain with every other word. "It ain't gonna be healthy for us to stay around this territory, with Red shootin' that sheriff."

"And you shootin' that little girl," Red reminded him. He didn't like the insinuation that all their troubles were the result of his shooting the sheriff.

"Hell, nobody cares about that little whore," Dubose retorted, "but you shoot a lawman and they'll have the U.S. Marshals and everybody else out after us. We've got to make ourselves scarce." His frustration at having had Blossom in his hand only to have to let her go would come back to take full control of his mind. But for now, the risk of a posse after them was foremost in his thoughts.

"I'm thinkin' it'd be best if we split up, especially if they get up a posse in Helena right now," Hog said.

"Not till we get me to a doctor and take care of this damn bullet hole in my shoulder," Dubose was quick to protest.

"We can't take you to no damn doctor," Hog blurted. "There ain't no town near here big enough to have a doctor, but Helena, and I don't think it'd be the smartest thing we ever did to go back there right now."

Ignoring the sarcasm, Dubose insisted, "Great

Falls—there's a doctor there. We've gotta go back there, anyway, to get our horses and everything else. We can split up after we get there."

"Damn, I reckon you're right," Red said. In the confusion of running for their lives, he had forgotten that most everything the three of them owned was in Great Falls. When they had raced down the Mullan Road to overtake the three women, they didn't bother to take packhorses, supplies, or cooking utensils, other than a coffeepot and some coffee and bacon. Dubose had not been willing to waste any time, confident that they would overtake the women before they reached Helena. There was also the matter of a substantial sum of cash hidden under the floor in Dubose's shack. "Yep, we gotta get back up to your place to get our stuff."

That settled, they waited until sure their horses were ready to travel, since there had been no sign or sound of anyone on their trail. "Ain't nobody comin' after us," Red commented. "Might not be any need to split up."

"That's what you say," Hog was quick to differ. "There ain't been time yet. Before the week's out, they'll be telegraphin' all over the territory, on the lookout for three gunmen, one of 'em with a bullet hole in his shoulder. You and Dubose can stick together if you want, but I like my chances better by myself."

"I reckon you're right," Red said, changing his mind again. "If we split up in three different directions, they won't know which way to look for us." So that was settled. Even Dubose agreed, as long as they stuck by him until he was able to get medical treatment. When the horses were rested, they started out for Great Falls, with still no sign of anyone following them.

Although anxious to get after the three gunmen, Hawk knew it was in his best interest to prepare for a long chase. So he went to Chad Benton's general store to replenish his supplies and ammunition and loaded them on his packhorse. Satisfied that he was supplied for whatever occurred, he stepped up into the saddle and turned Rascal toward the north road out of town. He felt sure the three men he chased had no intentions of hiding their trail at first, their immediate concern being to put distance behind them. To be sure, he went to the stable and picked up the tracks they had left when they came out of the alley and struck the road. As he expected, he found them and there had been no effort to hide them. It was an easy job to pick out the tracks of three galloping horses amid the older tracks of the usual traffic.

After a few miles, he crossed a busy stream and realized after only fifteen or twenty yards past it that he no longer saw the tracks he had been following, so he turned around and went back to the stream. As before, there was no attempt to hide their trail, so he had no trouble seeing it along the rocky bank. There was plenty to indicate that Dubose and his partners were heading back toward Great Falls, but he could not discount the possibility that they were taking the trouble to lead a posse in that direction while they intended to actually head off in another.

He followed the stream out until it connected with the Missouri and he determined it the place where they had rested their horses. Although he had not ridden Rascal as hard as the men he chased had driven their horses, he decided to give the buckskin a little rest, anyway. He found the idle time disturbing because it gave him opportunity to think about the tragic death of an innocent girl. *And she was just a girl,* he thought, even though she tried to play the part of a woman. Pretty soon, he started blaming her death on himself again, no matter that no one else held him responsible. "This ain't doin' me no good," he told himself after a while. "I'd best get my mind back on my business." He reminded himself that, if they decided to double back to see if a posse was after them and discovered there was only one man, they might wait for him in ambush.

When he failed to see any sign that he might be catching up with them, he had to conclude that the man he had hit with that one rifle shot was not hurt bad enough to slow them down. He felt sure now that they were going back to Great Falls, the place they had started out from. So it became a matter of getting there as soon as he could and hoping to find them at the shack Blossom had described. He wished now that he had paid more attention to where it was located. He hadn't a notion at the time that he would be trying to find it one day. If he could rely on his memory of the times he had ridden up this way, it was a good two days' ride from Helena to Great Falls. In an effort to gain on those he pursued, he planned to push his horses a little beyond what he would usually ask for in a day's ride. The buckskin would respond with little trouble, but he was restricted by the packhorse. He could only speculate that the outlaws were pushing their horses just as hard, and they had no packhorses to contend with.

After two hard days' riding, the three gunmen reached Luther Trotter's trading post. They found Luther sitting in a rocking chair on the front porch, smoking his pipe. Seeing that Blossom was not with them, he said nothing, but he feared that they had found her and Dubose had done what he had threatened. It would be a shame if he had. Luther had always liked Blossom, more so when she was Blossom Brown instead of Blossom Dubose. When he realized that Dubose was wounded, he could hold his curiosity no longer. "Well, I see you boys got back all right. What happened to you, Dubose? Did you find your wife?"

"Yeah, I found her," was all Dubose would offer. "What about that doctor? Is he still up in that lumber camp on the Sun?"

"Far as I know," Luther replied. "He ain't doin' no real doctorin', you know."

"I know it," Dubose said, "but he oughta be able to dig a bullet outta my shoulder."

"I expect so," Luther allowed. "I reckon he's patched plenty of 'em up after some of them wild fights up at that camp. A bullet, huh? You ain't said how you got shot."

"No, I ain't," Dubose snapped.

Hog laughed. Seeing no reason not to tell Luther what happened, he said, "We went deer huntin' and the damn deer shot back at us. We got us a buck and a doe, though."

Red laughed with him, but Luther, assuming the doe he referred to was Blossom, was not amused. Knowing the reputation of the three outlaws, he was not prone to alienate them, plus the fact that he enjoyed the money they spent in his saloon. So there was nothing he could risk saying that would show his disgust for the three of them. "If you're gonna go see Doc Sumner, you'd best get up there before dark if you wanna catch him sober," he said. It was not shallow advice. Doc had been a surgeon in the Confederate army during the War between the States. He was sent to the Confederate prison at Andersonville, where he operated on enough Union prisoners to turn any man to drink.

"That sure is a fact," Hog said. "Ol' Doc's been known to take a drink or two. You might better ride on up the river. Red and me can meet you back here at Luther's. Then we can ride out to your shack when Doc's done with you."

"I need to have you and Red go with me," Dubose responded at once. "In case Doc gives me some kinda medicine that knocks me out or some-thin', I need you boys to make sure none of that bunch up there tries anything." In truth, he didn't trust either of them not to ride off with his horses and everything of his in that shack while he was

getting doctored. Of special concern was the cash
box under one of the floorboards that held a few
dollars over six hundred. "We'll split up after I'm
done with Doc Sumner." This brought forth another hearty chuckle from Hog.

"You ain't worried about one of us taking more
than his share of the flour and bacon, are you,
Dubose?" Hog japed.

"I just think we'd best stick together till I'm
fixed up and then we'll make sure everybody gets
a fair share of the goods," Dubose stated calmly,
but there was no mistaking the threat in his tone.

"I don't have no problem with that," Hog said.
"Red, you got any problem with that?"

"I don't give a damn, one way or the other, but
let's get started," Red informed them. "I don't
intend to hang around here waitin' for somebody
to come lookin' for us. I'm ready to see other parts
of the territory."

"Couldn'ta said it better, myself," Hog said.
"Let's get goin'."

For the second day in a row, Luther Trotter had
a visitor he wasn't expecting. Sitting at a table in
the saloon half of the big, open room, he was
having a cup of coffee with Juanita Lopez when
Hawk walked in. "Well, I'll be . . ." Luther started.
"I ain't seen you in a coon's age. Last time you was
in here you was with an Injun and you was lookin'
to trade some pelts."

"That's a fact," Hawk said. It had been more
than a year since he had been to Great Falls, and he

remembered that Luther had not been willing to give much for the deer hides he and Bloody Hand had brought in. "How's business, Luther?"

"Not worth spit," Luther replied. "This place ain't attracted all the people everybody said would be comin'. Any coffee left in that pot, Juanita? Maybe Mr. Hawk would like a cup. Have you et your breakfast, Hawk? Juanita baked a pan of biscuits this mornin', so you caught us on a good day."

"I've had breakfast," Hawk said, and sat down at the table. "But I don't usually pass up a fresh-baked biscuit with some coffee." He had chewed on some deer jerky that morning early, but had not wanted to waste the time to go to the trouble of making coffee. He figured he was already almost a half a day behind Dubose and his two friends because of the arrangements he had made to be sure JoJo was going to get a proper burial, plus the time it took to ready his packhorse for what might turn out to be a long search.

Juanita got up to fetch the coffeepot and a couple of biscuits for him. Returning to the table, she placed them before him, paused, and asked, "Are you a morning person?"

He knew what she meant. "No. Thank you just the same, but I'm in a hurry this mornin'." She shrugged indifferently and sat back down.

"What's your hurry?" Luther asked. "What brings you up this way?"

"I'm lookin' for three fellows that had to come this way last night," Hawk said.

Before he could finish, Luther blurted, "Zach Dubose, Hog Thacker, and Red Whitley."

"That's right," Hawk replied, surprised by Luther's willingness to supply the information.

"Did you put the bullet in Dubose's shoulder?" Luther asked. When Hawk nodded, Luther said, "Good, then there won't be no charge for the biscuits and coffee. Too bad you didn't place that shot a little farther to the right."

"I intended to, but he was a little too far and he was on a gallopin' horse at the time." He was disappointed to hear the wound was not more serious.

"They was in here last night, braggin' about shootin' a man and a woman down in Helena. I swear, I was afraid Blossom was gonna end up dead. She ought'n never to have married that mean son of a bitch in the first place. Bertie tried to tell her." He looked toward Juanita for confirmation. She verified it with a nod. "I swear that gal had a lot goin' for her," he said, shaking his head.

"Blossom ain't dead," Hawk said. "He shot the girl called JoJo, and the man one of 'em shot was the sheriff."

"JoJo!" Luther exclaimed. "What the hell did he shoot JoJo for? Poor little homely gal, she had a lotta spunk, but she never hurt nobody. Just pure mean, that son of a bitch." Not waiting to be asked then, he volunteered what information he had. "They stopped by here last night, wantin' to know if Doc Sumner was still up at that lumber camp on the Sun River. Dubose was bellyachin' about gettin' that bullet outta his shoulder. I told 'em Doc was still there, so they bought a bottle of my corn liquor and took off right away, and I was glad to see 'em go."

"Blossom said Dubose has a shack somewhere around here. You know where that is?"

"No, I'm sorry, I don't," Luther answered, and looked toward Juanita, whose dull expression had shown growing interest as the talk progressed. "You, Juanita?"

"She say Hound Creek one time," Juanita answered.

"You know where that is?" Hawk asked, and Luther told him where it broke off from the Missouri. "What about that lumber camp? They might still be there." Luther told him how far the camp was up the Sun River. "Much obliged," Hawk said. "I reckon I'd best get a move on. Thanks again for the coffee and biscuits." As was his custom, he paused long enough to compliment Juanita on the biscuits, then he headed toward his horses.

Luther walked out with him and watched while he climbed up into the saddle. "Take that trail up the river," he reminded him. "About two miles, you can't hardly miss it." Hawk nodded. "Good huntin'. Come back to see us."

"Will do," Hawk replied, touching a finger to his hat in salute. He turned Rascal toward the Sun River. It was not a river he was unfamiliar with. In fact, he had just come from Walking Owl's camp on the Sun, but that was some distance west of the river's confluence with the Missouri. He had gotten a good look at all three men the day before in Sophie's Diner and now he knew the names of all three. Thinking back to the diner, he was sure he could take a fairly accurate guess as to which one of the three was called Hog, the heavyset boisterous one. He figured the dark, brooding one to be Dubose, leaving the wiry one with red hair to be Red Whitley. Hog and Whitley had to pay for their part in it, but Dubose was the one who killed JoJo. Hawk had witnessed that shooting, and he was afraid he would never be able to rid his mind of that picture.

As Luther had said, the sawmill was not hard to find. Brought up the Missouri by steamboat by a man named Samuel Guzman, it consisted of a single circular blade, run by a steam engine. It was set up under a large shed with two logging wagons beside it. Next to the shed, Hawk saw a small shack that he guessed was the operator's office. There were several men guiding logs into the blade and the only other structures were half a dozen tents set up close to the river. These were evidently the homes of the workers. The question now was where to find Doc Sumner, and Hawk figured someone at the mill should know. So he turned Rascal toward the building next to the mill.

His arrival caught the interest of the men sawing lumber, and work came to a stop when they all paused to eyeball the stranger riding the buckskin. Pretty soon a man came to the door of the office, no doubt to see the cause of the interruption in the saw's noise. Seeing Hawk, he stepped outside to meet him. "How do?" Guzman greeted him and received a nod in return. "You interested in buying lumber, or are you looking for work?" Guzman asked.

"Neither one, I reckon," Hawk replied. "I was hopin' you could tell me where I might find Doc Sumner."

"Well, I guess I can help you there," Guzman said. He turned and pointed up the river. "Last tent on this side of the river." For a few minutes he studied the broad-shouldered man wearing a deerskin shirt, until Hawk started to turn his horse away. "Are you a lawman?"

"Nope."

"Three fellows came by here last night looking for Doc Sumner. One of 'em looked like he mighta been shot. They friends of yours?"

"Nope."

"You know Doc doesn't really practice medicine anymore. Maybe you knew that," Guzman said.

"Yep. Much obliged." A gentle touch of his heels sent the buckskin off at a lope past the row of tents.

"He's a real talker, ain't he, Mr. Guzman?" the man standing by the steam engine commented.

"A regular chatterbox," Guzman replied. "Those three who came by here last night looked like they'd murder their mother to steal her broach, but that one looks like he didn't have a mother— looks like somebody chiseled him outta stone." It was an understandable observation, because JoJo's senseless killing had drained the gentleness and humor out of John Hawk.

He made special note of the horses grazing near the water and those tied close to some of the tents he passed, looking for a Palouse, but there was none. When he came to the last tent in the row, he found a man seated on a stool in front of it. He was dressed only in his underwear and he was staring at an empty whiskey bottle as if seeing an illusion. Hawk reined Rascal to a stop and dismounted, seemingly unnoticed by the man on the stool. "Are you Dr. Sumner?" Hawk asked.

"Does that bottle look empty to you?" Doc asked, ignoring Hawk's question.

"I reckon so," Hawk replied.

"Then, I guess I drank the whole damn bottle last night," he said. "Damn, I wish I could remember. What about you, my good man, did you bring any whiskey with you? A little hair of the dog, maybe?"

"No, sir, I'm afraid I ain't got a drop of whiskey with me," Hawk said.

"Damn," Sumner swore. "Those are the saddest words a drinking man can hear."

"Are you Dr. Sumner?" Hawk repeated.

Sumner looked at him as if discovering him for the first time. "You're the second time I've been asked that this morning. Dr. Samuel H. Sumner, at your service," he announced grandly, then released a heavy sigh. "What is it this time, young man? Gunshot? A boil on your ass? Rotten foot?"

"I don't need any doctorin'," Hawk said.

Before he could continue, Sumner interrupted. "Then what the hell did you come to the doctor for?"

"I'm lookin' for three men that came to see you last night. One of 'em had a gunshot wound."

"Left shoulder," Doc said at once, remembering then. He looked at the empty bottle in his hand. "Brought me a bottle of whiskey—good thing, 'cause I ain't much good without it. What is it you wanted?"

"I'm lookin' for 'em." Hawk could see that he was wasting his time with the doctor, who was obviously traveling a drunkard's path between the real world and the world that came in a bottle. He asked, anyway, "I'm thinkin' maybe you heard them say where they were headed after they left here last night."

"Can't say as I did," Sumner said. "But I removed that bullet and applied a bandage—did a right neat job." He got up from his stool then, still unsteady on his feet. "Now, if there's nothing more I can do for you, I think I'd best head to yonder woods."

"Much obliged," Hawk said, knowing he had wasted his time in coming here, but there had been the possibility that Dubose's wound had been bad enough to have kept him there overnight. He turned away and went back to his horse while Doc Sumner hurried to reach a stand of pines a few dozen yards behind his tent. He heard him curse in disgust before he reached the trees. *Reckon he didn't make it,* Hawk thought. *Well, at least I know one place where Dubose ain't. That doesn't leave but about a hundred places where he might be.* He headed for Hound Creek on the chance that Juanita had heard correctly when Blossom mentioned the location of Dubose's shack.

"It's a damn good thing you boys listened to me when I said we needed to keep some ready cash

hid, in case we needed some in a hurry, right?"
Dubose gloated, as they gathered around the loos-
ened floorboard to count the hidden stash. He
pointed his finger at Hog. "And you didn't wanna
do it. Now, who's the smart one?"

"Hell, I never said it wasn't a good idea," Hog insisted. "What I wasn't wild about was lettin' you
keep it. You messin' around with that whore at
Trotter's, I was afraid you and her was gonna take
a notion to take that money and run." He favored
Dubose with a sly grin. "And then me and Red
woulda had to track you down and take it outta
your hide."

"It's a good thing you didn't tell that whore you
had our money under the floor," Red commented,
"or she'da run off a long time ago. How much did
we put under there? She mighta found out about
it and helped herself to a little travelin' money."

"It's all here," Dubose said, and divided it into
three equal piles. "Two hundred dollars each with
one dollar left over and we can odd man out to see
who gets the extra dollar. I reckon we'd best get
our possibles together and cut outta here right
now. I know I ain't gonna hang around here. Blossom's most likely already told a posse where this
shack is, so I'm headin' down toward the Yellowstone. Then I'll decide where I'm goin' from there.
I ain't made up my mind yet."

"Me, neither," Red said. "How 'bout me ridin'
down there with you and we'll split up down there?"

Dubose shrugged. "All right with me."

"Might as well all of us ride down there together,"

Hog said. "I ain't decided where I'm headin', either, and we might be better off, the three of us together, in case there is a posse already comin' after us."

"Hog's right," Dubose decided. "They might get up a posse right away, but the three of us oughta stop a bunch of farmers and store clerks if they get on our trail. They ain't gonna want to get too far from home, anyway. I ain't worried about a posse. I just think it's time to get the hell outta here before they send some U.S. Marshals over here lookin' for us for killin' that sheriff."

"What was the name of the feller that owns that hog ranch on the Yellowstone where we holed up after hittin' that bank in Bozeman—where you got that fancy Palouse horse you're ridin'?" Hog asked. "Where that little yellow-headed gal with the buck-teeth worked. What was that feller's name?"

"Oscar Jacobs," Red answered when Dubose had to pause to try to recall. "Big Timber Hog Ranch," he said

"Right," Hog said. "That's the place. Why don't we ride down there? Hell, it was damn lucky for us before."

"Hell, that's about a four-day ride from here," Dubose said. He was recalling the card game where he won the Palouse gelding from a herder from Texas who was too drunk to know he was being dealt from the bottom of the deck. When he finally realized it, he made the mistake of calling Dubose out and wound up lying dead in the middle of the street.

Hog laughed. "I thought that was what we was

wantin' to do, to get the hell away from here, the farther the better. I know I ain't gonna stop at four days. I'm damn tired of this part of the territory. I'm ready to get back to where there's some people and somethin' goin' on. We came up here after robbin' that bank, but I expect they've give up lookin' for us back down that way by now."

"Lizzie Malone!" Red startled them. "That was her name." When they both responded with blank expressions, he said, "The bucktoothed gal at the Big Timber."

"Right . . ." Dubose responded, drawing the word out while he recalled. "Lizzie Malone. For a little woman, she was some kinda spunky."

"Look at him, Red," Hog japed. "He's really pining away for his wife, ain't he?"

Red laughed. "Yeah. About another day and he'll be askin', *What was the name of that woman I married?* Won't he?"

"You go to hell," Dubose said, "both of you. I ain't through with that woman till I fix her good for what she done."

CHAPTER 6

Trotter's directions were accurate—Hawk found
Hound Creek with no trouble. The task now was to
find Dubose's shack. There were several cabins
near the creek's confluence with the river, none of
which attracted Hawk's interest. They were obviously homes built by settlers, as witnessed by the
plowed fields and the presence of small children
playing near the creek. The place Hawk looked for
would stand alone, a good distance from any other
structures, no doubt tucked into the trees to avoid
being conspicuous. It was a good mile and a half
before he came to a bend in the creek with a dense
growth of trees on both sides. Instinct prompted
him to be cautious in approaching the bend, for it
was not possible to tell if there was a dwelling there
or not. So he turned Rascal away from the bank
with the intention of circling around the trees to
approach the bend using them for cover.

It was well hidden, for he didn't see it until he
had ridden into the trees. When he did, he immediately pulled his rifle and dismounted. Tying the

horses on a laurel bush, he made his way from
there on foot until reaching a point behind a large
cottonwood that allowed him an unrestricted view
of a small shack built of logs and the tiny clearing
it occupied. He waited there for a few minutes to
be sure. There were no animals about and no sign
of life from the cabin, so he decided it was empty.
He walked out from behind the tree and walked directly to the door, noticing as he walked the many
hoofprints close about the shack. They were recent
prints, enough to have been left by maybe half a
dozen horses, which would account for three men
with a packhorse each. He had found Dubose's
shack, there was no doubt about that, and he and
his two partners had already gone.

The door was closed, but there was no lock on
the chain holding it so. Bowing his head to keep
from bumping it, he stepped inside and stood for
a few moments looking around. He couldn't help
wondering how Blossom could have thought she
might be happy under such rustic conditions. His
attention was attracted to the hole in the middle of
the floor with the loose boards lying beside it. It
was a definite message, along with no lock on the
door, that the occupants were not coming back.
Further evidence were the few empty cartridge
boxes, discarded carelessly about. *No need to waste
any more time here*, he thought, and turned and went
out the door.

Now it had turned into a job of tracking, a job
he was damn good at, and the main reason he was
always assured of employment by the army. He
looked around the small yard briefly before going

back for his horses, hoping to find something unusual in one or more of the hoofprints. It always helped if there was a nick or mark of some sort to identify a horse in the event its tracks became mixed with others. It was of no importance at this point in the chase, but it might be later on if they joined with others on a common road. He found one print after only a few minutes that showed a V-shaped notch in the shoe that looked to have been done by a file. "That'll do," he announced, then knelt down to examine droppings that were fresh enough to have been left that morning. They didn't tell him exactly how much lead the outlaws had on him, maybe half a day, maybe more, he was not really sure.

Leading his horses, he walked along the creek until the many tracks came together to form a definite trail away from the shack. When he was certain this was his trail, he stood looking in the direction it was leading, a path across a wide, rolling prairie that would appear to be heading toward Judith Gap. It made sense to him because it was a direction that would take them toward the Yellowstone River, a journey of at least four days, with nothing in between here and there. He climbed up into the saddle and gave the buckskin a pat on the neck. "Let's get started, Rascal."

The trail left by six horses was not difficult to follow, for they were the only tracks he saw across the expanse of rolling terrain before him. Judging by droppings left occasionally by their horses, he couldn't see that he was closing any of the distance between the three and himself. There had been no rain for some time, so water opportunities, other than a couple of almost-dry streams, were rare. It had been quite a while since he had traveled this plain, but he remembered that Wolf Creek was about a day's ride from Great Falls. He had gotten a late start because of the time lost on Doc Sumner, but he still planned to make Wolf Creek in one day and maybe catch the outlaws in camp. It would be a long day for his horses, but he could give them a rest and good water there.

It was already after dark when he caught sight of the trees outlining the curves of the creek as it cut through the prairie. The three gunmen were not there, but near the bank of the creek, he found the ashes of their fire. They had stopped there, but evidently decided to push on, most likely planning to camp for the night at the Judith River. That was only about twenty miles farther, but it might as well be a thousand, for he couldn't push his weary horses any farther on this night. Dubose and his two friends were pushing their horses as hard as he was pushing his, running as if someone was chasing them. Having to camp here overnight resulted in putting him a full day behind. He thought about leaving Rascal's saddle on him and riding through the night, but scolded himself right away. The big buckskin had never failed him. He could not in good conscience run him to death. *Besides,* he told himself, *I'd have to leave my packhorse behind.* Frustrated, he pulled the saddle off the horse and left him to graze while he pulled out his coffeepot and a half-dozen slices of sowbelly. He went to his bedroll determined to rise before sunrise the next morning.

True to his intentions, he was awake and up before first light the next day, planning to rest the horses and eat breakfast by the Judith, twenty miles distant. With still no rain, he had an easy trail to follow east of the Little Belt Mountains, rising off to his right. When he reached the Judith, that trail led him straight to their campsite of the night before. From there, the trail followed the Judith for six or seven miles before leaving it to head straight south toward Judith Gap.

He made camp that night beside the Musselshell River at a point where two creeks formed a Y before joining the river. It was a camping spot used by Sioux and Crow hunting parties alike and one that he had camped at before while scouting for a cavalry patrol looking for one of those Sioux parties. He remembered the names of the creeks, Jawbone Creek and Antelope Creek, but he couldn't recall now which was which. As he built his fire on the ashes of the one the gunmen had built, he recalled another occasion when he had ridden with a cavalry patrol a day south of there on the Yellowstone. That patrol had nothing to do with Indians. It was a search for three white men who had robbed the bank in Bozeman. They never caught the robbers, even though Hawk had led the patrol right up to the door of a hangout for any manner of riffraff. It was known by all the soldiers as the Big Timber Hog Ranch, but it was not a place where soldiers were welcome. They definitely catered to those on the wrong side of the law. Rather than one building, the Hog Ranch was a compound of four cabins surrounding the main saloon, built like a fort, but with no wall around it. Lieutenant Meade had commanded that patrol and he decided Hawk had led them off on the wrong trail. Hawk was of the opinion at the time, and still was today, that Meade was concerned with breaking into a civilian business—that plus having been more than twenty days in the field with provisions for fifteen. He simply wanted to go home, as did his soldiers. Meade ordered the search but the three outlaws were not found. Hawk remembered telling him he was a damn fool for giving up the search. Meade never assigned him as a scout on patrols he commanded after that, which was fine with Hawk. As he sat there on this night some two years later, he tried to recall the name of the man who owned the complex. "Jacobs," he recalled, sure of it then. "Oscar Jacobs, that was the man's name." Bringing all that back to mind caused him to think of something that might be no more than coincidence. But if these three he was tracking now continued in the same direction, they might strike the Yellowstone near the same saloon where Lieutenant Meade gave up the police action—where the Boulder River joined the Yellowstone. "Helluva coincidence," he allowed. The more he thought about it, the more interesting it became. *Three men robbed that bank,* he thought, *and now I'm trailing three men again. And so far, it looks like they're heading to the same place I lost them last time.* "Helluva coincidence," he repeated.

He would know for sure if that's all it was by that time tomorrow because it was one day's ride to that hog ranch.

Unaware of the avenging scout, still one day behind them, the three men he trailed were sitting down to a hot meal, having arrived just thirty minutes before. Oscar Jacobs sat down to join them. "It's been a long time since you boys have showed up here," Oscar said. "I'd damn near forgot about you, figured you'd done got yourselves hung, or you were doin' time somewhere." He paused to signal his cook. "Pearl, bring me a cup of coffee when you come back from the kitchen."

"Got you a new cook since we was here last," Dubose commented.

"I reckon that's right," Oscar said. "I expect old Myra Beatty was doin' the cookin' last time you were here. Myra died, so I had to get me another cook. And this one's a good one. You tell me, how's that stew?"

"Just barely fit to eat," Hog replied with a wide grin on his face. "I don't expect I'll want more'n another plate or two."

Oscar laughed with him. "I'm gonna have to charge you double. How long you boys gonna be here? I've got a room ain't nobody in right now, make you a good rate on it."

"Not long," Dubose answered. "At least, I ain't. Red and Hog can decide for themselves."

That was good news to Oscar because he was at that moment recalling the last time the three of them had come to visit. A full cavalry patrol had followed, looking for them. Oscar's people had managed to hide the three of them, but only because the officer in command of the patrol didn't seem to want to thoroughly search the compound. "Who's chasin' you this time?" Oscar asked.

"Hell, what makes you think anybody is?" Dubose answered. "We're just relocatin' ourselves and as long as we were passin' this close, we thought you'd like our business. Like I said, I'll be movin' on in the mornin'."

"You boys splittin' up?" Oscar asked, visibly surprised. He nodded at Pearl when she set a cup of coffee before him. "You three have been runnin' together for a long time, ain't you?"

"That's a fact," Dubose replied. "And I expect we'll get back together again sometime. We just think it's a good idea to split up for a while."

Oscar understood at once. "You've got the law on your tail again. I swear, Dubose, the last time you boys were here I had soldiers turnin' the place upside down lookin' for you. Scared the hell outta my whores and sent more'n a few of my customers runnin'."

"Now, hold on, Oscar," Dubose said. "I told you, ain't nobody chasin' us, and for damn sure there ain't no soldiers after us. We're just taking precautions in case there *was* somebody after us, just bein' smart, that's all. Besides, that one time you're talkin' about, nobody found us, so you didn't get in any trouble with the army. And accordin' to my memory, I recollect that you got a mighty generous bonus for hidin' us."

Oscar calmed down a little at that. "I have to be a little more careful these days," he said. "There are so many more settlers movin' into this section of the Yellowstone that the army is even more particular about businesses like mine. And there's too many people that know about this place, more'n when you were here before."

"Well, you done a good job hidin' us that one time," Hog said. "That's why we came back this time, instead of takin' our business somewhere else. So we'll take that room tonight." He flashed Oscar a wide grin. "You still got that hole under the floor in your smokehouse?"

"Yeah," Oscar replied. "It's still there and we've had to use it a time or two."

The thought of it made Hog laugh. "Soldiers lookin' under every bed and behind every door, and we were settin' there right under their feet."

"It was mighty damn crowded, though, as I recollect," Dubose commented, "especially with you takin' up half the room."

"Is Lizzie Malone still workin' for ya?" Red asked. "If she is, I might wanna stay a couple more days. How 'bout you, Hog?"

"Reckon not," Hog replied. "I'm gonna head out in the mornin', too. I'm thinkin' I ain't seen my wife in a couple of years, not since we hit that bank. I think I'll see how she's doin'."

"Lizzie's still here," Oscar said. "She had a baby about five months ago." He chuckled. "Might be yours, only I don't reckon so, 'cause it ain't got red hair, and you've been gone longer'n that. She ain't been back but a month or two. She's livin' in the house with the red door, her and her young'un. She's a little bigger'n when you saw her."

"She wasn't much bigger'n a hickory switch last time I saw her," Red recalled. "Can she still eat corn on the cob through a picket fence?"

Oscar laughed. "Yeah, she's still got all her teeth, at least all her front teeth."

"Well, I'll stay with you for a day or two more," Red decided. He looked at Hog, still stuffing stew in his mouth as fast as he could. "I didn't know you was married. You ain't never said anythin' about havin' a wife."

"I ain't never said nothin' about a lot of things," he stated, and returned his attention to the almost-empty plate. There was a given amount of safety when riding with two other gunmen, but he had been thinking about their little partnership and the fact that they were forced to run again. They used to move around unnoticed, but now that they had killed a lawman, he feared they would begin to catch the interest of the federal marshals. That would mean there would be increased efforts to run them to ground. And if that happened, he liked his chances better apart from the other two. He wasn't sure if it would be of help to him if he did get caught, but he was hoping his ace in the hole was the fact that he didn't kill anyone in Helena. Red shot the sheriff and Dubose shot the girl, JoJo. It had been almost two years since he had seen his wife. Now might be a good time to go back to see how she was doing, that is, if she was still living in that humble little cabin on Stinking Creek outside Coulson. There wasn't much chance anybody would be looking for him there.

"Well, boys," Oscar announced, "sounds to me like you've been doin' some hard ridin' and you could use some relaxation. And you've sure as hell come to the right place for that. I got four houses out behind the saloon with three ladies in two of 'em, two ladies in one of 'em, and just one lady in the other one. That's the cabin with the red door, that's where Lizzie stays." He winked at Red. "Just don't get too rambunctious, or you'll get the baby to cryin', and that young'un can howl like a coyote." Turning to the others, he said, "Dubose, you and Hog can take a chance on the other cabins. Take a look. If you don't see nothin' that appeals to you, try one of the other cabins. Just like it was before, you pay your money, you get one ride. If you want all night, she'll tell you the price, 'cause it's a different price for different ones. I know I don't need to tell you boys this, but I've got a man that sees the ladies don't get treated too rough. That's him over there at the end of the bar." He nodded toward a mountain of a man, leaning against the bar, casually nursing a glass of beer. "His name's Ned, and he can throw a horse. So enjoy your stay, the saloon stays open all night."

"We plan to," Hog said while eyeing Ned. He had already speculated on the brawny, bull-necked giant stoically watching the crowd in the barroom. "Will he come runnin' if any of the women get rough on us?"

Oscar enjoyed a chuckle at that. "Yep, it's been known to happen."

* * *

Despite doing most of the talking the night before, Hog was the only one of the three who slept in the room they rented. Content with the huge supper and a few drinks of whiskey afterward, he walked up the stairs to the room, planning to get a good night's sleep, so he would be ready to get started early. The kitchen was open early, so he was among the few early risers to the breakfast table the next morning. He had almost finished when he saw Red walk in the door. "Red!" he called out when Red didn't appear to notice him.

"You already et?" he asked Hog when he came over to the table.

"Yeah, I'm fixin' to get on my way. It's a two-day ride to Coulson from here."

"Have you seen Dubose this mornin'?" Red asked. When Hog said he hadn't, he seemed surprised. "Was you fixin' to ride off without sayin' squat to anybody?"

"Tell you the truth, I didn't think I'd see either one of you this early, since neither one of you made it back to the room last night. And like I said, Coulson's a two-day ride. I didn't wanna get started too late." Eager to change the subject, he asked, "Did you tie up with that little bucktoothed gal?"

"All night long," Red replied with a satisfied grin. "And I aim to go back this mornin', but I got to have some grub first. That little gal can sure drain a man's strength."

Hog laughed. "Well, damned if you ain't a regular stud horse, all right."

"Sounds like it, don't it?" Red replied, this time with a grin more sheepish than satisfied. "For a fact, I went to sleep after the first ride and I wouldn'ta woke up for the second one if that baby hadn't set in to bawlin'. I ain't complainin', though, I paid her for all night, so that young'un helped me get my money's worth. I swear, I'd marry that woman if she was to ask me."

"You gonna stay here a spell?" Hog asked.

"For a while, I reckon, at least till Lizzie don't look so good to me anymore." He laughed, but then turned serious. "Tell you the truth, I ain't so sure about splittin' up like I was. Right offhand, I don't know where I'd wanna go."

"It's the smart thing to do," Hog tried to reassure him. "Once you shoot a lawman, you know damn well there's gonna be lawmen lookin' for you. And right now, they'll be lookin' for three men travelin' together. It's best we scatter till they've had a chance to give up on us, like they did after that bank holdup. Then maybe we can join up again."

"I reckon you're right," Red allowed. "Seen Dubose yet?" he asked, forgetting that he had already asked.

"Nope, but I expect he'll be draggin' in here before long—when that whore kicks him out, or asks for more money. But I'm about ready to make some tracks, so tell him I'll see him sometime." He got up from the table. "So long, Red." He turned and walked toward the door, eager to go before Red had a chance to ask to go with him to Coulson. Until that trouble in Helena cooled off, he preferred not to be caught riding with the man who shot the lawman.

It was late afternoon when Hawk rode through an open gate and followed a trail up to the large building in the center of a complex that included four small houses around it. Hawk remembered it from the time he had led a cavalry patrol up to the front door. There was no gate at that time, but everything else seemed as he remembered it. The nerve center of the complex was the saloon, so he guided Rascal up to a crowded hitching rail and dismounted, pulling his rifle as he did. He stood there for a few moments, looking over his saddle at the corral next to a barn beyond the houses, searching for a Palouse among the horses penned up there. There was no sign of the horse, and he at once feared he was too late, they had come and gone. That is, if they had come there in the first place. The obvious trail he had followed since leaving Hound Creek had soon disappeared when he came to an often-used freight wagon track that ran beside the river. He spent some time looking for the print with a notch filed in the shoe, but with no luck. Running on a hunch, anyway, he had come straight to the Hog Ranch. *If I'm dead wrong,* he thought, *at least I'll have a drink.*

"What'll it be, mister?" the bartender asked when Hawk stepped up to the bar. Hawk ordered a shot of whiskey and put his money on the bar. "First time in the Big Timber?" the bartender asked as he produced a glass and poured.

"I was in before, a while back," Hawk said while he scanned the room from one side of the large room to the other.

"Our policy musta been different when you were here back then," the bartender said. "Lotta things have changed, so I reckon you didn't know we don't allow no firearms inside the saloon or the dining room."

"No, I didn't know that," Hawk said as he continued scanning the faces at the tables, looking for any of the men he had seen in Sophie's Diner. "I'll leave 'em outside next time." He brought his attention back to the bartender. "I'm lookin' for some friends of mine—said they were gonna be here. Maybe you've seen 'em—Zach Dubose, Hog Thacker, and Red Whitley?"

The bartender immediately became cautious. "A lot of men come in here. I don't ask any of them their names. I didn't ask you your name. That just ain't anybody's business in the Big Timber Saloon." He paused for a few moments before asking, "Are you a lawman?"

"Nope," Hawk replied. When he did, he noticed the bartender's nod toward the kitchen door. In a few moments more, he was joined by a huge man with a sullen grin on his wide face.

"This gentleman was unaware of our policy of no guns, Ned. Maybe you can help him."

"Is that a fact?" Ned asked Hawk. Standing half a head taller and wide as the piano over against the wall, he leered down at Hawk. "I'll take that Winchester and the Colt and put it somewhere safe for you, then you can have 'em back when you're

ready to go." Accustomed to relying on his obvious
powers of intimidation, he continued to grin.

"Thanks just the same," Hawk replied, "but I
might be needin' 'em before I'm ready to go."

Ned, outwardly surprised by Hawk's apparent
disregard for his imposing physical image, was
stumped for a response at first. But after a moment,
he regained his sense of authority. "Look here,
mister, you ain't been in here long enough to get
drunk, so I reckon you're just downright dumb.
When I say I'll take your weapons, that ain't no suggestion, so if you don't want me to break your back
for you, you'd best hand 'em over right now."

Hawk looked the menacing hulk over for a
moment before replying. "All right, Ned, I understand that you've got your job and I respect that.
But I've got a job to do, too, and I've got a hunch
I'm liable to need my weapons to get it done. If the
men I'm lookin' for ain't here, then I'm sure not
gonna bother anybody else. And that's fair enough,
ain't it?"

Still scarcely believing the stranger's attitude,
Ned replied, "All right, you crazy son of a bitch,
you can't say I ain't warned you." He braced himself as if getting ready to attack.

"Hold on a minute, Ned, there ain't no need for
you and me to get into a tussle over this. These
men I'm lookin' for are outlaws and murderers.
They shot a young girl and the sheriff in Helena.
You oughta be helpin' me find 'em, if they're here."

Confused by Hawk's calm attitude, Ned could
only fall back on what he considered his responsibility, and that was to throw troublemakers out.

With no further warning, he suddenly lunged, intending to ram his shoulder through Hawk's midsection. His mistake was in underestimating Hawk's quick, animallike reflexes, for Hawk immediately sent him reeling with a sharp kick to the brute's knee while ducking to avoid his bull rush. Before Ned had time to recover, he went crashing headfirst into the edge of the bar. Stunned, he was knocked backward to land on his behind. Like a great cat, Hawk stood ready, watching for his prey's next move, poised to deliver the deciding blow with the butt of his rifle. He glanced at the bartender briefly to make sure there was no threat from him. There was none, for the bartender was as stunned as Ned, after seeing what he had previously thought unlikely. Hawk turned his attention back to Ned, who struggled as if trying to get up, before sinking back against the bar, unable to clear his head. Hawk again looked at the bartender and calmly said, "Now, that was damn unnecessary." He turned and walked back out the door.

Outside, he looked around him. His intention now was to search the four houses. He still saw no sign of the Palouse, but he didn't discount the possibility that there might be more horses grazing in the pasture behind the barn. He started with the closest house to the saloon and wasted no time in his search, aware there would be some efforts to intercept him. Not bothering to knock, he walked in the door to surprise two women sitting in a small parlor. "Don't mind me, ladies," he said, and went through another door that led to a couple of bedrooms, one with an open door, one with the door

closed. He opened the closed door to startle a
couple in bed. One glance at the confused man
and he knew he was not one of the men he sought.
"Pardon the intrusion," he said, and closed the
door again. Out in the short hallway, he saw a back
door, so he left the cabin through that door.

Knowing time was his enemy, he hurried toward
the back door of the next cabin. He could not be
sure how far he could get before some form of re-
taliation was set in motion against him. He was
counting on Ned being the total protection for the
hog ranch, but he could not be sure of it. His results at the second house were like those at the
first, with no sight of any of the men he chased.
Cabin number three had no customers, which oc-
casioned him to be offered an invitation to have
a drink with the two women there. He politely
declined, saying he was currently occupied with
a pressing endeavor, otherwise, he might have
accepted.

He was rapidly becoming discouraged after leaving the two women and it didn't help matters when
he could see the disruption he had left behind
him. Women and customers were outside in the
yard trying to find out what was going on. It was becoming apparent to him that he had been wrong
in thinking the three had come here. Standing in
front of the last possibility, he stared at the door,
painted a bright red, thinking it likely another
empty cabin. He held the Winchester ready to fire
quickly and walked in the door. There was no one
in the small parlor, and he paused when he thought

he heard someone crying. He stepped into the hallway to find the identical two-bedroom arrangement like the other cabins, and both doors were open.

With his rifle ready, he cautiously moved up beside the first door to peek inside. The room was empty except for a crib with a baby sleeping inside. He moved along the wall to the second door and he could hear the soft sounds of crying he had heard in the parlor. Making a sudden move inside the door, prepared to shoot, he was surprised to find a woman alone, sitting on the side of the bed. After a closer look, he saw the start of a fresh bruise on the side of her face, and her nose was swollen. When he saw her obvious suffering, he forgot for the moment his disappointment at finding none of the three he hunted in the complex. "Are you all right? It looks like you got some rough treatment."

"That redheaded bastard," she fumed. "He got mad when my baby cried again and took it out on me. He said he was gonna kill my baby."

Her statement immediately triggered his reactions. "You say, redheaded? Did he have red hair?"

His questions seemed beside the point to her, but she answered. "Yes, he's got red hair."

"What was his name?" Hawk asked.

She looked at him as if he might be simpleminded. "Red," she answered. "At least, that's what they called him."

"Was his name Red Whitley?"

"I think so," she said. "Yeah, that's the bastard's

name." She looked up at Hawk and asked, "Are you a lawman?" Hawk said he was not, so she continued. "He went out the window when he heard you come in the parlor. He started acting funny before that and he looked out the front window and saw people standing around the other houses. He thought the law was after him, so when he heard you come in the door, he went out the window. And he didn't pay me. He owes me for all night and he didn't pay me."

Hawk went at once to the window. There was no one in sight between the house and the barn. He was about to go out the window when a shot was fired and the slug ripped a chunk of wood from the side of the window frame, forcing him to duck back into the room. Another shot sent a bullet whistling through the open window to impact the wall opposite. "Get down on the floor!" he ordered Lizzie, and ran to the front door.

Outside, he circled around the house to a back corner. He was not sure where the shots had come from, so he was hoping the shooter would throw another one at the back window. A few seconds later, it came, but Hawk was still not sure where it had come from. His guess would have been the barn, but it didn't seem like it came from there. The only other possibility was a smokehouse beside the barn. He waited for another shot to confirm it, but none came. When, after a long minute with still no more shots, he feared Whitley must be on the run. With thoughts of losing him after coming so close, Hawk left the corner of the house and ran to the barn, thinking he might be in time to stop Whitley from galloping out the back.

Even in his haste to keep Whitley from escaping, he deemed it not worth the risk to go charging in the open door of the barn. So he stopped short of the opening and inched his way slowly along the wide door, listening for something that might tell him what lay in wait for him. There was no sound. He had to make a move, so he got flat on the ground, rolled over a couple of times, and came to a firing position on his stomach, clear of the barn door. There was no one in the barn, and there was no back door. Stumped, he suddenly thought to look up at the hayloft. *Too late*, he thought. *If he was hiding in the hayloft, I'd be dead right now.* He was left standing there, outsmarted, or outmaneuvered, he didn't know which. There was no place else the shots could have come from. He went back outside the barn and looked behind it at the wide pasture. His gaze settled on the smokehouse. It didn't seem likely, but it was the only place left, so he went to check it.

A small log structure, maybe twelve feet square, the smokehouse had no windows and only one door. He went to the door and found it had no lock on it, which struck him as unusual. Maybe there was no meat in it, he thought. He stood aside and suddenly threw the door open wide, waiting a moment for any shots that might come through it. But there was no one in the smokehouse. He went inside and looked around the dark interior. There were a couple of hams hanging there, but otherwise it was empty, so he turned about and started out, but stopped after taking a few steps. He backed up a couple of steps, then started forward again to see if he felt it again. He was sure then. He knelt down and felt around in the dirt that served as a floor until he found it, a slight ridge in the earthen floor that hid a trapdoor. It had evidently not seated itself firmly in place, due, no doubt, to a hasty entrance.

Hawk got to his feet and backed away from the trapdoor. With his rifle aimed at it, he spoke out. "All right, Red, you can come outta that rat hole now. You've run as far as you're gonna run."

There was a long silence before he heard the muffled response from inside the hole. "Who the hell are you?"

"Somebody who saw you shoot Sheriff Porter Willis down in Helena," Hawk answered.

"You a lawman?" Red called back.

"Nope. But if you come on outta there peaceful-like, I won't shoot. I'll take you over to Bozeman and turn you over to the army at Fort Ellis."

"So I can hang for killin' that son of a bitch? That don't seem like a good bargain for me. If you ain't a lawman, why don't you just mind your own business and get the hell away from here?"

"You might not hang," Hawk said. "Sheriff Willis ain't dead, so you got a chance to live if you come on out. I ride scout for Major Brisbin. He'll take my word for it, if I tell him Willis ain't dead."

"Is that so?" Red replied sarcastically. "You tryin' to take me for a fool? He's dead, all right. I shot him right in the gut. I'll tell you what, why don't you come down here and get me?"

This wasn't going well, as far as Hawk was concerned. He meant what he said when he offered to take Red to Bozeman, but he glanced over his shoulder at the small crowd of people that had gathered about fifty yards away in front of the saloon. "I could just starve you outta that hole. I doubt you took any grub in there when you jumped in, but I ain't got the time to fool with you that long. So I reckon I'll just set this smokehouse on fire and burn it down on top of you. You oughta roast just fine, just like a ham, baked in the oven."

Red took some time to think about that, but he still was not of a notion to surrender without a chance to save his life. "All right," he finally said. "I'll come out, but you'll have to help me. That damn door's so heavy I can't lift it by myself, not from in here. You need to grab that ring and help me lift it. All right?"

"All right," Hawk said. He hadn't seen a ring before, but he dug his hand in the loose dirt and, sure enough, there was a ring. *This must have been what I stepped on,* he thought. "I found it. Let me get my feet set in front of it and I'll raise it up." Then he tested the weight a few times to see how heavy it really was, lifting it no more than an inch or two, just enough to define the four edges of the door. Now that he knew the width, he quietly moved to the rear of the door where he guessed the hinges to be, propped his rifle against the wall, and checked to make sure his Colt was riding loose in the holster. Straddling the door, he bent forward and took hold of the ring. "All right," he called out. "You ready? Here we go." With one mighty tug, he jerked the door open wide. The result was as if he had opened the door to hell, itself, when a barrage of .44 bullets roared up out of the opening. Using the door for protection, Hawk waited until he counted six shots. A thought was triggered in his mind of something he had noticed on that day in Sophie's Diner, the first time he saw the three. When Red and his friends left the dining room and picked up their firearms at the door, one of them slapped on a belt with two guns. He couldn't be sure, but he was going to bet that it was Red who wore two guns. Most men only load five cartridges in their handgun, leaving the hammer resting on an empty chamber, so they don't accidentally shoot themselves in the foot. So he was going to assume that Red emptied one gun, thinking Hawk was standing in front of the door. When he discovered that he wasn't, he fired one shot from his second gun, so Hawk would feel sure he was empty. "You're wastin' my time, Red," Hawk said. "If you wanna live, throw both of those guns outta there, then climb on out."

"I ain't got but one gun," Red persisted, "and I just emptied it."

"Is that a fact?" Hawk came back. "And you didn't even think about reloadin' it? Like I said, you're wastin' my time, so if you don't throw two pistols outta there right now, I'm gonna empty my rifle into that hole and you can take a chance that none of the bullets hit you." He cocked his rifle so Red could hear it.

"All right, all right," Red quickly replied. "I'm

comin' out." He tossed his two pistols out of the opening. "I give up."

"Come ahead," Hawk said, and held his rifle ready to fire. In a moment, he saw Red's head and shoulders emerge from the dark hole. Anticipating a sudden attempt, he aimed his rifle at him, ready to react in case he was foolish enough to try something. Out of the hole and on his feet, Red suddenly wheeled around and fired a fraction of a second too late, for Hawk's bullet caught him square in the chest before he could aim the derringer pocket pistol he carried. He staggered backward out the smokehouse door, his shot striking one of the two hams hanging from the rafters to cause it to swing back and forth. Hawk walked out to make sure he was dead. He was. "I gave you your chance," he said. *This one's for the sheriff,* he thought as he looked down at the still body.

He picked up Red's weapons and cartridge belt. They were worth money in trade, and since he was not going to be receiving pay from the army for a while, he was going to need money to pay his expenses. He received a bonus when he thought to search Red's pockets, and found two hundred dollars. "Damn," he remarked, expecting to find a dollar or two. "I expect it's only right for you to pay my expenses for huntin' you three bastards down."

He looked toward the front of the little hog ranch complex to discover a somewhat larger group of spectators, the gunshots having brought additional gawkers. Leaving the body for someone else to deal with, he walked back to the cabin with the red door. Looking in the open window, he saw

Lizzie sitting on the floor, holding her baby. "You can get up now," he said. "It's all over. Come over to the window." She did as she was told, afraid not to. "Here, Red wants to settle up with what he owes you, plus a little extra for the whuppin' he put on you." He handed her fifty dollars.

She was speechless for a moment, but that didn't stop her from eagerly accepting the money he held out to her. "Thank you, sir," she finally managed. "Thank you!"

"He didn't say where his two friends were, did he?"

"No, he didn't say anything about 'em," she said. "I know they both left here this morning. I'm sorry I can't help you." He nodded and turned to walk away. "Thank you," she said again. "I don't even know your name."

"You probably don't need to know it," he tossed back over his shoulder, and kept walking. He saw no use in working on a reputation for himself, especially with the clientele of a whorehouse. There were most likely a lot of customers who considered themselves handy with a gun who might like to gain a reputation at his expense.

The spectators stepped aside to clear a path for him as he walked back to the front of the saloon, where his horses were tied. No one made a sound until he had passed. When he turned the corner of the saloon, coming to the front, he was disappointed to find Ned standing by the rail. *I ain't got time for this*, he thought. He did not hurry his step, but continued walking toward the massive brute, now sporting a bandage tied around his head. Hawk shifted his Winchester up to grip it with both hands. Ned watched him, but said nothing until Hawk reached his horse.

"I figured you might wanna know somethin' I heard those two friends of his talkin' about," Ned said.

Caught completely by surprise, Hawk nevertheless managed to maintain his indifferent manner. "Yeah? What was that?"

"They were talkin' about splittin' up, to make it harder for the law to track 'em down." This captured Hawk's attention at once, so Ned continued. "I don't know where the feller named Dubose was headin', but the other one, the heavyset one, told that one called Red that he was goin' back to see his wife in Coulson." He shrugged. "Anyway, I thought you mighta wanted to know that. They both rode outta here early this mornin'."

Hawk could hardly believe the huge man's contrite manner. "Much obliged," he said. "I appreciate the information." He climbed up into the saddle. "I'm sorry we got off to a bad start."

"Me, too," Ned replied. "When I thought back about what I heard them talkin' about, I got to thinkin' that maybe you had a good reason to come after 'em."

"You're right. A mighty fine young girl is dead because of them." He backed Rascal away from the rail. "And they shot the sheriff in Helena." He wheeled the big buckskin and rode away.

CHAPTER 7

Oscar Jacobs stood in the yard outside his saloon, talking to the working women still gathered there. "Who the hell was that fellow?" Oscar asked, but no one knew.

"He just walked through our cabin, polite as you please, looking for somebody," one of the prostitutes replied. "When he didn't find him, he went out the back, just as sudden as he came in."

"Well, I reckon he found who he was looking for," one of the other women said. "He shot that little redheaded fellow that was shacking up with Lizzie."

Oscar shook his head, feeling impotent for not having been able to prevent a threat to one of his customers. It was certainly not an incident he wanted to get around. Customers had always felt a sense of safety within his complex and an occurrence like the one just witnessed could hurt business. He took one look at Ned, still standing by the hitching rail, his head bandaged. He was still

unclear as to why Ned had not seen fit to detain
the man, or what had happened between him and
Ned in the bar earlier. His bartender's accounting
of the incident didn't make sense, either, so he
just shook his head again and went back inside
the saloon.

   Rascal and the packhorse had not really had
much rest since Hawk had ridden into the hog
ranch that morning, so he decided that was the
most important thing to do at the moment. He
needed time to think about what he should do at
this point, anyway, so he rode down by the river
until he found a place that suited him. He let his
mind work on what had happened so far that
morning while he gathered branches to start a fire.
One of the three men he hunted was dead—the
one who actually shot the sheriff. The one he
wanted the most was the man named Dubose, but
he had no idea where to look for him. He considered searching up and down the Yellowstone,
hoping to run across something or somebody who
might help him get on Dubose's trail. On the other
hand, he knew where Hog Thacker was heading,
and Hog was equally guilty of the fate that had be-
fallen JoJo. *But damn it*, he thought, *Dubose is the
one who pulled the trigger.* He worried over it while he
filled his coffeepot with water. No matter what,
he knew he would find no peace until he settled
with Dubose. Even then, it was unlikely he could
ever rid his mind of the image he saw on that day.
Even at the distance from which he witnessed the

shooting, he thought he could see the agony in JoJo's face when Dubose's bullet slammed into her chest.

He worried over the decision until it was time to start, then he told himself he would be foolish to abandon a search for Hog, when he knew where to look for him. Once he settled with him, he could spend the rest of his life looking for Zach Dubose, if that's what it took. He was not bound by any obligations to anyone or anywhere. Major Brisbin might wonder what had happened to him, but he felt sure he had a job with the army whenever he needed it. As long as Lieutenant Mathew Conner was stationed there, he would have a friend who would always vouch for him. So he set out for Coulson, knowing it to be about a two-day ride. By now, Hog had about half a day's ride on him, depending on how big a hurry he was in. Possibly, he might catch up with him before he reached Coulson. If not, then Coulson was not much more than a small settlement, and it shouldn't be too hard to find someone like Hog Thacker.

Ethel Thacker guided her mule between the two-story hotel built by John Alderson and the Paddle Wheel Saloon, following a path that led along Stinking Creek. She was tired. It had been a hard day, like every day at the hotel, where she was lucky enough to work. But today there were two beds destroyed with the contents of some drunken cowboy's stomach and bowels after a night in the saloons. The rooms had to be mopped as well as the hallway where one of them had tried to make it to the outhouse. She sorrowed in the thought that tomorrow would bring more of the same. Still, she was grateful for the job of cleaning lady for the hotel. Without it, she could not make it. If she were younger, or pretty, she wouldn't hesitate to sell her services as a prostitute, but the years had taken a toll on her and she had nothing to offer that a man would pay money for. At least she had a shack where she could go for peace and quiet every night. That was one thing Horace had done for her before he left one day and never came back.

She could not say that she missed him, but he didn't seem so brutal when they married. She was younger and homely, but he was not a man whom women found attractive in the least. So it seemed a workable arrangement for them both. It was such a short time before she became old and homely and Horace turned into the image that inspired his nickname, Hog. When he started running with Zach Dubose, it somehow brought out the brute in him and she knew they were getting more and more involved in illegal activities. Before long, Hog started leaving home for long periods, always returning with no more money than before, having spent in the saloons whatever he had stolen. She soon learned not to ask him why he managed to find money enough to come home drunk, but none to buy them food and supplies. To ask such questions usually brought physical violence upon herself. So when he failed to return after a month, she almost rejoiced.

Why her mind happened to be dwelling upon her abusive husband on this late summer evening, she could not say. Maybe it was an omen of the bad luck headed her way. When she rounded the sharp bend in the creek, she suddenly pulled the mule up short when she saw the strange horse tied up at the front of the shack. Not sure what she should do, she hesitated there for a long while watching the cabin. She pulled the shotgun she carried from the saddle sling. Even with a weapon, she was reluctant to ride on in and inform her visitor that the shack was occupied, for that was who she suspected, a homeless drifter who had discovered what appeared to be an empty shack. With the lock on the door, he should have known it was not abandoned. Maybe she should turn around and go back to the hotel. Mr. Alderson had told her before that he would make room for her behind the kitchen. But she felt like this shack was all she owned and she did not want to lose it. So she resolved to claim what was hers and inform the drifter that he had to leave.

She rode up before the shack, noticing the splintered doorframe, evidence of the door having been kicked in. Frightened by who might be waiting inside, she remained in the saddle and aimed her shotgun at the door. "You in the cabin," she called out in as husky a voice as she could affect, "come outta there with your hands up."

A long moment passed before the door opened a crack. "Put that damn shotgun down, Ethel, before you shoot yourself with it," the voice came back, a voice she recognized at once.

A cold shiver raced up her spine and her fingers went cold on the shotgun. "Horace?" All of a sudden her deepest fears came rushing back to her mind and she felt helpless to stop them.

"Who the hell else would it be?" came the reply from inside. "Put that damn shotgun down, or I'm gonna blow you outta that saddle." He opened the door wide and stood in the doorway, his ample body outlined by the fire in the fireplace behind him. "Where the hell have you been? I've been here since this afternoon. I come home and you ain't here. I wanna know where you've been and don't even think about tellin' me no lie."

In spite of her fear of the man, she stiffened her spine at the audacity of the brute. "You're some-thin', askin' me where I've been. Where have *you* been? You walked outta this cabin over a year and a half ago to go have a drink with that friend of yours, that *Mr.* Dubose, leavin' me with nothin' to eat. And now you come back here askin' me where *I've* been. What did you expect? I'd be waitin' here with open arms?"

"A man with a decent wife expects her to be ready with some supper when he comes home. Don't matter when he comes home. I've been ridin' hard for two days to get here and I'm hungry, so get down off that mule and fix me somethin' to eat."

"What if I ain't got nothin' to fix?" she replied as she got down from the mule and walked up to the door. "A woman with a workin' husband would have somethin' to fix. Did you bring some food with you, or is it always like it used to be, you don't come home with nothin' but whiskey on your breath?" She pushed past him and went inside to see if by chance he had brought some food with him. The only additional thing she saw was a half-empty bottle of whiskey on the table and her pantry looking as if it had been rifled by a bear. She turned to confront Hog, only to be knocked off her feet by a vicious backhand.

"Now," he commanded, "things are gonna get back to where they was around here. I can see you've forgot who's the head of this family, so I'll damn sure straighten you out."

She lay there for a few moments, the dreadful memories rushing to her brain with the throbbing in her cheekbone. Her nightmare had returned and she wanted to scream out against it. But she fought to contain it, having learned in the past that her crying seemed to infuriate him, bringing even more abuse upon her. She got up on her hands and knees while he stood over her like a conqueror over a fallen foe, waiting to deliver the fatal blow. "There ain't nothin' in the house to cook but some side meat," she finally whimpered. "There is some coffee and a little bit of flour. I can fry some of the meat for you."

He took a step back. "If that's all you've got, then it'll have to do." He continued to watch her closely as she got to her feet. "How come you ain't got no food? What was you gonna eat? You don't look like you've been missin' any meals."

"I eat at the hotel," she said.

"The hotel?" He almost exploded again. "How the hell can you eat at the hotel?"

"I work there," she explained, "so they let me take my meals there."

"Doin' what?" he asked, already thinking the worst and preparing to administer punishment for it.

"Cleanin' lady and help in the kitchen," she said. "How else do you think I could make it with you gone and not bringin' home any money when you *were* home?"

"Watch your mouth," he warned, then snuffed contemptuously. "I thought you mighta took to whorin'. You mighta made two or three cents, if you got a man drunk enough." He chortled over the thought of it. "You think I don't ever have any money to buy food? Well, I'll tell you what you're gonna do tomorrow. You're goin' to McAdow's store and buy somethin' to put in that damn pantry with money I'm gonna give you. Now that I'm home, I'm gonna need somethin' to eat. So get up offa the floor and find me somethin' to eat right now."

Surprised that he actually had money to spend on supplies, she got up to do his bidding, disheartened to find that he was planning to stay for a while.

* * *

At the time of Ethel Thacker's unhappy reunion with her husband, the man whose mission it was to track him down was encamped approximately twenty miles west of the little settlement of Coulson. Rascal and the sorrel packhorse grazed on a grassy slope between scattered growths of cottonwood trees, while Hawk sat near his campfire idly watching a strip of sowbelly roast. Come morning, he would ride on into Coulson, planning to first make the rounds of the saloons, thinking if anyone knew Hog Thacker, they would most likely be in a saloon. It had been quite some time since last he rode through Coulson. The town was little more than a post office and a sawmill, plus two saloons then. He had heard that there was now a hotel and another saloon along with a general merchandise store and some other businesses.

When the sowbelly looked to be done, he poured himself another cup of coffee before taking the meat off the spit he had improvised from a green cottonwood branch. As he ate, he pictured the man he had seen in the dining room, Hog Thacker. According to what Ned had told him, Hog had said he was going to visit his wife. In spite of his reluctance to do so, he allowed himself to wonder about the man's wife and if there were also children. He allowed himself to dwell on that for no more than half a minute before telling himself that all three of the outlaws were involved in the shootings of JoJo and Sheriff Willis. He'd be doing the world a favor if he killed Hog Thacker. He turned in that night with resolve to take care of business.

The next morning, he saddled his horses and

rode the remaining twenty miles into Coulson, planning to get some breakfast there. Signs of growth since he had been there were easy to see as he walked his horses the length of the short street. At a glance, he decided the Paddle Wheel was the busiest saloon at this late hour of morning, so he pulled Rascal over and tied up at the rail. He took a good look at a couple of men sitting on a bench outside the door before entering the saloon. There was some concern that he might not recognize Hog again. He had seen him only that one time up close. The next time, he had been flailing a galloping horse, riding low on the horse's neck on his way out of town.

Inside, he paused at the door to look the dozen or so customers over before walking over to the bar, happy to see a man standing at the end, drinking a cup of coffee. He was talking to a man dressed in a morning coat who was standing behind the bar, and Hawk figured he might be the owner, since the bartender was easily recognized by the apron he wore. Hawk moved down the bar closer to the two men talking. "Name your poison," the bartender greeted him.

"It's a little bit early for me to start on the hard stuff," Hawk said. "Can I get a cup of that coffee those two fellows are drinkin'?"

"Well, I don't see why not," the bartender said, "if you've got a nickel."

"That's reasonable enough," Hawk responded, and reached in his pocket to find a nickel.

The bartender walked over to the stove, where a large gray pot was resting, and returned with a cup of strong black coffee. "Want some sugar?" When Hawk declined, the bartender said, "Five cents, one refill for no extra charge." He paused there a few moments, studying the tall man in the buckskin shirt. "I don't believe I've ever seen you in here before, friend. You new in town or just passing through?"

"Passin' through," Hawk replied. "It's been a good while since I was in your town. I used to know a fellow that lived near here—thought I'd look him up, if he's still here—name of Thacker, Hog Thacker."

"Hog Thacker," the bartender repeated. "Can't say as I know anybody by that name. Little place like this, you'd think you'd remember somebody with a name like that." He turned to the man standing at the end of the bar. "Say, boss, you know anybody named Hog Thacker?"

His boss didn't take but a second to respond. "No, sorry. How 'bout you, John? Ever hear of anybody named Hog Thacker?"

John Alderson shook his head. "No, the only Thacker I know is a woman who works in my hotel, Ethel Thacker, but I don't think she's married. I don't really believe she's got any family at all."

"Much obliged," Hawk said. "I reckon ol' Hog's moved on. Well, no matter." He turned back to the bartender. "Know a good place to get some breakfast?"

Overhearing, Alderson answered before the bartender had a chance. "The hotel's hard to beat for breakfast, dinner, or supper." He looked at his

watch. "Breakfast is about over, but you can still get
something to eat if you don't waste much time."

"Much obliged, gentlemen," Hawk said. "I think
I'll hurry right on over there." He drained the last
of his coffee. "Good day to ya."

Outside, he climbed into the saddle and headed
toward the hotel, certain that he was on Hog's
trail. He hadn't expected anyone in town to know
Hog, since he figured Hog wasn't around that
much, and if there was more than one Thacker in
town, they surely would have known. The most important thing for him now, except getting some
breakfast, was to find Ethel Thacker, for she would
lead him to Hog.

Janet Combs looked up from the table where
she had sat down to have her usual cup of coffee,
now that the breakfast customers were gone. Her
first reaction to seeing the doorway filled with the
tall man in the buckskin shirt was to tell him he
was too late if he was looking for breakfast and
too early for dinner. As soon as he spotted her,
he walked over to her table, with a long, casual
stride she couldn't help noticing. "Good mornin',
ma'am," he said. "I can see I'm too late for breakfast, but I'd sure appreciate it if I could just buy
a cup of coffee. I just rode into town. I was hopin'
to make it in time for breakfast, 'cause I'd heard
this was the place to get the finest food in the
territory."

She didn't respond immediately, taking a few
moments to decide. He seemed so sincere and

polite that she finally gave in. "I guess we can give you a cup of coffee, since you're new in town." She hesitated a moment more. "I'm sorry we're already cleaning up the kitchen."

"I understand," he quickly replied. "I'll make do on that cup of coffee, and I apologize for botherin' you this late."

"How about a cold biscuit with a slice of ham?" she asked, surrendering to his polite respect.

"That'd be like a real banquet," he said with a wide grin.

"Alice," she called out, and waited a moment until a plump little woman stuck her head out the kitchen door. "Fix Mr. . . ." She paused and looked at him, questioning.

"Hawk," he said.

"Fix Mr. Hawk up with one of those leftover biscuits, please, and stick a slice of that ham in it. I'll get him some coffee." She gave him a smile as she got up to fetch the coffee.

He watched her as she went to the stove at the end of the dining room, where a pot was still warming, but he was not admiring her obvious feminine charm. He was thinking that he now knew that the cook's name was Alice and not Ethel. And he had already eliminated the lady getting his coffee. She was too young and much too pretty and polished to be the wife of someone like Hog Thacker. He decided that the woman he wanted to identify must be tending her duties in the hotel. At that moment, another woman came out of the kitchen. She was carrying a load of dishes to set up for dinner. He knew immediately that she was Ethel

Thacker. A stout, middle-aged woman, she wore a look of melancholy and fatigue. When Janet came back to the table with his coffee, he asked, "Is that lady with the dishes Mary Simpson? It sure looks like her, but that was a long time ago."

Janet turned to look to be sure it wasn't Alice who had come out of the kitchen. "No," she said, "that's Ethel Thacker." She turned back to him. "Who's Mary Simpson, a friend of yours?"

"She was just a friend of the family a long time ago." He didn't know anyone by that name—it was just the first to pop into his head. He took a long look at the woman, making sure he would recognize her outside the dining room. "No, I can see, now that I've looked a little closer. It ain't her, but she sure looks a lot like her. I don't know why I thought she might be in Coulson in the first place."

In a couple of minutes, Alice came from the kitchen with a plate containing two biscuits with ham. "I took a look at him," she said to Janet, "and figured he was gonna need more'n one biscuit."

Hawk took his biscuits and coffee to another table and sat down to eat. Before he was finished, Janet got up to refill her cup and walked the pot over to fill his. She stayed a few minutes to talk. "You have family with you, Mr. Hawk?" When he said that he didn't, she asked if he was looking for work.

"No, ma'am, I'm on my way back to Fort Ellis. I work for the army sometimes, scoutin'." She nodded as if to say she guessed as much. "I sure am glad I stopped in here, though," he went on. "You ladies sure know how to run a fine dinin' room, and I'll say these biscuits are the best I've ever had."

She flushed appropriately. "Why, thank you, sir, we're glad you think so. I hope you'll be back to eat with us again. We'll be open again at noon for dinner."

"I surely will," he said. "I'll most likely see you at noon. How much do I owe you for the coffee and biscuits?"

"I'll tell you what," she said, "I won't charge you anything. We'll just call it a welcome-to-town gift."

"That sure is mighty kind of you, ma'am, but I feel like I oughta owe you somethin'—as nice as you've been to me. Looks to me like you ladies work pretty hard, runnin' this place. Been here since before sunup, I expect. What time does your day usually end?"

Janet laughed at his earnest flattery. "Alice and I don't go home till after all the supper dishes are washed up, the floor swept, and the tables are set for breakfast."

"What about the other'n, the one that looks like Mary Simpson, doesn't she stay and help you?"

"Ethel?" Janet responded, amused by his interest in how hard the three of them worked. "She works in the hotel from breakfast till suppertime, then she goes home."

"Well, I'd best get outta here before you ladies put me to work sweepin' the floor or somethin'." He picked up his hat, struck for an instant by a stray thought that it didn't look right without the feather in the band. It immediately drew him back from the pleasant encounter with the ladies to the reason he was here. "Thank you again, Miss . . . I don't even know your name."

"Janet Combs," she said.

"Pleased to meet you," he said, then took his leave. Outside, he stood looking at his horse for a few minutes. So far, it looked as if it was going to be easy to find Hog Thacker. He just had to be sure he was there to see Ethel when she went home. That would be about five o'clock when the dining room opened for supper. In the meantime, he would take care of his horses, making sure they were watered good and fed a ration of oats to supplement their grazing.

Even knowing what he planned to do, he was still undecided about the best way to accomplish it. When he left the Big Timber Hog Ranch, his thinking was no more complicated than finding the man and shooting him down. Now that he was here in Coulson and had seen the sad, mournful countenance of the simple woman he intended to make a widow, he began to question the justice in the execution he had planned. There was no doubt in his mind that Hog deserved killing for his part in the death of JoJo Feeley. But did Ethel deserve to be made a widow? In his opinion, she'd be better off, but she might not think so. "Damn it to hell," he spat, bothered more than a little. Maybe he was wrong in saddling Hog with equal amounts of guilt in the shootings. Maybe he wouldn't have shot the girl, or the sheriff, if he could have prevented it. Maybe he should try to take Hog to Bozeman and hand him over to the army, like he had offered to do with Red Whitley. Let them decide what he deserved. "I'll think on it," he told Rascal. "But I might as well have another crack at that dinin' room at noon. It might be a long time before I get another chance for a good dinner."

"How long you thinkin'?" Waylon Burns asked when Hawk rode up to the stable.

"Maybe overnight," Hawk answered. "I ain't plannin' on bein' in town long. I wanna leave my packhorse here right now, but I'll need my buckskin."

"Whatever you say," Burns said. "I'll put him in a stall and you can stow your packs in there with him."

"How much for me to sleep in there with my horses?"

"A dollar extra," Burns replied.

Hawk thought that was a bit steep, but he didn't complain. He was operating on money he had found on Red Whitley, so he paid Burns and left the sorrel there while he killed time looking the town over until the dining room opened again. He was one of the first to enter when Janet turned the OPEN sign around. "Well, well," she greeted him, "you meant it when you said you'd be back."

"I surely did," he replied. "I stayed in town just so I could eat here again."

"Sit down at the long table," she said. "We serve dinner and supper family style, so you'll get more to eat at that table." He did as she suggested, pulling a chair back near the middle of the table.

She caught his arm before he could sit down and led him to the end of the table. "The meat platter starts at this end and today it's pork chops and sometimes there aren't any left but the small ones when it gets to the other end."

"Much obliged," he said.

"You want coffee or water?" She went to get it when he chose coffee. After that, when patrons started arriving, she and Alice became too busy for any more visiting. He marveled that the two women could manage it, but they kept the bowls filled and the coffee hot. It was well worth the charge of fifty cents. When he finished, he paused only a moment to catch Janet coming out of the kitchen with a tray and told her he enjoyed the meal. "You coming back for supper?" she asked.

"I reckon not," he said. "I wish I could, but I've got some business to tend to this evening. I ain't used to eatin' two big meals like that in one day, anyway."

"Well, it was nice to meet you, Mr. Hawk. Maybe you'll have occasion to pass this way again. I hope you'll come back to see us, if you do."

"You can surely count on that," he said as he started for the door.

At a couple minutes after five, according to his watch, Ethel Thacker walked out of the hotel. He watched her as she walked down the short street to the stable and went inside. After a few minutes passed, he decided to move from the bench in front of the post office in case she went out the back of the stable. But she appeared at that moment, walking with Waylon Burns, who was leading a mule. At the door, Burns handed the reins to her, but did not offer to help her up into the saddle. Instead, she exchanged a couple of words with him, then walked back up the street, leading the mule. Thinking it best not to let her see him sitting in front of the post office, he started to get to his feet, but she stopped at the general store, tied her mule at the rail, and went inside. She remained in the store for what seemed a long time before she came back outside, carrying a couple of sacks that appeared to be full. He continued to watch as she tied her purchases to her saddle and waited until she climbed on the mule and turned it away from the rail. He let her get out of sight when she turned from the road to pass beside the stable before he climbed aboard Rascal and followed.

He caught sight of her as soon as he turned at the stable, and had to rein Rascal back to allow her to extend her lead, although he would not have expected her to be wary of someone following her. Plodding slowly on her mule, showing no sign of being eager to get home, she rode away from the river until she came to a creek. Instead of crossing, she turned and followed a path that ran beside it. He estimated a distance of about two miles when he lost sight of her again when the creek made a turn around a formation of rocks. When he got to the bend, he pulled up sharply, for he could see the rough shack about fifty yards ahead. Very slowly, he backed Rascal up until concealed by the rocks, where he dismounted and tied the buckskin to a bush growing out of the rocks.

Shadows were already lengthening as he moved up close enough to the shack to see Ethel slide off her mule and lead it to a lean-to attached to the back of the cabin, where a couple of horses were tied. The door of the shack opened wide, but no one came out to help the woman unsaddle her mule or to carry her purchases inside. With no plan for his approach, Hawk decided to wait until it became a little darker before he crossed the opening between the cabin and the cottonwood he now took cover behind. He was counting on sur-prise to make his attack easier.

"Where the hell have you been?" Hog met his wife at the door. "I thought you mighta took that money I gave you and run off somewhere. Much longer and I was fixin' to saddle my horse and hunt you down."

"I had to go to the store to buy all the food you wanted," she explained, casting a wary glance in his direction to determine how much he had been drinking. She was disappointed to see a new bottle on the table beside the empty one that had been half-full when she left that morning. He tended to become abusive when he got drunk. From the first, he had been a mean drunk, never a happy drunk like Mr. McAdow. And as the years went by, his mean drunks only got worse. If he went that way tonight, it was going to be even harder for her, since he had been away for such a long time and she had enjoyed his absence. She dreaded the thought of it and hoped that she could avoid the worst of it, if she could get some food in him before he finished that bottle.

"Well, get your ass goin'," he ordered. "I ain't had nothin' to eat but them biscuits you made last night and a few little ol' strips of bacon."

"It won't be long," she said, trying to sound cheerful. "I'll cook up those beans that have been soakin' since this mornin'. I bought some cornmeal. I can make you some corn bread, and I bought a quarter of a ham. We'll have a fine supper real soon." She put more wood on the fire in the fireplace. "I need to split more wood for the fire, too," she muttered under her breath. To him, she said, "Maybe you won't drink any more of that whiskey, so you can enjoy your supper."

"How much likker I drink ain't none of your business," he immediately responded, his nostrils seeming to flare in anger.

"I know, I know," she quickly cried. "I'm just wantin' you to enjoy your supper."

"Well, get at it, and damn quick," he ordered. He sat down at the table and poured himself another drink. The whiskey he had already consumed began to have a numbing effect on his brain now and he began to close his eyes frequently for short periods. Noticing, she stole glances at him, hoping that he might fall asleep, but he would suddenly jerk his head up, his eyes blinking open to stare stupidly at her. Seeming to be awake again, he said, "I swear, you was always a homely woman, but damned if you ain't got worse-lookin' every year.

Thank God for whorehouses." The thought of it made him laugh. "There's this little bucktoothed gal at the Big Timber Hog Ranch that ol' Red gets all hot and bothered over. She ain't no bigger'n a willow switch—got yeller hair. I get up that way again, I think I'll take a ride—see if she's as good as Red says she is."

She said nothing, suffering his insulting rantings in silence. At least, it was preferable to the times when he felt the urge to pummel her purely for his entertainment. She had endured both before, but it was just so much harder now since his recent absence. She hoped that he would just pass out, as he had done so many times before. But each time he nodded off, he would jerk upright several moments later until finally his chin dropped to rest on his chest and he began to snore. She went to work on the corn bread, thinking that a good plate of beans and corn bread would help sober him when he woke up. She didn't notice when the cabin door came open until she felt the cold draft of air. When she turned to go and close it, she was confronted with the formidable figure standing in the doorway. She started to scream, but couldn't make a sound, her voice was so constricted. Then she realized where she had seen him before. "You," she said, "at the dinin' room. What do you want?"

"Him," Hawk said, pointing at the unconscious Hog at the table.

"Are you a lawman?" she asked when her fright over his sudden appearance subsided to the point where she could again talk.

"No, ma'am," he said. "I'm just wantin' to see justice done. I'm awful sorry to break in on you like this, but your husband and two friends of his are responsible for the murder of a young woman named Joanna Feeley and shootin' the sheriff in Helena."

She could not prevent the horrified gasp that escaped her lips. She had long suspected the three outlaws were capable of uncontrolled violence, but now it was no longer speculation. Hog had finally brought it home with him. "Was the young woman close to you?" Ethel asked.

"Yes, ma'am, she was," Hawk replied, his gaze concentrated on the still-sleeping outlaw. "She was very special."

"What are you going to do with Horace?" Ethel asked.

"Well, to tell you the truth, I wasn't sure. I planned to kill him till I saw you and talked to your friends at the dinin' room. Then I decided I didn't want you to lose your husband, so I decided the best thing to do is for me to take him back to Helena to let him stand trial. The sheriff that was shot ain't dead, so maybe they'd go a little easy on your husband, especially since he ain't the one that killed the girl. That was Dubose." She seemed so calm, now over her initial fright, that he wasn't sure what to make of her. Perhaps she was at peace with the turn of events, maybe expecting this day to ultimately arrive. But his attention had to be returned to Hog because he was making snorting noises in preparation to waking up. "I promise you, I won't be hard on him, but I'm gonna have to tie his hands." She nodded, her eyes seeming to focus on something or some time far away. Satisfied that she was going to be calm, he propped his rifle against the wall behind him, took a coil of rope he had brought with him, and began to fashion a loop to put over Hog's wrists.

Suddenly Hog woke up when Hawk removed the .44 from his holster. "What the hell . . . ?" he demanded.

"Just hold still," Hawk said, "and there won't be any need to get rough."

Completely confused, Hog's first thought was that his wife had betrayed him. He looked at her and wailed, "Ethel!"

Equally confused, Ethel found herself thrown into a whirlwind of events and questions of loyalty. Seeing Hawk, now with Hog's pistol in hand, she wasn't sure of his intentions. "That's enough! Stop right there," she cried. Startled, both Hawk and her husband turned to see her standing there with the shotgun she had brought in from her saddle. It was leveled at Hawk. "Put the pistol on the table," she ordered calmly. Caught flat-footed, Hawk didn't want to do that, but it was obvious that she meant business. "On the table," she repeated sternly.

"Ma'am, you don't wanna do this," Hawk pleaded, but there was no wavering in the intense look in her eye as she motioned with the shotgun toward the table. He placed the pistol on the table.

The events having just taken place were enough to sober Hog. "Hot damn! Good work, Ethel. Shoot the son of a bitch."

"No," she said. "He wasn't gonna shoot you, so he's just gonna get on his horse and ride back the way he came."

Hog was stunned. "The hell he is!" He snatched his .44 off the table and turned in time to catch the full blast of the shotgun in the chest. His eyes wide in disbelief, he dropped the gun as he stumbled backward to land on the floor.

Not sure if he was next, Hawk stood dumbfounded, trying to read the intent in the woman's eyes as she continued to stare down at her dying husband. He was not sure if she even remembered he was there. After a long moment, she looked at the shotgun she was holding and, seeming confused, she handed it to Hawk. He propped it against the wall beside his rifle, then turned back just as her knees gave way. He caught her by the elbow to keep her from falling and guided her to one of the two chairs at the table and she sank down onto it, drained of energy. "I should have done that a long time ago," she said softly. Hawk understood her words were to herself and not directed at him. He could only imagine the hell it must have been for her, living with a man like Hog.

He knew he should do something for her, but he didn't know what. Seeing the whiskey bottle on the table, he poured some of it in the glass beside it and handed it to her. She stared at it for a moment, then drank it, only to spew half of it back out of her mouth. "That ain't gonna work," he decided. "How 'bout some coffee?" She nodded vigorously. He went to the fireplace, hoping the pot sitting in the coals was not empty. He was in

luck, but it smelled as strong as iron. She sat there
for a long time, sipping the hot coffee, before turning to look at the body of her husband for a few
moments. Then she turned back to stare at the cup
in her hand. Hawk studied her face more closely,
noticing then the many old scars, evidence of past
violence at the hands of her husband. "Are you
gonna be all right now?" She nodded. "I swear, I
didn't come here with the intention of killin' your
husband unless he didn't give me no choice."

"You didn't kill Horace, I did," she said. "I believed you when you said you'd take him in for
trial. He was gonna shoot you and I couldn't let
him do that. He was an evil man and there have
been many times when I wanted to shoot him for
the way he treated me. But I didn't have the
courage, till now, when he was fixin' to shoot you.
I'm done, he's the devil's problem now." She ut-
tered a long, weary sigh. "So now I reckon you can
tell the law that Hog Thacker's dead and turn me
over to the sheriff, or whoever you were gonna
turn Horace over to."

Hawk found it difficult to believe she felt de-
serving of punishment for ridding the world of
Hog Thacker. He knew he had bungled this whole
encounter with the outlaw and it was primarily because he had felt empathy for his widow. "I don't
intend to take you anywhere," he said to her. "Does
anybody know about your husband, I mean here in
Coulson?"

"No. They think I'm a widow. It was one of the
reasons Mr. Alderson gave me a job. Horace didn't
want anybody to know about him."

"Good," Hawk said. "Now you really are a widow and rightfully so. We're gonna bury your late husband and then I'll take you anyplace you wanna go away from here. Have you got family somewhere you can go back to?"

"No," she said. "No family. I don't wanna go anywhere. I wanna stay here and keep my job and my house. This is the only place I've found peace when Horace was gone."

"All right, if that's what you want," he said. "I'll dig his grave away from the cabin, so you don't have to see it every day. You need to go through his pockets to see if there's anything you wanna keep. I'm thinkin' he might have a good bit of money on him, or in his saddlebags. His partner Red did." He paused and waited for her to respond, but she was obviously hesitating. "You want me to search him?" he asked. She nodded at once. So he quickly unbuckled Hog's gun belt and pulled it out from under him. He picked Hog's .44 up, returned it to the holster, and placed it on the table. "If that shotgun is the only weapon you've got, you might wanna keep this handgun, too."

When he had finished searching the body, he dragged it out of the shack, which was no small task. Hog had been a large man and the job of getting his body up on Ethel's mule was even more difficult, but Hawk managed it and took the body down the creek to find a burying spot. Digging the grave was a considerable job with the small spade he found in the lean-to with the horses, so he went no deeper than what he figured enough to keep predators from digging it up. When he returned to the shack, he was astonished to find Ethel cooking supper. "You must be hungry, after all the work you've been doin'," she said. "I've got some beans and ham in the pot, and the corn bread's about ready."

"I hadn't even thought about eatin'," he replied, amazed that she was so calm, after what she had just gone through. "But since you've already cooked it, I reckon I could eat and thank you very much." She motioned toward the table and he sat down while she filled a plate for him. After pouring him a cup of coffee, which he noticed was from a fresh pot, she sat down with a plate for herself. They ate in silence for a while until Hawk, feeling uncomfortable with it, commented, "This is good eatin'. You're a mighty fine cook."

She paused and looked up at him. "You think so? Horace said I was the worst cook he'd ever seen."

"Well, he was wrong," Hawk said, and pointed his fork at her. "It's a damn good thing that man is out of your life."

"I agree," she said with a slight smile gracing her homely face.

He was still amazed by her attitude, but he was convinced that she truly felt the freedom she had longed for, to be released from a grave mistake she had made when she was younger. He no longer worried about her—she was going to be all right. After supper, he fixed the door Hog had damaged as best he could with the few tools she had.

* * *

He spread his bedroll in the front corner of the tiny shack and stayed the night at her insistence. "There's no sense in you sleepin' in the woods somewhere when I've got a warm fire and a roof here," she said. It seemed awkward to him, but somehow it didn't seem wrong.

They were both up early the next morning, she to go to work, and he to head back down the Yellowstone. Even though she ate her breakfast in the hotel dining room, she offered to fix him something before she left. But he declined, saying that he would get breakfast at the hotel as well. "I'll have me one more big meal before I start back. I'll ride into town with you. I've gotta pick up my packhorse at the stable, anyway." It occurred to him then that Ethel had now acquired two horses and a saddle that might be hard to explain. He would have suggested she tell folks that he had brought it to her, but Waylon Burns knew that he had only the one packhorse with him and no extra mounts.

"Don't worry about it," she said. "I won't ride a horse to town for a while after you're gone. And I'll make up some story to suit everybody. I ain't worried." He couldn't help noticing her uplifted spirit, even cheerful. He guessed that maybe she felt finally free after so many years in her abusive marriage.

He rode with her until they reached the point where she would normally leave the path by the creek and head toward the stable. They agreed it best to arrive at the dining room separately, so he paused there for a while and let her go on alone.

"Don't you worry about me, John Hawk," she said in parting. "I think the Lord sent you here to set me free and I'm grateful. You be careful goin' after Zach Dubose. That man's ten times as evil as Horace was."

"You take care of yourself, Ethel," he said. Then he paused there to watch her as she rode on into the stable to give her time to turn her mule over to Waylon Burns, before riding in to get his pack-horse ready to travel.

"Well, look who's here, Alice," Janet Combs remarked when Hawk walked in the door of the dining room. "I guess our cooking hasn't scared him off, after all. He's back to try it again." She made it a point to speak loud enough for him to hear it.

"Good morning, ladies," Hawk greeted them. "I had to see if that was just a good day in the kitchen yesterday, or if the food's that good every day." He expected to see Ethel sitting there eating, but she was not. Then it occurred to him that maybe she ate with Janet and Alice after the dining room was closed. As happened the day before at the noon meal, Janet and Alice became too busy with the breakfast crowd to have much opportunity to make small talk with him. That was just as well, he thought, because he didn't want to spend a lot of time jawing. He was ready to shake the dust of Coulson off his feet, now that the question of Hog Thacker was settled, and get on with the search for Zach Dubose. The problem now was where to start looking for Mr. Dubose. He hadn't a clue. Where would he head? Where was he from?

"You look like you're doing some really deep thinking." The comment came from behind him, startling him for a moment, enough to make him flinch. Janet walked around to take a seat in the chair opposite him and placed her coffee cup on the table. "Your breakfast all right?"

"It was just fine," he said. "I'm gonna rate your dinin' room the best in the territory."

"Thank you, sir," she said sweetly. She took a sip of coffee while eyeing him intently over the rim of her cup. "The word should get around, if you tell everybody you meet about us, as much as I'll bet you travel." She didn't wait for him to answer. "You're getting ready to leave Coulson right now, aren't you?"

"Yes, ma'am, I reckon so," he said.

"Well, you be sure and stop by to see us when you're next in Coulson." She got up, picked up her cup, and went to the kitchen.

Alice was already starting to clean up the kitchen. She cocked an eyebrow at Janet when she walked in. "Well?" Alice asked.

"He's just another drifter." She paused and looked back through the door at him as he pushed his chair back and grabbed his hat. "Probably got a wife and six kids somewhere."

CHAPTER 8

"That's two of 'em," he said aloud as he rocked in rhythm with the big buckskin's stride. "One to go." The one remaining was the problem, for he had no idea in which direction to search for him. If he had even one small clue to pursue, he would follow it no matter how long it took him. But he had none.

He had held Rascal to a steady pace for all of that day and the faithful horse deserved a rest, so when he came to a wide stream lined with trees, he followed it back away from the wagon road. He continued up the stream until he found a place that suited him, with grass for the horses and wood for a fire. Early the next morning, he was on his way again, and by five o'clock mess call, he rode into Fort Ellis. "Well, I'll be damned," Lieutenant Mathew Conner exclaimed when he walked out the headquarters door to see Hawk tying Rascal at the rail. "Where the hell have you been? I thought you had finally gotten shot by one of those Blackfoot bucks you call your friends."

"Hello, Conner," Hawk returned. "I see they ain't court-martialed you outta the army yet. You must be behavin' yourself for a change."

Conner laughed. "Yeah, I figured I'd better lay low around here for a while. The major's getting a lot of heat from regiment on rounding up all the bands of Indians still refusing to come into the reservations. So I figured it wasn't a good time for me to cause any trouble." He grinned mischievously. "I'm about ready to bust out, though. What about you? You've been gone for a helluva long time. You musta had trouble finding your friend Walking Owl."

"I found him, but Brisbin ain't gonna like what Walkin' Owl thinks about comin' in to the reservation. I'm on my way to give him my report right now."

"He ain't in right now," Conner said. "You just missed him. He's gone home to supper, so you'll have to wait till morning. Come on, you can eat supper with me at the officers' mess and you can tell me where you've really been for so long. Hell, ol' Meade's already saying you've gone Injun again. I didn't say so, but I agreed with him for once. I figured you might have found your Blackfoot friends and decided to go back to living like an Indian for a while just to get the taste of the army outta your mouth. I told 'em you'd be back when you ran outta money to buy cartridges. Where the hell's your lucky feather?" he blurted, just then noticing it missing.

"I gave it to a young woman, not much more'n a girl," Hawk said. "She wanted it." The question brought his mind back to the issue that troubled him. Mathew Conner had been a friend to him ever since he first started working as a scout, but he couldn't explain to him the frustration he felt at the present time. The pledge he made over a dying young woman to avenge her murder was still the only path he could travel. And with no clue where to start his search, it was a path without light. Any time he closed his eyes, he could still see Joanna's face and the pain in her eyes.

"Hawk," Conner charged, "where are you? You looked like you drifted off somewhere in your mind. Damn, man, you've been spending too much time alone in the woods with the deer and the bears. What were you thinking about just then?"

"Oh, nothin' much," he answered, and quickly changed the subject. "Supper's a good idea, but I'll have to take care of my horses first."

"All right. Why don't you just come on over to the officers' mess when you're done. You won't be long, will you?"

"Nope," Hawk answered as he stepped up into the saddle.

"You're one of the scouts, ain't you?" The mess sergeant asked. "Hawk, ain't it?"

"That's right," Hawk replied, and reached for a tray.

"This is the officers' mess," the sergeant informed him. "Scouts usually eat with the enlisted men. That mess hall is on the other side, over by the barracks."

Hawk was about to tell him that Lieutenant Conner had invited him to eat supper with him, but Conner walked up at that point to intercede. "Mr. Hawk is my guest, Sergeant."

"Yes, sir," the sergeant responded at once. "I'm sorry, Mr. Hawk, I was just trying to make sure everything was proper and . . ." He trailed off, unable to think of what he should say.

Conner laughed, finding the incident humorous. "I don't blame you, Sergeant. Ol' Hawk looks like he might be thinking about scalping somebody."

"Yes, sir . . . I mean, no, sir, he looks just fine." He looked at Hawk. "No offense."

"None taken," Hawk replied.

"Fill your plate and come on over to the table. My food's getting cold," Conner said.

Hawk took advantage of the opportunity to dine with the officers, an occasion that, like the sergeant had pointed out, was not the usual routine. None of the other officers eating seemed to be bothered by his presence there, with the exception of one, Lieutenant Meade. As far as the chart of responsibility was concerned, the scouts were officially commanded by Meade. But there had been some friction between the lieutenant and the imperturbable scout, ever since they had a disagreement during a search for three bank robbers at the Big Timber Hog Ranch. It seemed ironic to Hawk now that the three bandits were never caught, for he was totally convinced that he had recently seen the demise of two of the three. He noticed that Meade was watching him as he went to Conner's table and sat down. Conner noticed it, too, and commented, "Looks like your old friend Meade is glad to see you back."

"Looks that way. I expect he'll wanna come over and say howdy." Hawk was well aware that he would be out of a job with the army, if it were up to Meade. He also knew, however, that as long as Major Brisbin commanded the fort, he had a job.

Conner laughed at Hawk's comment, but in short order Lieutenant Meade got up from his table and headed straight for them. "Uh-oh, looks like you were right. Here he comes."

"Well," Meade said upon approaching the table, "I see you finally returned from your trip to find that Blackfoot village." He nodded toward Conner. "Mathew."

"Harvey," Conner returned the acknowledgement.

Returning his attention to Hawk, he said, "Since I command the complement of scouts, I would have expected you to report to me as soon as you got back."

"That would be my fault," Conner quickly interrupted. "You weren't there when Hawk came to report, so I invited him to have supper while he waited for you."

Well aware of Conner's friendship with Hawk, Meade favored the indifferent scout with a smug smile. "Is that a fact?"

"Yes and no," Hawk answered. "I was really lookin' for Major Brisbin first, since he told me to report directly to him when I got back. Then

I reckon I woulda looked for you, to let you know, too."

"I see," Meade said. "Well, did you find Walking Owl's camp?"

"I did, but it wasn't much use tryin' to get him to come in to the reservation," Hawk replied. "All his young warriors have gone north to Canada. There wasn't anybody left in Walkin' Owl's village but old men, women, and children, and he said they'd rather die like free men in the land as they have always known it than go like white man's cattle to the reservation."

"It didn't do much good to send you to find him, then, did it?" Meade smirked.

"Reckon not," Hawk replied. "I expect the old chief knows what's best for his people."

"Damn Indians don't have a clue about what's best for them," Meade said. "I'll give Major Brisbin your report. There's no need for you to bother him with it."

"Thanks just the same, Lieutenant, but I expect I'll report to him, since he told me to. Sort of a courtesy kinda thing, you know?"

Meade didn't make any kind of reply. He just stood there, glaring at Hawk for a long moment before glancing at Conner. "Mathew," he finally said, and turned to leave.

"Harvey," Conner returned. Then he watched him until he walked out the door before turning back to Hawk. "How the hell did you and ol' Harvey Meade get to be such big friends?"

Hawk shrugged. "I told him he was a damn fool a couple years ago."

"That oughta do it," Conner said. "Listen, I'm escorting the payroll for two quartz mills up in Butte day after tomorrow. I was gonna take Ben Mullins along as a scout, but why don't you come along instead? I haven't told Ben yet, so that won't cause any problem. Five days, there and back, give you a chance to get back to work and I expect you could use a payday. Whaddaya say?"

"What about Meade?" Hawk replied. "He might not okay it."

"Hell, Meade's taking a patrol out in the morning to Three Forks. He won't even know you went with me."

"All right," Hawk said. "I'll ride scout for you— day after tomorrow, right? That'll give me time to get my horse some new shoes and rest him up a little. I've been workin' him pretty hard for the last few days and he's showin' signs of havin' trouble with one of his hooves." He thought maybe a routine patrol might be what he needed, might give him some time to decide where to start looking for Zach Dubose. As it was now, he might as well throw a stick up in the air and start searching in the direction it pointed when it landed.

"Good!" Conner said, and pushed his chair back to get up. "I guess I'll see you in the morning when you come in to report to Major Brisbin." He flashed a mischievous grin and confessed, "I'd invite you to meet me later on for a round of drinks, but there's this lady friend of mine who's expecting me to call on her tonight to give her some spiritual guidance while her husband's away in Helena."

* * *

As Conner had told him, Lieutenant Meade led a patrol out early the next morning, so Hawk waited until after he had gone to report to Major Brisbin. The major was disappointed to hear the results of Hawk's journey to find Walking Owl, but was not really surprised. "I thought it was worth a try," the major said. "If that old chief would listen to any white man, it would have been you." He thanked Hawk for taking the assignment, leaving Hawk feeling slightly guilty for not having given the chief any argument extolling the wisdom of going to the reservation.

When he left the headquarters building, he saddled Rascal and set out for Bozeman, four miles away. He was afraid he had not been paying enough attention to Rascal during the past few days, with everything else that had been going on. But lately he noticed the horse shifting weight from one leg to another as if to relieve pain or pressure in his feet. That was unusual for Rascal, and Hawk suspected the buckskin might have a "hot nail." If that was the case, it could be causing the horse a lot of discomfort. He had just recently had Rascal shod in Helena by Grover Bramble, and Grover had always done good work. But he remembered the circumstances on that day when Grover was in a hurry to get home early. He thought about having the farrier there at the fort take a look, but he was partial to the blacksmith in Bozeman. The army blacksmith might do an adequate job, but when it came to Rascal, Hawk preferred something above adequate. And Ernest Bloodworth had been shoeing the big buckskin for the past few years with never a complaint from Hawk. He could have gotten Rascal shod at the fort free of charge, but he felt it worth the money to take him to Bloodworth.

It was in the middle of the morning when Hawk rode into Bozeman. He received a friendly "Good morning" from Ernest Bloodworth when he pulled up at his shop. After they took a look at Rascal's shoes together, they agreed that the buckskin's hooves appeared to be in good shape, but Bloodworth suspected that the nails were driven too close to the center of the foot. Hawk decided to walk across the street to Grainger's Saloon while Bloodworth examined all Rascal's hooves.

"Well, lookee here," Fred Grainger blurted when Hawk walked in the door. "Mr. Hawk, it's been a while since you've been in. I thought maybe you weren't working for the army anymore." Hawk walked up to the bar. "What happened to that feather you always wore in your hat?"

"I lost it somewhere up near Helena," Hawk replied, thinking that he was always being asked about that feather now. And every time he was asked, he recalled a vivid picture of the time he had actually lost it and the guilt he felt for not having fulfilled his promise. "I reckon I'll have to find me another one," he said, if only to stop the questions. "You got any coffee? I ain't quite ready to start drinkin' yet."

"I sure do," Grainger replied. While he got Hawk's coffee he rattled on, "I don't reckon I'll ever forget the last time you were in here and that fellow called you out. You sure as hell gave him something he wasn't expecting. You ever run into him again?"

"Nope, not anymore," Hawk said, not wishing to discuss his troubles with the cold-blooded murderer Roy Nestor. Grainger was obviously eager to recall the incident in his saloon, but Hawk quickly changed the subject. "You got anything to eat with this coffee, a piece of jerky or somethin'? I didn't eat breakfast this mornin'."

"I got some jerky," Grainger answered, "and some hardtack."

"That'll do," Hawk said. "Just somethin' to hold me till I get some dinner at Sadie's Diner." It was enough to steer Grainger away from rehashing the incident in his saloon, so he ate a couple of pieces of beef jerky and downed a couple of cups of coffee. He paid Grainger and hurried out, saying he had best check on his horse.

On his way out the door, he passed one of Grainger's regulars coming in and he could hear Grainger greeting him. "See that fellow going out . . . ?" He had no desire to become famous, so he decided that maybe he would go down the street to the Trail's End Saloon next time.

"It's a good thing you brought this horse in," Bloodworth said when he returned to his shop. "I found one nail too close to the center in his left front foot. It was startin' to irritate him, but we got to it before it caused an infection."

Hawk waited and watched while Ernest Bloodworth finished shoeing Rascal, then went up to

Sadie's Diner for dinner. Sadie remembered him as the customer who had said that her cooking was the best in the territory. It was good for an overly generous plate of beef stew. She even sat down to chat for a few minutes when she had the time. He paid her and told her again that it was by far the best stew in the territory.

Back at Fort Ellis, he turned Rascal out to graze while he checked over the packs he had stored in a corner of the tack room where he usually kept his saddle. He wouldn't take his packhorse on this patrol because he could carry enough food and his small coffeepot in his war bag on his saddle. The troopers riding in the patrol would be ordered to take rations for five days, the same for Lieutenant Conner. They could do it in five days if there was no trouble along the way, even though a good portion of the trip would be through a lot of mountain country. When all was ready, he spread his bedroll on an empty cot in the enlisted men's barracks after supper in their mess hall. The seven-man patrol pulled out the next morning right after "Stable and Watering" call at six o'clock on the way to pick up the courier with the payroll at the Bank of Bozeman.

The patrol pulled up at the bank long before it opened for business, and Lieutenant Conner dismounted to go and meet the courier. A slightly built man wearing a business suit and riding boots walked out of the bank to meet Conner. His first comments were to express surprise to see an officer, seven soldiers, and a scout when he just expected Major Brisbin to send a couple of guards. He was carrying an oversized pair of saddlebags, which he placed on a horse tied at the rail after he greeted the lieutenant. He introduced himself as John Durham, a special assistant to W. A. Clark, the owner of several quartz mills. He questioned Conner on the wisdom of an escort of this size, wondering if it might trigger suspicions from anyone with a mind to steal. Conner assured him that it would take a sizable raiding party to pull off such a raid. Durham didn't appear to be pacified by Conner's assurances, but he climbed on his horse and the escort was under way. After that, there was very little said between Durham and the lieutenant, since Mr. Clark's courier seemed intent upon the trail ahead and behind, and less interested in passing idle chitchat. Hawk wondered if the fellow had been held up before, or if he was just naturally nervous and no doubt feeling the weight of his responsibility.

Following Hawk's recommendation, Conner pushed the column a few miles farther than usual before stopping to rest the horses at the forks where three rivers met. Hawk went on ahead to scout the riverbanks to make sure no hostile Indian hunting parties were camped there. Blackfoot hunting parties had been reported in the mountains surrounding Butte, along with Kutenai and Flathead. Of these, the lieutenant was more concerned about the Blackfoot. In spite of Hawk's close ties with them, their reputation as a warring tribe was enough to give Conner reason to be cautious.

Hawk had selected a good spot to rest the horses by the time the escort caught up with him. "I figure when we make camp for the night, we oughta be near the Jefferson River," Hawk said to Conner when the lieutenant had dismounted. "You can give the men a good break here to fix some breakfast and rest up, then you'll have an easy half day to the Jefferson. That'll get us to Butte plenty early tomorrow afternoon."

"Sounds good to me," Conner said. He studied his friend's face for a long moment. It seemed to him that Hawk's mind was somewhere else ever since he came back. He was doing his job as a scout, there was no complaint there, but his mood appeared to be unusually serious. "What's eating at you?"

"Nothin'," Hawk replied. "What makes you think somethin's eatin' at me?"

"You ain't been the same ever since you got back two nights ago, but I guess you just don't wanna talk about it."

"Reckon not," Hawk said. "Right now, I expect we'd best see about the horses and get a couple of fires goin', so we can eat breakfast."

"All right," Conner said, giving up for the moment. "But I'll get it outta you by and by." He turned and handed his reins to Corporal Johnson, who promptly handed them off to one of the other men with instructions to take care of the lieutenant's horse. There was no opportunity to press Hawk further because of the presence of John Durham, who naturally had his coffee at the lieutenant's fire. That suited Hawk just fine because he didn't want to discuss his problems with Conner, or anyone else. To take his mind off Zach Dubose, he occupied it with a study of the nervous little man with the huge payroll. Maybe it was the size of that payroll that caused Durham to be so jumpy. A pale man of almost delicate features, he was clean-shaven except for a neat mustache so thin that it looked as if it had been drawn with a pencil. Hawk would have bet he had never seen the outside of a clerk's office. He wondered how he had ever drawn an assignment like the one he was now on.

When the horses were thought to be sufficiently rested, the escort moved out again, headed for Three Forks, where they went into camp for the night. To satisfy Mr. Durham, Conner sent Hawk out to scout the area around the campsite to make sure there were no would-be bandits about. Conner was more concerned with a coincidental encounter with a Blackfoot war party. When Hawk returned with a report that there was no sign of anything within a wide circle around them, Durham was only partially placated. Hawk was reminded of his thoughts upon first meeting the little man and his obvious nervousness at the time. It was almost like he expected to be ambushed, even though he had commented that he thought his escort was composed of more soldiers than he had thought necessary. He decided to take another look around after everybody was in bed for the night, *just for the hell of it,* he told himself.

Shortly after dark, everyone turned in with the

exception of the one soldier who drew the first two hours of guard duty. Conner had seen no reason to post more than the one sentinel, primarily to make sure a party of Sioux raiders had no opportunity to steal the horses. After the camp quieted down with the exception of a small chorus of snoring, Hawk rolled out of his blanket and walked over to the private posted near the horses. "Can't sleep?" the sentry asked him when he approached.

"A little too much on my mind, I reckon," Hawk replied. "So I thought I'd look around down the creek bank, see if there's a muskrat lookin' to find a cook pot."

"Hell," the private said, "you coulda took my place. I wouldn't have any trouble sleepin'."

"I reckon I could have at that, but Lieutenant Conner most likely trusts you not to go to sleep more'n he'd trust me. I'll give you a little whistle when I come back so you don't shoot me." He walked past the guard and soon faded into the darkness under the trees.

I don't know why he needed that rifle, the private thought. *He'll sure as shooting raise hell if he shoots at a muskrat and draws everybody outta their blankets.*

Halfway of the opinion that he was wasting good sleep, Hawk circled back to scout the column's back trail. He was curious to see if there might be a chance they were being tailed. If they were, and their followers' intention was to steal the mine payroll, they would have to be a large party of bandits to even think about attacking a patrol of soldiers. Thinking his suspicions confirmed after scouting the path they had ridden into their camp and finding no sign of anyone, he decided to start back.

"That snivelin' little bastard didn't know what he was talkin' about," Bevo Brogan complained. "How many you make it?"

"I'm countin' seven sleepin' and that one standin' guard by the horses," Johnny Dent replied. "Is that what you make it, Slim?"

"That's about right," Slim answered. "What are we gonna do?"

"He said there would be a couple of guards and that's all," Bevo said. "And it looks like they sent half the damn soldiers from Fort Ellis. We can't go down there and take all them on."

"That little shit is totin' a helluva lot of money in those saddlebags he's usin' for a pillow," Johnny reminded them. "I swear, it's hard for me to turn tail and ride away and leave all that money behind." The three of them remained there on the opposite bank of the creek, watching the sleeping camp for a while longer, reluctant to give up on such a prize, but not eager to engage a cavalry escort. They didn't know the exact amount of the payroll Durham carried, but they had been promised a thousand dollars each to kill the guards and steal it. "You know, they may have us outnumbered, but we oughta be able to fix that. We could shoot most of 'em before they could get outta their blankets. We could cut them odds down till we outnumbered them before they know what's goin' on."

"Maybe," Bevo said, giving it serious thought.

"I don't know. We'd have to be damn sure on every shot."

"Hell, we can get close enough, so we can't miss and they won't know where it's comin' from, dark as it is," Johnny Dent insisted. "I say we can do it."

"And while we're at it, we can put a bullet in Mr. John Durham and thank him for puttin' us onto this little job," Bevo said. "I'm thinkin' if he's willin' to give us a thousand dollars apiece, there's gotta be one helluva lot of money in those saddle-bags."

"And then it's off to Texas," Slim said. "Hell, I'm for it."

"All right," Bevo crowed. "It'll be the three of us against the U.S. Army. That sounds like a fair matchup to me." He got serious for a moment then and warned his partners. "We've got to be damn good and sure we don't miss with our first shots. We've got to make sure there's three less soldiers when they come outta them blankets. If we do that, we're bound to get a couple more before they know what hit 'em."

"We need to get a little bit closer, so we can't miss," Slim said, and pointed to a mound of grass close to the edge of the water. "Maybe behind that hump yonder. That'd give us protection from any-thin' they throw at us." The other two agreed, so they moved cautiously down to the mound and got set to aim their rifles at the unsuspecting soldiers.

"We need to all fire at the same time, so pick your targets, so nobody's shootin' at the same one," Bevo said. "I'll take that one standin' guard. We gotta take him first, for sure. Go ahead and pick your target." Slim and Johnny each picked one of the sleeping targets. "All right," Bevo went on. "Soon as you shoot, cock and shoot another'n as fast as you can and we might get the whole bunch before they can fire a shot. Remember, everybody at the same time on the first shot. I'll count to three and we'll cut loose."

"Do we shoot after you say three, or at the same time you say three?" Slim wanted to know. Slim was known to be simpleminded, so the question didn't surprise the other two.

"You rest your finger on that trigger and when you hear the word *three*, you squeeze it, all right?" Bevo said. When Slim said, "All right," Bevo started the count, "One . . ." was as far as he got before the lethal warning.

"You say *three* and you're a dead man." The deadly promise came from behind him, causing Bevo to freeze.

Confused, Johnny turned and fired his rifle, but his shot screamed harmlessly up through the trees when a slug from Hawk's Winchester slammed solidly into his chest. Reacting then, Bevo spun around, but not before Hawk had cranked another round into the chamber and stood with his rifle pointing squarely at the startled man's face. "Hold on!" Bevo shouted, and dropped his weapon. If Slim Perry had any notions about taking a shot, they were promptly rejected when the sentry came running to investigate. Slim dropped his rifle and stood with his hands up.

"Everythin's under control," Hawk called out to the rapidly approaching guard. "We've got a couple of prisoners here with their hands up." His only concern at the moment was the prospect of getting shot by the sentry. By this time, there was a minor state of chaos in the camp behind the sentry, as the other soldiers scrambled out of their blankets, thinking they were under attack. "Everythin's under control!" Hawk repeated, but this time it was a yell.

"Is that you, Hawk?" Lieutenant Conner called out from the small tree he had taken cover behind. "What was the shooting about?"

"Yeah, it's me. Tell your men to hold their fire." He looked at the sentry. "What's your name, soldier?" The sentry responded, still excited about what had just taken place, although he was not yet sure exactly what that was. Hawk called out again. "Me and McQueen are bringin' in a couple of prisoners, so hold your fire."

"Come on, then," Conner called back, and he and the other men gathered back at the campsite they had just abandoned. That is, all but one soul. The courier, John Durham, never left his bedroll, but had remained cowering there throughout the attack gone bad. He crawled out of his blankets only when all the soldiers returned from the various trees and logs they had scrambled to for cover. He still lingered behind the men as Hawk and Private McQueen marched Bevo Brogan and Slim Perry into the camp. "Well, I'll be damned," Conner swore, then turned to the soldier closest to him. "Build up that fire, so we can see a little better." While the soldier jumped to obey, being as anxious to see as the lieutenant, Conner kept his eyes on the prisoners. "Is that it?" Conner asked. "Where are the rest of them?"

Hawk directed the prisoners to sit down, so Bevo and Slim did as he ordered and sat down by the fire, which was rapidly gathering strength. "There's another one back on the other side of the creek I had to shoot."

"Another one?" Conner asked. "And that's all? You mean you're telling me three men were planning to attack an army escort more than twice their number?"

"Looks that way," Hawk answered.

"See, we figured we could cut down the odds if we was to shoot most of you while you was asleep," Slim volunteered.

"Shut up, Slim," Bevo blurted out, shocked by his simple partner's confession.

Addressing Bevo, Conner asked, "How did you know this payroll was going to Butte on this particular day?"

"Ask him," Bevo answered, pointing at Durham, who was trying not to be conspicuous. Everyone turned to stare at him.

Obviously flustered, Durham emitted a small choking cough before responding. "Why are you looking at me? I've never seen this man before."

"Lyin' son of a bitch!" Bevo exclaimed. "I ain't takin' the blame for this all by myself!" His anger rising now, he charged, "You said there'd likely be two guards ridin' your ass up to Butte, not a whole damn patrol. And Johnny Dent layin' dead back on the other side of the creek," he added. Finding the story more than a little interesting, Hawk recalled his initial thoughts about Durham's nervousness from the beginning. Then he remembered how Durham, himself, had commented that he hadn't expected so many in his escort when they picked him up at the bank.

Barely able to talk above a squeak now, Durham insisted, "The man obviously has a mental problem. I've never set eyes on him before and he certainly doesn't know me."

"Is that so?" Bevo replied, determined that if he was going to pay for the attempted robbery, the man who planned the whole thing was going to share the blame. "I know your name is Mr. John Durham and you were a whole helluva lot more anxious to know me and Johnny Dent when you set yourself down at the table in the Trail's End Saloon back in Bozeman."

"That's right," Slim piped up again. "I wasn't with 'em that night. They came to get me later to help 'em out."

Hawk almost laughed. If they got those two in front of a judge, it would be a helluva job to keep the simpleminded one from confessing every detail, and possibly owning up to several other crimes. "This is downright entertainin'," he said to Conner, "but I think I'll go back and check on that fellow I shot and see if I can round up their horses."

"You want me to send a man to help you?"

"No, no need," Hawk replied. "I'll be back shortly." He whistled softly and in a few seconds, Rascal walked up to be saddled. Hawk didn't bother with the saddle, however, but jumped on the buckskin's back. He figured it would be easier to find the three horses with Rascal's help and this time he'd cross the creek on horseback. His trousers were going to be a long time drying out as it was, since he walked Bevo and Slim across before.

He found Johnny Dent's body in roughly the same position he had left it. It appeared that Dent had made a few futile efforts to get up, but he hadn't made much progress before the devil called him. Hawk relieved the body of its weapons and cartridges, with an eye toward selling the weapons. He had an idea that Connor would not insist that they be confiscated by the military, knowing that Hawk had to count on resources outside his modest pay as a scout. He would leave it up to Conner as to whether or not to bury the body. If it was up to him, he'd leave it for the scavengers to feed on.

Knowing the horses couldn't be far away, he rode back away from the creek until he heard one of them give an inquiring whinny to Rascal and he found them tied in a clump of bushes. When he led them back to camp, he saw that Conner had given orders to tie the two would-be assassins hand and foot and leave them by the fire to dry their trousers. Conner was in the process of deciding what to do with Durham. As far as sleep was concerned, it was apparent that this night was shot, for there was already coffee boiling in the ashes of the fire. None of the soldiers were inclined to go back to bed as long as there was so much going on.

With a thought toward picking up an extra horse, Hawk wanted to identify the one that belonged to the dead man. He was pretty sure where he would get an honest answer, so he stopped by the fire long enough to ask Slim which horse belonged to the dead man. The red roan, he was promptly told. With any other officer, the horse would become government property, but with Conner, there was always a chance he might let Hawk take possession of it. He took the horses over with the army mounts and pulled the saddles off the three he had picked up.

"To tell you the truth, Durham," Conner was saying when Hawk walked up to listen, "I've never quite had a situation like yours before." He was obviously not sure what he should do with W. A. Clark's trusted assistant, whether to tie him up with his accomplices, or trust him to be on his good behavior until they reached Clark's offices at the quartz mill. Whereas it might seem fit to let Clark deal with him, it might be protocol to place him in jail and notify the U.S. Marshals Service to send a deputy to transport him back for trial. To his knowledge, there was no jail in Butte, however. As for Bevo and Slim, their crime was an assault on a U.S. Army patrol. They would be taken back to Fort Ellis to stand trial.

"I tell you, Lieutenant, you're making a huge mistake," Durham pleaded. "It's my word against the word of two craven outlaws, who obviously intended to steal this payroll and kill every one of us. Surely you won't take the word of an outright outlaw over one who was trusted enough by my employer to carry this money. This is not the first time I have been entrusted to carry the payroll."

He looked with pleading eyes from Conner to Hawk and back again.

"There's always a first time, I reckon," Hawk commented, firmly convinced that Durham was guilty of the conspiracy to steal the payroll.

"Here's what I'm gonna do," Conner finally decided. "I'm taking your two accomplices back with me to Fort Ellis to stand trial. If you'll give me your word that you won't try to escape, then I won't put you in restraints. But I'll be taking possession of those saddlebags holding the money. When we get to Butte, I'll turn you and the money over to your company and they can do whatever they think best." Durham looked sort of sick about the decision, but had to figure it was better than being trussed up like his conspirators for a full day of riding ahead of them before they reached Butte.

Upon reaching the headquarters of W. A. Clark's quartz enterprise, Lieutenant Conner, along with two troopers, escorted Durham into the office, where they were met by Clark's second-in-command. "Well, hello, John," Marshall Talbot greeted Durham. "I see you made it all right. With that escort, I can see why there wasn't much danger of trouble." He flashed a wide smile toward Conner. "Thank you for your help, Lieutenant. We're always grateful for the army's protection on these payroll runs." It struck him then that something didn't seem right. Instead of responding to his greeting, Durham remained silent and continued to stand behind the lieutenant and between the two soldiers.

"There was a little trouble on the ride up here," Conner began. He introduced himself, then went on to inform Talbot about the attempted payroll holdup. He handed the astonished Talbot the saddlebags carrying the money. "Like I said, we have two of the three accomplices in our custody and I see it as my responsibility to take them back to Fort Ellis for trial. I'm turning Mr. Durham over to you to punish as you see fit. I don't know of any precedent for his actions, so I'm not interested in taking him to a court."

Durham pleaded to the obviously flabbergasted Talbot. "Marshall, this is all some terrible mistake. I don't know why these outlaws who attempted to steal the payroll said that I was a part of it. It's such an absurd accusation, I would hope you know me better than to believe such a tale."

Totally at a loss as to what action he should take, Talbot was struck speechless for a long moment. Who could he believe? He wasn't sure. It was inconceivable to think John Durham capable of such a crime, but the accusations made by the lieutenant were hard to refute.

Knowing the quandary he had created for the milling company, Conner found the situation almost amusing. For his part, he didn't really care what the company did about Durham, he just wanted to be rid of him. So he said, "The army's responsibility ends with the delivery of the payroll and your employee. Good day, sir." He turned and walked out.

Outside, he climbed on his horse and laughed when he said to Hawk, "We sure left that fellow in a pickle. He doesn't have a clue about what to do with ol' Durham." He wheeled his horse and started back. "Let's get the hell away from here before they try to give him back to us." Hawk heard him chuckling to himself as he nudged his horse to lope away from the mill. Hawk followed, leading the red roan that had belonged to Johnny Dent. Behind him, the troopers escorted Bevo and Slim, their hands tied together behind their backs.

CHAPTER 9

They descended the trail they had arrived on, down from the hill and the diggings to the town of Butte, which was little more than a ghost town since most of the gold and silver miners had given up and moved on. There were a few dreamers still working the veins, but the only productive operations were now the less-precious mines, like W. A. Clark's. In the town, there was a post office, a general store, and a saloon, the latter of which drew the interest of the soldiers. Lieutenant Conner was a favorite among the enlisted men, not only for his fair-minded manner, but also because of his carefree disregard for strict military protocol. Consequently, it was not surprising that Corporal Johnson pulled up alongside of him and suggested that it would be good for morale if the men were allowed the opportunity to have a drink of whiskey. "We've delivered the payroll safe and sound and stopped an attempted robbery," he said. "It sure would go a long way with the men, if you were to let 'em have a drink or two. I'd go with 'em to make sure it didn't go any further than that."

"Oh, you would, huh?" Conner japed. "You'd make that sacrifice? Well, who's gonna make sure you limit yourself to one or two?" He let Johnson struggle for a reply for a second or two before giving in. "I wanna find a good spot to camp down here in the valley and we'll stop here for the night. When the camp is squared away and the horses are taken care of, you can let the men go into town, half of 'em at a time. I want guards on our prisoners at all times. Understood?"

"Yes, sir, understood," Johnson eagerly replied. "Thank you, sir."

"I don't want anybody failing to show up here before I'm ready to ride in the morning, Corporal. Is that understood? I'll send Hawk to look for them with orders to kill."

"Yes, sir," Johnson said. "I'll tell 'em," he said, and fell back to give the men the good news.

Hawk found a suitable place to make camp not too far from the town by a small stream. The rickety remains of an old sluice box bore evidence of past placer mining, but the water was now clear and there was grass enough for the horses. Since every man was supplied with rations for himself, there was normally no particular time when they ate it. On this occasion, however, Conner ordered every man to eat his supper before walking to the saloon. That way, he figured there was half a chance a couple of drinks on a full stomach wouldn't hit them too hard. "How about you?" Conner asked Hawk. "You wanna go have a drink, too?"

"Reckon not," Hawk replied. Thinking of the usual results that followed the release of a group of soldiers to the temptations of a saloon, he decided it might be best to have a few sober men left to keep an eye on things.

As soon as the chores were done, someone cut some branches into long and short sticks to see who went into town on the first shift. One of the men, a religious man named Solomon, had no desire to visit the saloon, so there were only six sticks cut and Solomon held them for the others to draw. The prisoners watched all this in silence until Bevo felt the urge to complain. "Hey," he yelled. "What about me? I could use a drink of likker. Ain't you gonna take care of your prisoners?"

"Why, hell," Corporal Johnson replied, pretending to be shocked. "Where's my manners? Course, you'll have to promise you'll come back."

Bevo sneered, but made no further comment. Slim, on the other hand, was baffled when Bevo failed to reply. "I promise I'll come back," he volunteered, in honest sincerity.

"Slim, you ain't got the brains of a pine knot," Bevo said.

"I wasn't really gonna come back," Slim whispered. "I was just gonna let him think I was."

Morning came early and painfully for the majority of the seven soldiers after a night of drinking with little or no sleep. Whereas he had been kindly indulgent in permitting his men to visit the saloon the night before, Lieutenant Conner showed no mercy in his marching orders on the morning after. The result was a slovenly column of cavalry that escorted their two prisoners through the mountain pass east of the town on the long march back to Fort Ellis. Of the numerous complaints, none was as legitimate as that from the prisoners, for they had spent the night sitting at the base of a tree, their arms and legs tied around the trunk. Conner confided to Hawk that it had been a mistake to let the men visit the saloon, thinking he could trust them to have a couple of shots and return to their duties. Hawk shrugged and said there was no real harm done, since all the men came back to camp. "You didn't make a mistake in trustin' the men. It's the whiskey you can't trust."

It was Conner's intent on the return march to simply use the same rest stops and camping sites they had used on the trip to Butte. So the first stop was at the Jefferson River to rest the horses and to make some coffee to doctor the aching heads that needed relief. "Lord, I hope to hell we don't encounter a Blackfoot war party," the lieutenant expressed to Hawk as they drank a cup of coffee. "We couldn't put up much of a fight." With the exception of the guard, Private Solomon, watching the prisoners and Hawk and himself, the rest of his command was trying to catch up on the sleep they had missed the night before.

"The Blackfeet ain't on the warpath now," Hawk said, "at least the village Bloody Hand belongs to ain't."

"You keep telling me that," Conner replied. "But I know they like to fight. It'll just be a matter of time and I hope this ain't the time—not while I'm commanding this gang of drunks." Hawk laughed, not really worried about the possibility. He glanced over at the two prisoners, seated on the opposite side of the fire from Private Solomon. They were drinking coffee and eating some strips of bacon, their wrists bound together by rope, since the patrol had no handcuffs or chains. "It's a good thing they had some bacon and jerky with them," Conner said, "or we wouldn't have anything to feed them."

"If you ain't in a hurry to get back, there's got to be plenty of deer up in those hills. I could take a little ride up there this evenin' and see if I could find one. That'd be plenty of meat for everybody. I expect your boys would enjoy some fresh roasted venison, too."

"That is a tempting thought," Conner said. "I'm not in any hurry to get back, but I hate to have the men lie around here for the rest of the day and put us a half day behind." He knew that the best time of day to hunt deer was in the morning or evening when they were more likely to come out to feed.

Hawk thought about that for a moment while the possibility of some fresh meat began to take hold in his mind. "I reckon I could go out now and see if I can run up on somethin', but I need to rest my horses, too. Tell you what, why don't I hang back here till Rascal's ready to go back to work? You boys can go on ahead. You don't need me to lead you back. I'll catch up with you at Three Forks, same place we camped before, and we'll see what kinda luck I'll have."

"I don't know," Conner replied, thinking it over. "There isn't any reason not to do it." If Hawk was as successful in the hunt as he usually was, the men could enjoy a feast without being a half day behind. "All right, that sounds good to me."

While Hawk and Conner were making plans for a deer supper, Private Solomon was relieved at guard over the prisoners by a reluctant Private Rakestraw. Unlike Solomon, Rakestraw had taken advantage of the opportunity to buy whiskey the night before in a quantity sufficient to turn his head into a gigantic bass drum on this morning. Two of the men had had to help him stagger back to camp the night before, and now that drum was pounding inside his temples. It was no secret that Corporal Johnson had put him on the guard detail to teach him a lesson on the evils of overindulgence.

Rakestraw's hungover state was recognized at once by Bevo Brogan. He studied Rakestraw's attempt to keep the bright sun from piercing the pupils of his eyes, trying to watch the prisoners through eyelids that were little more than slits. "Hey, stud," he said, "how 'bout takin' your knife there and cuttin' up this slab of bacon, so I can eat it?"

The question seemed to make Rakestraw's head pound harder. "Just chew it off," he replied.

"That's what I've been tryin' to do, but my teeth ain't too good. That's why I need it cut up."

Listening with great interest, Slim had to remark. "I never knowed your teeth weren't no good."

"Shut up, Slim," Bevo barked, then back to Rakestraw, he said, "It wouldn't take much. If I had my knife, I could cut it up in a jiffy, even with my hands tied together." He waited for a few seconds with no response from Rakestraw. "If you was to let me borrow that knife on your belt, I could save you the trouble. I'd just need it long enough to cut some of this bacon so's I wouldn't have to tear it off with my bad teeth." Rakestraw still hesitated. "You can watch me the whole time, hold your rifle on me, and I'll give the knife right back."

"All right," Rakestraw gave in. "Just cut it up and shut up about it." He drew the knife from his belt, tossed it toward him, and watched for a minute or two while Bevo made a big show of cutting the bacon with both wrists firmly tied. In a few more minutes, he grew tired of watching and tired of trying to force his eyes to remain open. The next thing he was conscious of was someone shaking him by his shoulders.

"Damn you, Rakestraw," Johnson cursed. "Wake up! Get on your feet! You sorry drunk, get over there and stick your head in the water. How the hell did you stay on your horse till we got here?" He gave the stumbling trooper a shove toward the river's edge and yelled, "McQueen! Get over here and keep your eye on these two birds."

A more-than-casual observer, Bevo Brogan watched the changing of his guard with Rakestraw's knife tucked neatly away up his shirtsleeve. He glanced over and shook his head at Slim when the simpleton nodded excitedly and grinned, looking as if about to say something. In a little while,

Conner gave the order to mount up and the
column moved out on the trail to Three Forks, all
save one. Hawk watched them depart before turning Rascal toward the northeast and heading for
the line of hills in the distance, leading the red
roan gelding that had once belonged to Johnny
Dent.

It was still an hour before sundown when Hawk
rejoined the soldiers at Three Forks. He rode into
the camp with the carcass of a six-point buck riding
across Johnny Dent's saddle. His arrival was met
with great enthusiasm in spite of the fact that most
of the men had already eaten their meager rations of bacon and hardtack. And there was no
shortage of volunteer help in skinning and butchering the deer. Corporal Johnson took charge of
most of the butchering after Hawk skinned the
deer, and Solomon promptly took on the actual
cooking duty. Even Rakestraw, whose head was
finally down to normal size, was eager to help, although lamenting the fact that he had lost his
knife. "I left the dang thing back yonder at that last
camp," he complained. A large campfire was built,
started up with the burning branches of two smaller
fires, and before much longer, fresh strips of venison were roasting over the flames.

"This escort detail turned into a damn Sunday
picnic," Lieutenant Conner was prompted to say to
Hawk, as they stood back to watch the men take
over.

"I had a taste for deer meat," Hawk replied.

"And you needed extra food for those prisoners you have to feed. They sure as hell didn't have much with 'em."

"That's a fact," Conner admitted. "I sure as hell didn't bring along provisions for prisoners." He glanced over at Bevo and Slim, eagerly consuming the portions of venison that Solomon had brought them. "They won't get that kind of feed where they're going."

"Reckon not," Hawk agreed.

Almost as if he had heard the lieutenant's comment, Bevo Brogan turned to look in his direction, the trace of a smile parting his whiskers. "That was downright thoughtful of them boys to put on this big feed for our last night as their guests," he said when their guard walked over to the fire to get another piece of meat. When Slim stared at him with one of his typical wide-eyed expressions of confusion, Bevo smiled broadly, without his usual harsh response to his partner's childlike reactions. Before Slim could ask what he meant, Bevo said, "Me and you are leavin' this little party tonight."

"We are?" Slim responded, instantly excited. "How we gonna do that?"

"Look at 'em," Bevo said, nodding toward the soldiers gathered around the fire. "Eatin' their bellies so full of that deer, ever' one of 'em's gonna be sleepin' like a baby tonight. Then we'll just slip on outta here and say good-bye to the army. And this is the best place they coulda picked to camp.

We can run straight down the valley to Nevada City."

"Hot damn!" Slim exclaimed, then paused when he thought further. "How we gonna do that? We'll be tied to a tree again, just like last night." Bevo didn't answer, but looked back at the guard to make sure he wasn't watching them. Then he let the knife slide down his sleeve until the tip of the blade fell into the palm of his hand. With a shift of his eyes, he directed Slim's gaze down to the knife blade. Slim's mouth dropped open, losing the generous bite of venison he was currently working on, but he managed not to exclaim.

Lowering his voice to a whisper again, Bevo said, "We'll wait till they're all asleep and cut ourselves loose. Then we'll get to the horses and be gone from here."

"What about the guard?" Slim whispered. "They'll have a guard watchin' us."

"We'll just have to wait and see," Bevo said, having already been thinking about that problem. "Maybe he'll go to sleep, too. If he don't, then I reckon I'll have to use this knife to make sure he don't make a sound."

"Maybe he'll go to sleep," Slim echoed. He thought about what Bevo proposed. It might work if they were lucky. Thinking about other things that could cause a problem, he asked, "What about that big feller in the buckskin shirt?"

"What about him?" Bevo asked.

"We might notta been caught in the first place if he didn't wander around in the woods at night. I ain't sure he ever sleeps."

"He better hope he ain't walkin' around tonight,"
Bevo answered him. "Now, hush up, that guard's
comin' back."

Bevo's predictions turned out to be pretty accurate. Although most of the men stayed awake
much later than usual, eventually their full bellies
drove them to their blankets for a deep sleep. In
spite of his excitement about the daring escape
they had planned, Slim also succumbed to the
sandman's call. *I ought to leave him here,* Bevo
thought when Slim began snoring before the first
guard was relieved by a second right at midnight.
Shortly after midnight, he relaxed the pressure in
his left arm that held the knife firmly against the
tree trunk. He had pressed the knife inside his
sleeve hard up against the trunk to keep it from
falling out when his hands had been tied to Slim's.
It was difficult to suppress a grunt of relief when he
could finally move his arm to free the knife and
he had to raise up enough for the knife to drop to
his hand. But as soon as it did, he began sawing on
the ropes that held Slim and him to the tree. Their
luck seemed to hold, because the guard that came
on then was already having a great deal of trouble
staying awake. Bevo pretended to be asleep when
the new guard came close to check on them. With
Slim's steady snoring, it appeared to the soldier
that he had nothing to worry about concerning his
prisoners.

Bevo maintained his patience as the guard
made an attempt to remain alert, but he soon set-

tled down to await his relief. In a short time, he
began to snore. A slow smile crept across Bevo's
face as he looked back at the sleeping soldiers. It
was just as he had envisioned it, but he had to look
again at the blanket belonging to the scout to
make sure he was in it. He was, so Bevo sawed away.
Still snoring, Slim didn't even wake up when his
hand was suddenly free and his arm dropped to
the ground. Bevo paused when he heard the guard
grunt and seem to be talking in his sleep. After a
moment, the guard settled down again and Bevo
clamped his free hand over Slim's mouth and nose
and held tightly until Slim suddenly jerked back,
trying to breathe. "Don't make a sound," Bevo
whispered, and held his hand over Slim's mouth
until he was sure he was awake. "Help me get our
hands untied."

It took a few moments for Slim to understand
what was happening, but when he did, he could
hardly contain his excitement. In a matter of minutes, they were free of their bonds. "We gotta get
to the horses," Bevo told him. "You go ahead, I'll
be right behind you." He waited to see that Slim
sneaked away toward the horses that had been tied
to a line between two trees at the water's edge.
When no cries of alarm rang out, he crept up carefully behind the guard, who was sleeping with his
back against a small tree. Reaching around the
tree, he suddenly grabbed the guard's mouth,
jerked his head back, and slit his throat, almost in
one motion. He picked up the guard's rifle, took
one more look in the direction of the sleeping
camp, then hurried over to join Slim.

"What was you doin'?" Slim whispered when Bevo got there.

"Makin' sure that guard didn't wake up."

"Damn, Bevo, you reckon you oughta done that? It they catch up with us now, they're liable to hang us."

"Reckon so, but if that guard happened to wake up before we could get outta here, he woulda had the whole camp on us. And we need time to get saddled up." He had no intention of leaving their saddles and saddlebags behind. Time was important, but they had a long run to Nevada City and it would be damn difficult without guns and supplies. So they took the time to reclaim their saddles and saddlebags, hurrying as much as they could, and when they were ready to ride, the camp was still sleeping. The last step they took to slow down pursuit was to untie the other horses. Then they herded them down toward the river ahead of them. When they were well clear of the camp and there was still no sound of alarm behind them, they let the horses scatter, then cut back to head south.

Hawk awoke with a start, thinking the camp was under attack. He grabbed his rifle and rolled out of his blanket ready to defend himself. He realized then that the alarm that had awakened the whole camp was the outcry of the soldier relieving the guard. Upon running to discover the trouble, he immediately saw that the prisoners were no longer tied to the tree. Looking toward the river then, he saw that the horses were also missing. "What the hell's going on?" he heard Conner demand.

"It's Anderson," he heard another soldier reply to the lieutenant. "He's dead! They cut his throat and escaped! I found him like this when I came to relieve him at guard."

One of the other soldiers came running up to report. "They drove the horses off with 'em!"

Conner was too concerned about the loss of one of his men at that moment to think about the loss of his horses. But before long, he couldn't help worrying about the mark this whole incident would leave on his record. Starting with his decision to let the men go to the saloon on the first night before starting back. Then letting them feast on venison the next night might make him the favorite officer among the men, but it might also cause him to lose his commission. Now if his men had to walk back to Fort Ellis because his prisoners stole his horses, he might find himself eating in the enlisted men's mess hall. Guessing his friend's predicament, Hawk tried to reassure him. "I doubt they stole your horses," he said. "They were most likely in too big a hurry to try to drive a herd of horses. I expect they just wanted to run 'em off to keep you from catchin' up to 'em. They won't go far." To demonstrate, he whistled, and in a few moments, Rascal appeared from the shadows and trotted up to be saddled. "I'll see if I can round up the other horses while you decide what you're gonna do." He knew that Conner was left with a critical decision to make. The two would-be robbers were now murderers because they had killed a soldier. There was no question but that the two men must be pursued and brought to justice. But Conner's patrol was not supplied with provisions to mount a long chase. They were already down to practically nothing and he couldn't afford the time it would take to return to the fort to be resupplied. Hawk stepped up into the saddle, wheeled the buckskin around, and paused. "I can try to track those two down. I'll move faster than a patrol and I won't be as easy to spot. Just wanted you to know you have that option. I'll go round up your horses now. I can't do much trackin' till daylight, anyway." There was no way of knowing if the two fugitives purposefully did it or not, but by riding out with the army mounts they would effectively lose their tracks among those left by the other horses. He would need daylight to try to distinguish between the two. It would be time lost, but he didn't see any choice in the matter. He gave Rascal a nudge and went after the horses.

As he suspected, the army's horses had not wandered far. He found them gathered together in a pocket of fir trees near the riverbank no more than a quarter of a mile from the camp. He grabbed the reins of a couple of them and started walking them back and, as he hoped, the others fell in behind him. He found Conner standing by the fire, waiting for him, and while the men took charge of their horses, he dismounted to talk to him. "Whaddaya wanna do?" Hawk asked.

"Damn it, Hawk," Conner started. "This thing has put my ass in a vise. I've lost one of my men on a simple escort patrol and I've let two prisoners escape." He looked at his friend and shook his head. "And none of it should have happened. It's all my fault. I got sloppy with the discipline of the patrol, and I'm going to have to answer for it." He grimaced as if reluctant to go on. "We're not provisioned to go after those two murderers and I can't take the time to go back for supplies. So I'm going to take you up on your suggestion. I know your job is a scout and not a lawman, but I know you'll find them. When you do, I only want you to report their whereabouts. I can't ask you to make any attempt to capture them. The army doesn't expect you to risk your neck, trying to arrest murderers. Just tell us where they are, all right?"

Hawk shrugged indifferently. He hadn't given any thought toward what his actions would be if he actually was able to track them. He was just leaving that to take care of itself, depending upon what circumstances he found himself in. "Don't worry, I won't stick my neck anywhere I think it might cost me my head."

"All right," Conner said. "While you see if you can find them, I'll ride on back to Fort Ellis and see if I can make out a report that doesn't look as bad as it is."

Daylight found the patrol mounted and ready to depart for Fort Ellis with a final word from Conner to Hawk. "Good luck, and remember, I don't expect you to make any arrest."

"I don't have any authority to arrest anybody,"

Hawk answered. He watched for a moment while the patrol pulled out, leading Private Anderson's horse with his body draped across the saddle. Hawk promptly turned and went to the trees where the horses had been tied the night before. The tracks were easily picked up where they had been herded away from the trees before scattering some few hundred yards farther along the river. At this point, he took time to study the tracks carefully, searching for two sets of tracks that would continue to veer off together and maintain a more or less definite direction. After a while, he found what he felt he was looking for, so he stopped to examine the tracks more carefully, trying to determine if the two horses that left them were carrying riders. From the depth of the impressions left in the sand near the water's edge, he decided they were the two he sought. He stood up and looked across the river to see what might lie ahead in that direction, but he knew he would have to find where they came out on the other side to know for sure. What he hoped to determine was a general direction that might give him a clue where they were heading. He figured there weren't many choices for directions they could run. Either north or south, for to go east or west would likely lead them into an army patrol.

When he crossed the river, he found their exit tracks right away. They had made no effort to lose anyone who might be tracking them, but struck out to the south, following the Madison River. Since they stuck close to the river, it made tracking them fairly easy, that and the fact that it was dark when they made their escape, so they were not as conscious of the tracks they were leaving. Since their trail continued down the valley, he had to wonder if they had a destination or were just running. There was not much in the way of towns down this valley between the Tobacco Root Mountains and the Madison Range. It was once a more heavily traveled trail to Virginia City before that town dried up, but there was nothing much to attract outlaws, unless their intention was to get lost. *Maybe that's what these two had in mind*, he thought.

It was late in the morning when he came to the ashes of a small fire. They had driven their horses a long way before resting them, which didn't surprise him. By this time, his horses were ready for a rest as well, so he stopped to let Rascal and the roan drink and graze on the many shoots by the water. Realizing he was hungry as well, he dined on some strips of roasted venison, left over from the night before. When his horses were rested, he continued on down the valley.

It had been some time since he had ridden the trail to Virginia City, so Hawk was mildly surprised to sight a small collection of structures in the valley ahead. Some wooden structures and a few tents, the settlement looked to be close to the onetime homestead of a man named Ennis. As he neared the settlement, Hawk determined the largest of the buildings to be a trading post with a stable behind, so he guided Rascal toward it. Maybe he could get some information on the two he pursued and he could pick up some coffee beans, too. He was just about out.

Rufus Tubbs stood in the doorway of his store watching the rider approaching. He squinted in an effort to make out his features, but he could not recognize him. He was the third stranger to come this way since that morning. Looking to be a sizable man, riding a buckskin horse, he wore his hat square on his head, not cocked to one side or the other. This was an important detail to Rufus. He figured a man that wore his hat cocked to the side didn't have his mind set on where he ought to be heading. He walked out on the porch and waited until Hawk pulled up by the hitching rail. "Afternoon," he called out in greeting.

"Afternoon," Hawk returned. "Wonder if I might buy some coffee beans from you?" He stepped down from the saddle.

"Sure can, neighbor," Rufus replied. "Come on in the store." He stepped aside while Hawk walked inside. "Don't believe I've ever seen you in these parts before. You just passin' through, or is Ennis where you was headed?"

"Just passin' through," Hawk replied. "The last time I rode this trail, there wasn't any town here."

Rufus chuckled. "Ain't much of one here now, but we're growin'. There's folks findin' out that cattle do pretty well in this valley. Where you headed?" He scooped coffee beans into a sack until Hawk motioned for him to stop.

"Virginia City, I reckon," Hawk answered after a

moment's pause. At this point, it was hard to guess the two fugitives he trailed could be heading anywhere but the old gold rush town.

Rufus studied the formidable man wearing a buckskin shirt for a long second before he followed his hunch. "Lookin' for two men, one of 'em sizable, the other'n wormy—both of 'em with their hats cocked over to the side?" The question caught Hawk by surprise. He had planned to eventually broach that subject, figuring the man might not volunteer the information.

"Maybe I am at that," Hawk answered. One of the fugitives was big and the other was a slight little man. That much was right on the money. He hadn't paid much attention to how they wore their hats, though.

"They came through here this mornin'," Rufus went on. "Maybe they was headin' to Virginia City, they didn't say. But if I was lookin' for 'em, I'd most likely head to Nevada City. That's where most of them outlaws on the run are headed for. What did they do, anyway?"

Still astonished by the flow of information pouring out of the talkative man's mouth, Hawk answered the question. "They killed a soldier. What's in Nevada City?"

"Not much of anything anymore. A few honest folks still hangin' on, since the gold played out," Rufus said. "There's a saloon and a hotel, a stable, even a general store hangin' on, but not much else. You bein' a lawman, I figured you'd know all that."

"I reckon that's the problem. I ain't a lawman."

Rufus looked truly stunned. "You ain't?" he blurted.

"Nope."

Rufus was speechless for a long moment, so sure had he been. Then the thought struck him that Hawk might be a friend of the other two. "But you said you was lookin' to catch up with those two fellers. I just naturally thought . . . Dang it! Are you sure you ain't a lawman?"

"I'm pretty sure," Hawk said. "But if I catch up with those two, I'll turn 'em over to the law. Like I said, they tried to rob a mine payroll up in Butte and they killed a soldier after they'd been captured. I ride scout for the army out of Fort Ellis."

"That's the same thing as a lawman in a way, ain't it?" Rufus replied. "I'm pretty good at readin' people. I mean, I knew those two fellers were outlaws the minute they walked in my store." He extended his hand then. "I'm Rufus Tubbs. I own this store."

Hawk shook his hand. "Pleased to meet you. My name's Hawk. Now tell me about this place up in Nevada City."

"I can tell you anything you need to know about Nevada City. Anywhere else on that gulch, too. I used to have my store in Nevada City, back before the gold ran out, but it ain't much more'n a ghost town now. I moved my business down here in the valley five years ago." He went on to tell Hawk about the arrival of an outlaw element a couple of years before, that soon turned what was left of the town into a hideout for anyone on the run. "A feller I know that had a blacksmith shop up there, came through here about a week ago, headin' for Bozeman. He said the outlaws walk all over the town like they own it. He said they've took over the hotel and the saloon. He figured he'd pack up and git before he caught a stray bullet from one of their drunken brawls."

That surely sounded a likely destination for the two he was tracking and not one for him, if he had any choice. It complicated his job only because instead of two outlaws to deal with, it sounded like there might be a hell of a lot more. They held further advantage because they could recognize him before he had an opportunity to get close. By nature, he was a stubborn man when it came to doing something that needed to be done, so it never entered his mind to turn around and go back for an army patrol. The two he was after might well be gone by that time. *We'll just have to see what's what*, he thought.

Rufus was happy to tell Hawk where the best trail into Nevada City forked off from the one leading to Virginia City. "It's about ten miles from here," he estimated, "most of it rough country. Stop by on your way back down, if you make it outta there alive."

"Thanks," Hawk said. "I'll try to do that." He thought about what he might have to do and decided he'd be better off without his packhorse. So he made arrangements with Rufus to leave the horse in his stable.

"I'll take good care of him for ya," Rufus promised. "How long should I give you?"

Hawk understood that he asked the question to determine how long he should wait before claiming the horse and packs as his property. "Better give me about three days, just in case it takes longer than I figure."

Rufus grinned. "I'll tell you what, I'll give you a week, and I hope to see you again. You be careful up there with them outlaws."

CHAPTER 10

He rode into Nevada City just as the sun disappeared behind the mountains to the west, leaving the town in the last traces of dusk. He saw the lights of the saloon at the opposite end of the street beyond the darkened doors of empty buildings that had no doubt been thriving shops and businesses in days long past. Near the middle of the street, the two-story hotel stood, the front doors wide open. A solitary figure smoking a pipe sat slouched in a rocking chair. He said nothing as Rascal padded slowly by, but stared openly at the tall rider. Hawk continued along the street, heading for a stable he saw beyond the saloon. A general merchandise shop owner paused to give Hawk a cautious look while closing a padlock on his front door.

There were two men in a fistfight in the street in front of the saloon. A handful of spectators watched as both men reeled in a circle. They were obviously too drunk to do each other much harm, but were just drunk enough to provide amusement for the spectators, who egged them on. Hawk did not recognize any of them as the two he looked for, and he hoped that the fading light was not enough to make him easily recognized. He continued on to the stables and the corral beside it. The husky man, called Bevo by his smaller partner, had ridden a sorrel with two white stockings on its front legs. Hawk wanted to see if he could spot the horse, so he rode around to the side of the corral before dismounting. As soon as he turned to look over the dozen or so horses milling about, he froze, stunned by the sight of a heavily spotted horse at the water trough. All thoughts of Bevo and Slim were immediately forgotten at the sight of the horse that looked like the gelding Zach Dubose rode. Without realizing it, Hawk tensed, his feet spread wide, his knees flexed, ready to react to attack from any quarter. He turned suddenly when, out of the corner of his eye, he glimpsed the dark figure of a man approaching from the back door of the stable. He cautioned himself to calm down when he didn't recognize the man.

"Howdy," Loafer Smith called out. "Didn't mean to startle you. You looked kinda jumpy there. If it's the law you're worried about, there ain't none in Nevada City."

Hawk responded with a forced chuckle. "I reckon I just didn't see you back there. I was just admirin' that Palouse over there. You don't see many with that pattern of spots on 'em."

"That's a fact," Loafer said. "That gelding belongs

to me, so I hope rustlin' horses ain't your line of work."

"Nope," Hawk replied. "I ain't got any thoughts about stealin' horses. Ya just don't see one like that very often."

"They ain't as rare as you might think. A couple of weeks ago, a fellow came through town with a horse that was the spittin' image of mine. I swear, if we'da took their bridles off, we coulda swapped horses without even knowin' it."

Thoughts were bouncing around in Hawk's brain like bullets ricocheting inside a rain barrel. There couldn't be that many horses that looked exactly like the one he was looking at now. He cautioned himself to be casual. "I knew a fellow that had a horse like yours—thought maybe it was his. That's the reason I stopped to admire yours. Zach Dubose, I ain't seen him in I don't know when. But it couldn'ta been Zach. He's up around Great Falls."

"Coulda been him, I reckon," Loafer said. "I don't rightly recall his name." He paused, then said, "Like I said, that was a week or more ago. I don't know if he even told me his name. He wasn't here but a couple of days."

Hawk couldn't help wondering if Loafer was purposefully losing his memory, just as a natural precaution, but he decided to continue pressing for information. "I'll bet ol' Zach woulda hung around a little longer, if he knew I was comin' this way. He'da been glad to see me. I owe him some money from a little business we did a couple of years back." He affected an amused chuckle and winked at Loafer. "Course, maybe I'm just as glad I missed him, 'cause I spent that money a long time ago. He didn't say where he was headed when he left here, did he?"

"Not that I recall," Loafer answered, then thought about it for a few seconds. "He did ask me how to get to the old Montana Trail. I told him most any trail you took outta Nevada City that was headin' west would strike the Montana Trail, just dependin' on how far you ride."

"I expect you're right," Hawk agreed. He didn't know for sure, he had never ridden the Montana Trail, but he had heard of it. It was a wagon road that a lot of folks used to haul freight before the railroads ran track into the territory. It ran north and south, starting in Salt Lake City, passing through eastern Idaho, and into Montana, up as far as Fort Benton. Along with the freighters with their mule trains and oxen, many settlers drove their wagons on the road. "I hope he's got some of the boys with him. They're havin' some trouble with the Bannocks up that way, aren't they?"

"Not no more," Loafer said, "not since the army went up there and massacred about half of 'em. The Nez Perce ain't causin' no trouble right now, either. You thinkin' 'bout headin' up that way? That feller you're talkin' about, Zach Dubose, was that his name? I wouldn't be surprised if he didn't cut across the mountains to pick up that trail. A lotta boys on the run have found 'em a new place to hide out down in Utah Territory."

"No," Hawk quickly assured him. "I ain't headin' that way at all." The longer he had talked to Loafer, the more he became convinced that he had nothing to fear from him, but there was no use in telling everyone what you were going to do. He might be completely wrong, but he had a strong feeling that the man Loafer talked about might be Zach Dubose. Maybe his hunch was so overpowering because it was the first sign of Dubose he had struck. So convinced was he that during the conversation with the stable owner he had all but forgotten what had led him to Nevada City in the first place. He immediately brought his mind back to the problem at hand. "No," he repeated. "I sure ain't goin' over that way. I'm supposed to meet a couple of fellows here. One of 'em's ridin' a horse like that one yonder with the two white stockin's."

Loafer paused for a moment to look at the horse Hawk referred to before he responded. "Yep, two fellers brought that sorrel and another'n in this mornin'. S'posed to leave 'em here for a couple of days." He paused again to study Hawk carefully then asked, "Are you a lawman?"

"That's the second time today I've been accused of lookin' like a lawman," Hawk replied. "No, I ain't a lawman."

"I ain't as dumb as I look," Loafer said. "These two fellers you say you're supposed to meet, I got an idea they ain't wantin' to meet you. I need to tell you there's a few honest folks still in this ghost town, folks that ain't on the run for committin' a crime. I'm one of 'em. I'm still here because, so far, I get paid for takin' care of whoever comes in here wantin' to board their horses. I ain't got no family to worry about, so I'll stay here as long as I do get paid. Those fellers you're askin' about are two of the sorriest-lookin' jaspers I've seen come into this town. And I expect you've got good reason to be lookin' for 'em. It ain't none of my business what your reasons are, so I don't wanna know. What I'm tryin' to tell you is I ain't gonna tell anybody that you're lookin' for somebody. I'm an honest man. I don't cheat anybody, outlaw or lawman. I'm just tryin' to make a livin', but I hope you do what you came here to do, young feller."

Hawk was astonished. He hadn't expected such a lengthy speech from the simple stable owner. Loafer was obviously convinced that Hawk was a lawman, regardless of claims to the contrary, and he wanted to make sure he understood that his was an honest business, regardless of his customers. He was also convinced that despite his eloquent denials Loafer was a willing source of information. "These two that just rode in, are they at the hotel?"

"Ain't but two places they all go," Loafer said, "hotel and the saloon. Some of 'em will hole up in an empty shop or somewhere when the hotel's full. But right now, there ain't enough of the bastards in town to fill the hotel."

"Much obliged," Hawk said, and extended his hand. "What do folks call you?"

"Folks call me Loafer. My given name's William Smith," he replied, shaking Hawk's hand.

"Pleased to meet you, Loafer. My name's Hawk." He stepped up into the saddle, his mind still not made up as to what he should do. When he rode into town, he was not sure how he was going to be able to capture Bevo and Slim, then ride out of town with them without having to battle a gang of outlaws. Lieutenant Conner's instructions to simply locate the fugitives, then let the army or the Marshals Service take over the arrest, seemed to make more sense, considering the odds in the outlaws' favor. Dynamiting the whole operation was the chance discovery of Zach Dubose's trail, which was far more important to Hawk than settling with Bevo and Slim. He wasn't sure where the closest telegraph was, even if he decided to wire Fort Ellis, so that would be more time lost while Dubose was going who knew where. He had to caution himself before deciding what to do. It was definitely an extremely long shot to ride off into Utah Territory with nothing to go on but the word of this man. *I need time to think before I make the wrong move,* he told himself. "I need somethin' to eat, too," he said aloud. "I just remembered I ain't had anythin' since sunup. How 'bout that little diner back up on the other side of the hotel? Who runs that?"

"Belle Lewis," Loafer replied. "She's been here since the first tent went up in this gulch—used to be a whore, till she got too old. She's a pretty good cook. I eat there, myself." He paused, watching Hawk's reaction, then he added, "She don't get much business from many of the other boys. They mostly eat at the saloon. Don't wanna get too far from the whiskey, I reckon." He chuckled in appreciation of his humor.

"Much obliged," Hawk said again, and wheeled Rascal to head back up the street. There was much he had to work out. Maybe he could think better with a little grub in his belly. Although finding himself in a quandary, he counted himself lucky to have run into Loafer Smith, not only for putting him on Dubose's trail, but for giving him at least one man in town he could trust. There was still the matter of Bevo Brogan and Slim Perry, the original reason for his landing in Nevada City. According to what Loafer told him, they were probably holed up in the hotel with no telling how many other men on the run from the law. At the moment, he didn't know how he might catch them apart from their fellow outlaws. He decided to come up with a plan over a hot meal, hoping a full stomach might activate an empty brain.

The light was rapidly fading now as he rode past the saloon again, his hand resting on the butt of the Winchester in his saddle sling. The fistfight had ended and the spectators had filed back into the saloon to talk about it over drinks. He continued past the hotel and pulled up in front of the small building with the sign over the door proclaiming it to be a diner. There were no horses at the rail where he looped Rascal's reins, causing him to wonder if he was too late for supper. He pulled the Winchester out and went in the door.

Inside, he found two people seated at a small table by the kitchen door. They were eating supper. They looked up in surprise when they saw him. When he hesitated, unsure if the diner was open, the woman greeted him. "Lookin' for some supper? Come on in, stranger, and set yourself down. I got some lamb stew on the stove." She got up and started for the kitchen, talking as she went. "I raised that lamb, myself. Jake, get the man a cup of coffee." The man she addressed as Jake pushed his chair back and slowly rose to his feet. Then he shuffled over to a sideboard to pick up an empty coffee cup and take it to a stove where the pot was sitting. After filling the cup, he stood motionless before Hawk, waiting for him to choose a table. He set the cup down when Hawk pulled a chair back from the end of the long table, never uttering a word, then went back to his supper. Hawk wondered if he was a mute.

In a few moments, the woman returned with a bowl piled high with stew and placed it on the table before him. Then she stood back, smiling, as if waiting for a comment from him. "Looks good," he offered, which seemed to satisfy her.

She stood over him, however, waiting for him to try the stew. "I bet you ain't had no lamb for a long time," she began. "Nothin' but pork and beef. A feller from down in the valley brought me that lamb's mama 'bout a year ago. He didn't know she was carryin' a baby. I didn't either till one mornin' out it popped. Well, I'd seen many a baby born, so I took care of it and raised it till it looked ready for my iron pot." She glanced over at the man busy eating his supper. "Ain't that right, Jake?" Jake looked up from his plate and nodded. She continued with her story. "'Bout a month after that lamb was born, I lost the mama. One of them drunken son of a bitches down at the saloon shot her." When Hawk failed to comment on that, she paused a moment, then said, "Well, I reckon you're gonna

let your stew get cold, if we don't stop gabbin'."
She went back to join Jake then.

Hawk studied the plump, matronly woman with
her lined face and gray-streaked hair for a moment
after she sat down. He tried to imagine what she
must have looked like when she was in her youth-
ful prime. *She might have been a fine-looking woman,*
he decided. Since she was still watching him, he
determined not to make a sour face if her stew
wasn't good. To his relief, it was very good. He gave
her a smiling nod.

"Who is it?" Bevo Brogan whispered low while
seated on the floor of the empty room, his back
against the wall, a half-full whiskey bottle on the
floor beside him. "Take a look."

Slim Perry was standing near the door of the
abandoned harness shop they had taken tempo-
rary residence in. He drew his .44 and sidled up to
the window to peek through the ragged remnant
of a curtain. "It's Loafer. Wonder what he wants."

"Hell, open the door and find out."

"Whatcha want, Loafer?" Slim asked when he
opened the door.

"I thought you boys might be interested to know
there's a stranger in town askin' questions about
you," Loafer said.

This captured their attention right away and
caused Bevo to scramble to his feet. "Soldiers?" He
blurted the first thought that came to mind.

"No," Loafer answered. "Ain't no soldiers. Ain't
but one man."

"One man?" Bevo exclaimed. "Lawman?"

"He says he ain't, but he sure looks like one to me. Claimed he was supposed to meet you two fellers here—askin' me all kinds of questions—even asked about that feller that came through here a while back, ridin' a horse like that Palouse he saw in my corral."

"What did he look like?" Bevo asked, thinking at once of the scout who had captured them.

"He's a sizable man, wearin' a buckskin shirt." He remembered then. "And he's ridin' a buckskin horse."

"It's that son of a bitch that shot Johnny," Slim blurted, "that damn scout ridin' with the soldiers. He's the one that sneaked up on us when we was gettin' ready to rob that payroll."

"That's him, all right," Bevo said, certain that Hawk had tracked them down. "And you're sure there wasn't no soldiers with him?" Loafer shook his head. "Maybe settin' back hidin' behind your barn?" Loafer continued to shake his head. "He came up here, in this place, all by his lonesome?" It was difficult for him to think that one man would dare to come after them by himself—a squad of soldiers, maybe, but not one man. "Hell," he said to Slim, "we couldn't have asked for anythin' better'n this. We owe that son of a bitch a killin', and he's come to the right place to get it." Turning back to Loafer, he asked, "Where'd he go after he left your place?"

"Belle's place," Loafer said with a satisfied grin. "He went to get hisself somethin' to eat." He grinned again, finding that amusing. "I expect that's where he is right now."

Excited now, Bevo grabbed his gun belt and slapped it around his waist. "Come on, Slim, let's catch him before he gets outta there."

"Hell, Belle's cookin' might save you boys the trouble of killin' him," Loafer said, laughing outright as he followed them out the door. "I told him I ate there."

At that particular moment, Hawk was having similar thoughts about Belle's cooking. At first taste, the lamb stew seemed very good, but upon finishing about half of it, he began to hear rumbling noises in his stomach accompanied by an uneasy feeling. He suddenly suspected that the lamb he was eating was tainted, turned bad, and it was too late because he already had a belly half-full. "Bread!" he blurted, startling the couple at the small table. "Have you got any bread?"

"Bread," Belle echoed. "I didn't give you no bread? Jake, get the gentleman some bread."

Jake went in the kitchen and returned a minute or two later with a chunk of bread from what had been a large loaf. Hawk, desperate to quell the eruption threatening deep down in his gut, didn't wait for the bread to reach the table, snatching it off the plate while it was still in Jake's hand. He bit off hunks of the stale bread, hoping it would help by absorbing the stew inside him while the two astonished spectators watched. "Outhouse!" he finally blurted when it was clear the bread was not going to work. Still speechless, both spectators pointed to the kitchen door. He didn't wait, but, grabbing his rifle, he dashed through the door, through the kitchen, and out the back door. He made it to the outhouse without a moment to spare. He could never remember ever having felt so sick in his life before as the lamb decided it would use the upper and lower exits simultaneously as it departed his stomach.

In a few minutes, although it seemed an eternity, he felt he had some measure of control again. He decided at that moment that he was going to break his usual practice of complimenting the cooking no matter how good or bad. In fact, he saw no reason to go back inside the diner at all. He just wanted to get to a cool stream and clean himself up a little and had no intention of paying for his supper. Outside the outhouse, he stopped and took a moment to breathe in some of the cool evening air. Then he started to walk around to the front of the diner where his horse was tied, but stopped when he saw three men in the street, walking toward the diner. Even in his present state, he recognized Loafer, but the two walking with him caused him to freeze in his tracks. Bevo and Slim, he was sure of it, and they had obviously not seen him. *That low-down son of a bitch,* he thought when he realized Loafer had double-crossed him. Suddenly the troubles inside his body were temporarily forgotten, replaced by the call to fight. He remained motionless until the three entered the diner.

Loafer held back when Bevo and Slim suddenly kicked the door open and charged in, guns drawn, to see no one but Belle and Jake, still seated at the table. Astonished for the second time in less than fifteen minutes, they could only sit there, gaping. Outside on the porch, Loafer, still grinning with anticipation for the showdown he had orchestrated, sobered immediately when he felt the cold barrel of the Winchester against the back of his neck. "One peep outta you and I'll blow a hole right through the back of your head." Loafer felt the handgun he wore slowly rising out of his holster. Hawk motioned toward a bench at the edge of the porch. "Get over there and sit down."

"Yes, sir, ain't no trouble outta me," Loafer pleaded. "I got no hand in this game." He promptly did as he was told.

"You got a hand in it, all right," Hawk threatened. "And I ain't decided what I'm gonna do about it. But I promise you this, if you don't sit there with your mouth shut, you're a dead man, 'cause you'll get the first bullet. You understand?"

"Yes, sir, I understand," Loafer answered. "Mouth shut, I ain't movin' off this bench till you tell me to." He had never seen a man as angry as Hawk obviously was, with no idea that a huge part of his fury was instigated by agony left from his encounter with Belle's lamb stew. Reasonably sure that this time he could take Loafer at his word, Hawk turned his attention to the two would-be assassins whose loud demands could be heard through the open door.

"Where is he, you crazy ol' bitch?" Bevo demanded, and used his .44 to motion at the half-finished plate of stew on the table. He failed to read the message conveyed by her wide-open eyes at the sight of the avenging stranger behind him.

"I'm right here," Hawk said softly. Both Bevo and Slim froze, stopped by the deadly promise in his tone. "Both of you drop your weapons and I'll let you live to go to trial for killin' that soldier."

Caught with their backs to him, both outlaws hesitated to try to turn and shoot, but when Hawk offered to take them back for trial, Bevo was emboldened to challenge him. "You arrestin' us? You ain't no lawman, you can't arrest nobody. How you gonna ride outta here without gettin' shot? Lawmen ain't welcome around here, and somebody actin' like one is dead meat."

"You're runnin' outta time," Hawk said. "I've told you what your choices are, so drop those pistols on the floor."

"If me and Slim turn at the same time, you ain't gonna have time to get both of us. Did you think about that?"

"That's right," Slim finally piped up. "You can't get both of us."

"I thought about it," Hawk answered Bevo. "I reckon we'll just have to see who the sun shines on tomorrow, but one of you ain't gonna see it."

Bevo made his decision. "On three," he whispered to Slim. "One . . ." was as far as he got before Slim, his nerves stretched beyond controllable limits, whirled around to shoot. Hawk fired before he was halfway around, cutting the simple outlaw down. Then, without losing a second, he instantly stepped to the side, using the doorframe for protection as he cocked his rifle while Bevo's hurried shot snapped through the empty doorway. Hawk stepped back and shattered Bevo's breastbone before he could cock his pistol again. He slumped to the floor, his eyes wide in disbelief. In a few seconds, the shock of the bullet in his chest turned to pain and he realized he was dying. Clutching his chest, his final words were meant for his partner. "I said 'on three,' you dumb shit. You kilt us both."

Hawk turned back toward the end of the porch, but the bench was empty, Loafer having taken advantage of an opportunity to run. Knowing his tendency to spread the news now, Hawk presumed he didn't have time to dawdle. He stepped inside to make sure both men were dead, then glanced at the man and woman sitting like statues at the table. "Sorry 'bout the mess," he said, then hurried out the door. There was still the problem of getting out of town before a mob of lawless men decided to avenge two of their outlaw brothers. Hawk climbed into the saddle and took a quick look around him to select his best route of escape. He figured Loafer would have headed straight for the saloon to tell about the shooting, so he decided his best bet to escape would be to head in the direction the mob was coming from. "Rascal, now's the time to do your job," he said as he wheeled the big buckskin and galloped off behind the diner to race along the alley behind the buildings. He experienced a small stab of pain in his gut as he galloped past Belle's outhouse and it occurred to him that he had forgotten the misery he had been in. That caused him to think that maybe he owed Belle his thanks for her part in saving his life, or maybe it was the lamb that should get the credit.

Glancing between the buildings as he passed behind them, he could see men running up the street toward the diner and he admonished himself for pulling such a boneheaded stunt. In all honesty, he might have very well decided to forget about attempting to capture Bevo and Slim in the face of such odds. If he had simply reported to the military where the fugitives had fled to, then he would have completed his job. As far as killing both men, he had to believe he was given no choice, circumstances having been what they were. Maybe there should be guilt to be considered for having killed two men. He would let higher powers decide that issue. Besides, the two outlaws were destined to be hanged, if they had made it to trial. His concern now was to save his own neck.

Once he left the town of Nevada City behind, he reined Rascal back to a pace the big horse could maintain for a while. There were many trails coming into the once-bustling town. He picked one that looked as if it might take him east, out of the mountains, and back to the valley where he had left his packhorse. When he felt sure he was not being followed, he stopped to give Rascal a drink at a busy stream near the valley floor. Suddenly reminded of the rancid taste in his mouth from his episode in the outhouse, he dropped on his stomach beside his horse and did his best to rinse the episode from his memory.

His mind returned to focus on Zach Dubose. He felt sure the rider of the Palouse that Loafer had talked about was Dubose. He had to be. It was the first possibility he had come across since Dubose had eluded him at the Hog Ranch in Big Timber. If he found a town that had a telegraph, he would wire Fort Ellis the news of the demise of the two fugitives they sought for the murder of Private Anderson. He didn't have any evidence to prove they were dead, but he knew Lieutenant Conner would take his word for it. Then maybe he could convince Major Brisbin. At this particular time, Hawk didn't care if they believed it or not. He had something more important to him to pursue, and the first order of business was to fetch his packhorse.

"Looks like I ain't gonna own me a packhorse," Rufus Tubbs greeted him cheerfully when Hawk reined Rascal up to the rail. "I kinda had an idea you'd be showin' up. You didn't find them two outlaws?"

"I found 'em," Hawk replied. "They didn't wanna come back with me, so they stayed in Nevada City."

Rufus felt no need to ask for additional clarification of the matter. As far as he was concerned, he had accurately judged the earnest young army scout the first day he walked into his store. "Well, since you've settled that, where are you headed now, back to Fort Ellis?"

"Nope, I just came back this way to get my packhorse. Then I reckon I'll head back west to see if I can strike the Montana Trail, up from Utah. I've been told if I head straight west, I can't miss it. You agree with that?"

Rufus laughed. "Well, I reckon that's pretty much the general idea. If you want directions a little more specific, I can help you out. Where you thinkin' about headin' after you strike the trail, north or south?"

"South," Hawk answered. He had no idea where Dubose might be heading, but he doubted he would turn north, since that would take him back to Butte.

"In that case," Rufus said, "the best way to go is to take a trail about a quarter of a mile back up the valley. It's an old trail used by the Bannock Indians when they traveled over into this valley to hunt. It'll be easy to find the trailhead. There's a big old rack of elk horns nailed to a fir tree." He paused to chuckle over that. "It was nailed up by a white man—Injuns didn't need a sign. Follow that trail. It'll lead you past the foot of the Tobacco Root Mountains, west to strike the Ruby River in about half a day's ride. Another half a day oughta get you to the Beaverhead River. Follow that river and it'll take you to strike the Montana Trail farther south."

"Much obliged," Hawk said. He settled up with him for boarding his packhorse and bought a few supplies from him in case his search might take him into the winter months, for summer was already fading. Then he struck out to find the fir tree with the elk antlers.

The Indian trail was as easy to find as Rufus had said it would be, and his estimates on the distances turned out to be reliable, for Hawk struck the

Ruby around noon. After that, it was not as simple as Rufus predicted, for the trail seemed to end at the Ruby. After resting the horses, Hawk decided he was going to have to find this old Montana Trail on his own. So he headed a little more south to ride around the southern slopes of the Ruby Mountains, trying to work his way back to the west across rolling treeless terrain. Like Loafer had said, if he kept going west, he was bound to strike the Montana Trail eventually. And when he did, he was sure he would recognize it. It was bound to be scarred with the tracks left by the countless settlers and their wagons, as well as mule trains and oxen, pulling heavily loaded freight wagons. "Then, I reckon I'll just head south and see if we can pick up Mr. Dubose's trail," he informed Rascal. Even as he said it, he couldn't escape the feeling that he was embarking on a hopeless mission, searching for a needle in a haystack. "Why would Dubose head down through this wilderness?" He questioned the sense of it. "Maybe I'm makin' a big mistake." It struck him then that he had in fact blundered into a huge waste of time. He had carelessly accepted another of Loafer's stories as truth when he should have realized that the Palouse he had seen in the stable was the one he had been following all along. There was no second horse, and the realization that he had been so stupid to have thought that there was made him feel like a blithering idiot.

CHAPTER 11

"Mornin', Zach," Loafer Smith said when he turned to discover Dubose coming in the door of his stable. "You comin' to get your horse?"

"Yeah," Dubose replied. "I reckon I've had about enough of that damn saloon. I need to head for somewhere to hell away from Nevada City. My shoulder feels damn near as good as new. Ain't no need for me to lay around here no more." He unconsciously reached up to feel the healed-up wound behind his shoulder. "Besides, damned if every lawman in the country don't know this is the place to look for an outlaw."

"Maybe you're right," Loafer said, then chuckled. "I know one lawman that's headed west across the mountains, lookin' for that old Montana Trail and headin' for Salt Lake City." He laughed again. "At least I think he's a lawman. He said he wasn't."

Dubose had to laugh at the thought as well. "I ain't forgot what you done," he said. "So I'm payin' you a little extra for your trouble." That brought a wide grin to Loafer's face. Dubose paused to think about Hawk. It seemed to him one hell of a coincidence that he showed up here, looking for those two small-time outlaws, at the same time asking about him. He had to agree with Loafer, the man had to be a lawman—or maybe a bounty hunter—to even know about him. But then there was the way the relentless tracker took care of the problem of Bevo and Slim, shot them down with little regard for taking them in to collect a reward. He wondered then if Hog or Red had crossed paths with Hawk, and if so, did they end up the way these two did? He couldn't rule out the possibility that maybe it was one of them that told Hawk to look for him here. When he left Big Timber, he didn't tell them where he was heading, but they had hidden out here before. They might have guessed he would head for Nevada City. *The double-dealing bastards*, he thought.

How can this one man keep showing up everywhere I go? Dubose asked himself. He ran after he killed Bevo and Slim, but he would have been a fool not to. Nevada City was now considered outlaw territory, and any lawman coming here to make an arrest was dead meat. He might have found himself in a standoff with at least a dozen outlaws, all of them out to kill him. If Loafer did as good a job as he bragged about, then Hawk was riding south on the Montana Trail, but that didn't mean he wouldn't come back. Whoever he was, it was plain to see that Zach Dubose was the next one on his list. So he planned to be long gone in case Hawk decided to come back to Nevada City, instead of going to Utah, chasing air. So far, there was no sign of him this morning, so maybe Loafer was right. "You sure it was the same man askin' about me that killed those two last night?"

"I'm sure, all right," Loafer answered. "I was standin' right behind him on the porch there at Belle's when he killed 'em. That's the reason I'm sure he's a lawman, 'cause he tried to arrest 'em and take 'em to trial, but they drew on him. And I'm here to tell you, he didn't waste no time takin' care of 'em—cut 'em down like winter wheat— didn't even think about woundin' 'em. I tried to warn them two, just like I did you. But instead of layin' low, like you did, they decided to go after him." He chuckled again, unable to resist joking. "Hell, he ate some of Belle's cookin', and if that wasn't enough to kill him, nothin' can."

Dubose forced a grin. "You might be right about that. That's another favor I reckon I owe you for, warnin' me about Belle's Diner." He reached in his pocket and pulled out a roll of bills. "How much do I owe you for takin' care of my horse?" When Loafer told him his board bill had added up to four dollars, Dubose started peeling off several bills, and Loafer went to fetch the Palouse gelding.

"I saddled him for you," Loafer said when he led the horse out of the stable. "You can check your cinch to see if it's the way you like it."

"It's fine," Dubose said after giving it a tug. He handed Loafer the money and stepped up into the saddle. "I 'preciate your help. There's a little extra there for tippin' me off about that lawman." He gave the Palouse a nudge with his heels and headed toward the street.

"Much obliged," Loafer called after him, then hurriedly counted the bills Dubose had handed him. In a second, his grin turned into a disappointed frown. "Four, five, six, seven," he counted. "Seven dollars," he snarled. "You cheap son of a bitch, I saved your ass from gettin' shot and you pay me three dollars for that! I hope to hell that lawman catches up with you."

It had been two days since Zach Dubose had departed Nevada City, and Loafer was still complaining to everyone who came in the stable about his meager reward for his part in saving his life. Some he complained to said that perhaps Dubose didn't have any more than those few dollars. But a couple of those who had rooms over the saloon where Dubose was hiding out were sure that he was carrying a sizable sum of money. "I know damn well he was," Loafer whined. "I saw the size of that roll of money he was carryin' in his pocket." He was still mumbling to himself about it that night when he climbed up in the loft to throw some hay down. Descending the ladder again, he reached for his lantern and struck a match to light it.

"I don't see that spotted horse of yours anywhere."

The voice came out of the dark like a shaft of steel through Loafer's heart, freezing the blood in his veins, just at the moment he struck the match. Then he saw him in the flare of the match, standing

next to a corner post, his rifle cradled, ready to
fire. He feared he was looking into the face of
death. "Hey, wait a minute," Loafer stuttered. "I
didn't know Dubose was here when you asked me
about him!"

"Loafer," Hawk started impatiently, "why do you
wanna start lyin' to me again? That damn horse is
gone, so that means Dubose is gone, too. Right?"
Loafer nodded, then let out a little yelp when the
match burned down to his fingers and he dropped
it. "Stomp it out," Hawk ordered, his tone soft and
patient now, as if addressing a child. Loafer did as
he was told, stamping out the small flames that had
already caught in the hay. "Now, how long has he
been gone?"

"Two days come this mornin'," Loafer dutifully
reported.

"Where was he headed?"

"I don't know," Loafer replied. "I swear to God,"
he quickly added when Hawk cranked a cartridge
into the chamber of the Winchester. "I'm done
lyin' to you, mister. He didn't say where he was
goin', just said that since you were headed west, he
was goin' in the opposite direction." When Hawk
paused to consider that for a moment, Loafer
pleaded, "There ain't no reason for me to lie to
you. I swear, he's gone and he didn't tell me
nothin' else." Remembering then how mad he had
been at Dubose for the skimpy reward he got for
saving him before, he became suddenly more talkative. "No, sir, the son of a bitch wouldn't say where
he was goin', but when he left here he took that
trail headin' out between the blacksmith shop and

that old empty store next to it. My guess is that he'll follow the Madison River north when he gets to the valley, 'cause I doubt he'll wanna keep ridin' straight through those mountains on the other side."

Hawk was not yet ready to trust Loafer, but he felt he was probably right about the direction Dubose was headed. And he agreed that Dubose would not likely head up into the mountains on the other side of the Madison. Men like Dubose needed the saloons and the whorehouses to satisfy their needs. So it was reasonable to assume he would likely show up in one of the towns along the Yellowstone on his way to wherever he thought was his safe haven. It was Hawk's hope that he would pick up his trail in one of those towns. At any rate, he was finished with Nevada City, so his next priority was to get out of town without alerting anyone else. He felt he could safely assume that Loafer had informed every outlaw in town about the presence of a "lawman" before, and would inform them again as soon as he got the chance. He wasn't ready to discount the possibility that one of them might take a shot at him if they had the opportunity. And that included Loafer. "All right, Loafer," Hawk said. "I was thinkin' about puttin' a hole in you for wastin' my time with that tale that sent me off on a wild-goose chase. But I'm gonna let you live to lie another day. I'm gonna relieve you of that six-gun you're wearin', then I'm gonna make you comfortable while I ride outta here."

Loafer made no effort to resist while Hawk disarmed him and tossed the weapon over into a stall. Then he marched Loafer over to the side of another stall where he had seen a rope coiled. After tying Loafer's hands together, then tying them to the rail of the stall, he stuck the knife Loafer had carried firmly into the rail. When he was satisfied with the situation, he said, "Now, if you're as handy with your hands as you are with your mouth, you can just reach that knife. And if you're careful, you oughta be able to saw through that rope before too long."

Making no comment during all this, Loafer felt compelled to ask one question. "I'd just like to know, are you a lawman?"

"No, for a fact, I'm not," Hawk answered. "I'm just doin' somethin' that needs doin'."

His answer made it a little easier on Loafer's conscience to say what was on his mind. "I hope to hell you catch up with that no-good son of a bitch. And you ain't gonna hear a peep outta me till you're long gone."

"I 'preciate that, Loafer," Hawk said, and walked out of the stable. A few seconds later, Loafer heard the sound of his horse's hooves as Hawk rode away.

Taking the trail that Loafer had indicated, Hawk rode out of Nevada City without being seen by any of the few drunks lolling on the steps of the saloon, making his way along under a three-quarter moon that made it easy to follow the narrow track. Rascal and his packhorse had worked a full day already and Hawk knew they needed rest. So when he crossed a lively stream a few miles away from the town, he decided he'd risk the possibility of any pursuit. In his opinion, it wasn't much of a risk, anyway. He didn't expect the gaggle of lawbreakers hiding out there to possess the zeal to organize a posse. But just in case, he followed the stream back until he found a place that offered some cover, and where a small fire would not be seen from the trail. The night passed peacefully and he was on his way early the next morning.

It was still early morning when he approached the trading post beside the Madison River where he had boarded his packhorse before. He had no reason to stop there again other than the possibility that Dubose might have. And if so, maybe he could confirm his assumption that the outlaw had headed north and not into the Madison Mountains. He spotted Rufus Tubbs standing on the porch of his store at almost the same time Rufus turned to watch him. As he narrowed the distance, he could see the smile on Rufus's face.

"Well, howdy, Mr. Hawk," Rufus called out when Hawk reined Rascal to a stop. "Didn't expect to see you back this way. I thought you'd be halfway to Eagle Rock by now."

"Rufus," Hawk returned in greeting. "No, I changed my mind about findin' that trail. I'm headin' back the way I came before."

"Well, step down and light awhile. I was just fixin' to go inside and have myself a cup of coffee. I believe summer's about run its course. The air's already gettin' a little nippy. Whaddaya say? You could use a cup, couldn't you? Won't cost you nothin'."

"Well, now, that sounds to my likin'," Hawk replied, and stepped down. He was in a hurry to catch up with Dubose, but he knew the chase would be measured in days and not in minutes. When he rolled out of his blanket that morning, he chewed on a strip of jerky, but that was all the breakfast he'd had. He hadn't even built a fire for coffee because he had an idea he might buy that at Rufus's store. Wrapping Rascal's reins loosely around the rail, he followed Rufus inside.

The little iron stove in the middle of the store was glowing cherry red and the gray coffeepot was sitting as close to the edge of the top as it could get without falling off. Otherwise, it would be hard to keep the coffee from boiling away. "Leanne," Rufus called. In a moment, a young girl came into the room. "Leanne, honey, pour us a cup of coffee." He looked at Hawk. "You had your breakfast?" He didn't wait for Hawk's answer, instead looking back at the girl. "Have you got any more of them corn cakes you and your mama made this mornin'?" The girl nodded. "Bring us a couple of 'em." She turned immediately to do his bidding.

"She doesn't talk much, does she?" Hawk commented.

"No, she's good about that. It don't come natural, though, 'cause her mama can't seem to shut up for more'n two or three minutes a day."

"Bannock?" Hawk asked.

"Nez Perce," Rufus answered. "I took her and her mama in after that big fight at the Big Hole. Her daddy was killed in that battle with the soldiers. So many of the survivors scattered and Leanne and her mama ended up over in this valley. I took 'em in and I reckon her mama was just satisfied to stay."

"Leanne," Hawk said. "Is that her real name?" It didn't sound like a Nez Perce name to him.

"Nah, her mama told me her Injun name, but I never could say it right. I don't know what it means, but it sounded like Leanne to me, so that's what we call her."

In a few moments, the girl returned with the corn cakes, her mother following close behind her. Rufus had not exaggerated, the round little woman chattered away from the moment she walked in the room. Still talking, she went to the stove, wrapped a heavy cloth around the handle of the coffeepot, then brought it to the table and poured into the cups Leanne had placed there. She never stopped talking during the entire procedure. It sounded to Hawk like scolding, so he asked Rufus what she was saying. "Damned if I know," Rufus replied. "I don't speak no Nez Perce."

Hawk nodded to the woman, who was eyeing him openly. "Thank you, ma'am." She paused for a moment, then smiled at him. But it was only for a moment, then she directed more of what sounded like scolding at Rufus.

It seemed to tickle Rufus. "Ain't she somethin'?" He took a bite of the corn cake. "She can sure cook, though. So can her daughter. It beats what I'd been cookin' for myself before she moved in with me. You get used to the talkin'—kinda like hearin' the wind blow—don't pay no attention to it till it stops. Then you sit up real sudden and snort, *What was that*? It's what you get used to, I reckon." He chuckled at the thought. "That's a damn good corn cake, ain't it?" Hawk said that it surely was. Rufus went on. "Leanne mighta made 'em. I can't tell the cookin' apart—don't know which one does it sometimes. She's gettin' past the time when a young girl oughta be matin' up with a young man. I expect if they was still with their village, she'd already been married, as pretty a gal as she is."

Hawk was beginning to suspect an ulterior motive for the invitation to have coffee and corn cakes. He cast a suspicious eye in Rufus's direction. "Listenin' to you, a man might think you've got one too many women in your house. You ain't tryin' to get rid of Leanne, are you?"

Rufus almost blushed. "It mighta sounded like that, I reckon, but it wouldn't be no trouble to get rid of Leanne if I didn't care who got her. I read you as an honest man, so I just thought I'd mention her in case you didn't have a woman somewhere and you were lookin' for a good one."

With all that was going on in his hunt for outlaws, it was almost inconceivable to think that he was being offered a woman—and without the woman's say-so in the matter. Leanne was an attractive girl, he guessed. He had really not paid that much attention to her, and looking at her now, he felt sorry for her. He was reminded anew of JoJo, although their situations were not the same. "No," he finally responded, "I don't have a wife. I 'preciate you thinkin' I was good enough for Leanne, but I wouldn't ask a woman to put up with the life

I lead. I'd never be home, so she'd likely be a widow, or just the same as one with no husband there. You know why I came here already, and now I'm huntin' for another man who's gonna lead me God knows where."

"'Preciate your honesty," Rufus said, then dropped the subject as if it had never been brought up. "Have another cup of coffee." He turned to the girl. "Leanne." She brought the pot and looked at Hawk as if to say thank you for not taking her from her mother. Hawk decided she might be younger than Rufus let on. "You say you're after another feller?" Rufus continued. Hawk nodded. "Wouldn't by any chance be a man ridin' one of them spotted horses the Nez Perce breed, would it?"

"It would," Hawk replied. "He was here?"

"Two, no, three days ago," Rufus said. "Stopped in here wantin' to know if I had any chewin' tobacco—heavyset fellow, had a mean look about him—bought every last plug I had and a slab of bacon. From the look of him when he walked in, I was halfway afraid he was fixin' to rob me. I stayed close to the shotgun I keep under the counter, but he paid. He pulled out a roll of money big enough to choke a hog."

"Did he head up the valley?" Hawk asked.

"When he left here, he did, as far as I could see, anyway. I told Mama to keep Leanne in the back room till he was gone. What are you chasin' him for?"

"He killed a young girl, about the same age as Leanne."

Hawk's answer sobered Rufus for a moment. "My Lord," he exclaimed, then he pressed Hawk again. "I know you're a lawman. I ain't ever heard of any army scout goin' after outlaws before and that's all you've been doin'. If you ain't a lawman, you're a bounty hunter. Now, tell me if I'm wrong."

"Like I told you before, I ride scout for the army outta Fort Ellis. Things just happened to put me on this path, things I didn't want to happen. I'll be goin' back to my job with the army as soon as I get finished with the fellow ridin' that Palouse horse." Once again, he felt the discomfort of filling the role of a lawman. The only living things he wanted to hunt were things fit to cook over a campfire. He had already been away from Fort Ellis too long, but he couldn't give up on the hunt for Zach Dubose now that he was finally on his trail. He had made a solemn commitment to the memory of the young girl called JoJo, and he took that promise as seriously as any he had ever made. And now that he had a trail to follow, no matter how slim it was, he would not let himself quit the chase. With those thoughts weighing heavily on his mind, he bid Rufus farewell and started out to follow the Madison River north.

Following the river was a common trail that had been used enough to show some old tracks as well as some that he decided could be as fresh as three days old. When he had ridden for what he estimated to be about twenty miles or so, he began looking for places that offered good stops for horse and rider. He found several, and the third one he checked had the ashes of a small fire near the bank of the river. Thinking this might be the spot Dubose picked to rest his horse and cook some of that bacon he bought from Rufus, Hawk reined Rascal to a stop and dismounted. Freeing his horses to drink and rest, he began a closer search of the area around the ashes in hopes of discovering some imperfection in the shoes on the Palouse that would give him some means of distinguishing the horse from others. He couldn't find anything that stood out, however. He had no guarantee that he was looking at the Palouse's hoofprints, anyway. He was still going on a gut feeling. He found tracks that could be fresh enough, they were going in the right direction upon leaving the place, and the ashes from the fire were not too old. What it all boiled down to was he had no choice but to assume he was on Dubose's trail.

When the horses were rested, he set out again along the river, keeping an eye sharp to pick up any tracks leaving the trail. There was nothing to indicate Dubose had anything in mind beyond simply following the river to Bozeman, until reaching a point where it took a more northeastern direction to reach that town. Hawk missed it at first, but soon discovered the tracks he had been following were no longer there, causing him to backtrack to find where he lost them. It took some careful study of the trail, but he eventually found the point where they left the common trail. *No wonder*, he thought when he found the faint impressions where the trail passed over a heavily grassed area. They had

escaped his notice, but as he looked ahead in the
direction they pointed, they told him that Dubose
had left the river and continued straight north to
Three Forks and not to Bozeman. So he turned
Rascal in that direction with a slight feeling of confirmation that he was following Dubose for sure.
He thought of the Hog Ranch Dubose and his two
partners had gone to before when they left Great
Falls. He had considered the possibility that he was
heading there again, since Dubose might be convinced that the man chasing him was riding down
toward Utah Territory on the Montana Trail. If
that was the case, then why not go to the hog ranch
again on his way to wherever? According to what
both Loafer and Rufus had said, Dubose had plenty
of money. It might give Hawk a chance to catch up
with him if he decided to stop awhile and spend
some of that money. At least he had hoped so, but
now he wasn't sure what Dubose had in mind,
since it seemed obvious that he was heading for
Three Forks and not Big Timber.

The sun was hovering low over the mountains to
the west when Hawk rode into the settlement of
Three Forks. With eyes peeled for any sight of the
spotted horse he had become so familiar with, he
held the big buckskin to an easy walk as he passed
the blacksmith and the general merchandise store.
Continuing on toward a stable, he involuntarily
jerked Rascal to a halt. There, in the corral with at
least a dozen other horses, he saw it—*the Palouse.*
His hand automatically fell to rest on the stock of

his Winchester as his eyes darted back and forth to discover any immediate threat. But there was no one in sight, until a man walked out of the stable, and upon seeing Hawk, stopped in front of the corral to greet him. "How do, stranger. What can I do for you?"

Although there was no doubt in his mind that the horse he now saw was the horse Dubose rode, he did not see the man, himself. That left the only possibility of his whereabouts to be the general store he had just passed because he could see that he was not in the blacksmith's shop. He quickly looked back the way he had come in case Dubose had seen him ride by the store, but there was no sign of anyone behind him. He was aware then that the stable owner was waiting for an answer to his question. "Maybe you can tell me where I can find the man that owns that Palouse over yonder."

"You're lookin' at him," the man said, at once somewhat guarded in his tone. "What's your interest in that horse?"

I'll be damned, Hawk immediately cursed to himself, thinking he was about to be met with the same stunt Loafer had pulled in Nevada City. He struggled to hold his temper. "Had that horse a long time, have you?"

"As a matter of fact, I traded two good horses for that Palouse just a couple of days ago," the man answered. "Fair and square, so if you've got some kinda claim on that horse, you're gonna have to show me some kinda proof and you're gonna have to make up what I lost."

Hawk, surprised, paused to think about that. He

hadn't expected it, but it looked as if Dubose had become concerned enough about being tracked down to finally get rid of that spotted horse. That was not good news because that horse was the only clue Hawk had to find him. His task just became more impossible. He was aware then that the man was again standing there waiting for him to speak. "I've got no interest in the horse," he said. "I'm just tryin' to find the man who traded him to you."

"Oh," he responded, then sheepishly hastened to explain. "No offense, mister, when you asked me about him, I thought maybe that horse was stolen. I sure got the best end of the trade, and the feller I traded with had a look about him. You know what I mean? Like he mighta been the kind that'd steal a horse." When Hawk simply nodded his understanding, the man went on. "My name's Raymond Fuller. This here's my stable."

"John Hawk. Mr. Fuller, you got any idea which way that fellow went when he left here?"

"Well, I know he rode out toward the east, headin' for Bozeman, I reckon," Fuller said. "That's one helluva fine horse. I was tickled to get him." He hesitated then before asking, "He ain't stolen, is he?"

"Not that I know anything about," Hawk said. "But I wouldn't be surprised, knowin' the man who traded him to you." To give Fuller some reassurance, he added, "If he did steal it, it was a long way from here and a long while back." He shook his head, thinking about this unfortunate turn of events. "I'm just damn sorry to find out he got rid of that horse. It was the only real hope I had of findin' him."

"Maybe you ain't outta luck after all," Fuller said, a wide smile spreading across his whiskered face. "Like I said, I gave him two horses in trade. One of 'em's a sorrel he was wantin' for a pack-horse, but the other'un he threw his saddle on was a dappled gray that wouldn't be too hard to spot. That horse wasn't but about four years old, so it's still a pretty dark gray."

"Much obliged," Hawk said. "I 'preciate the in-formation."

"Not a-tall," Fuller replied. "I'm always glad to help the law. Hope you catch him."

There it is again, Hawk thought. "Thanks," he said without going to the trouble of telling him he wasn't a lawman. He turned Rascal toward the wagon road that led to Bozeman. He had to consider him-self lucky that Dubose had a liking for horses with unusual markings, otherwise he would have a much smaller chance of spotting him. It was about twenty-five miles from Three Forks to Bozeman, a good half-day's ride, and he knew of only one small trading post on the road between. It was owned by a fellow named Lem Wooten and it was halfway to Bozeman. Hawk had often stopped there in the years since he began working as a scout for the army, so he could count on Lem to help any way he could. His concern now was for his horses. They could use a rest, but he decided he would push on and rest them at Lem's. There was a creek there and good grass for Rascal and the packhorse, and since Lem was a good friend, the possibility of a meal cooked by Lem's wife.

It was approaching hard dark by the time Hawk saw the lights in the small store by the creek. His arrival was announced well in advance by the two large dogs that slept on the front porch of the log structure. In a matter of a few seconds, the front door opened a crack and Lem called out. "Who is it?"

"John Hawk, Lem."

The door opened wide, revealing Lem Wooten, holding a shotgun. "Hawk," he responded. "Come on in, boy!" He stepped out onto the porch to call his dogs back. "You ridin' alone? I don't see no soldiers with you."

"Yep," Hawk replied, "nobody but me. Figured I was close enough to your place, I'd just camp here tonight."

"Well, you know you're sure welcome. I expect you ain't had your supper yet. We've done et, but Lucy can fix you up somethin'."

"Thanks, Lem, but I wouldn't wanna put Lucy to the trouble. I've got some bacon in my packs and a little bit of coffee," Hawk said, knowing Lem would insist, and counting on it.

Lem insisted. "No such a thing. Lucy'd be down-right insulted if you didn't let her fix you somethin' to eat." He looked back toward the open door and yelled, "Lucy, it's Hawk and he ain't et."

"Tell him to give me a minute and I'll rustle up something," Lucy called back.

Lem turned to relay her message to Hawk. "Take care of your horses and she'll have somethin' ready for you by the time you're done." By that time, two small children, a boy and a girl, moved up on either side of their father to stare at the man called Hawk, who was close to being a legend in their young minds.

"Much obliged, Lem. You sure Lucy won't mind?"

"Not a-tall," Lem replied. "We ain't seen you in a coon's age. Where you been?"

"Oh, here and there, I reckon. I'll pull Rascal's saddle off and turn him out to graze. I wish I had some help with my packhorse, though." He winked at Lem when he said it.

"I'll help!" Eight-year-old Martin immediately exclaimed, and pushed away from his father.

"I figured you'd be too busy," Hawk teased. "Come on, then." He strode toward his horses with the small boy trying to match him stride for stride.

After the horses were taken care of and Hawk's overnight camp was set, he and young Martin returned to the house. Lucy and her ten-year-old daughter, Mary, greeted Hawk cordially. They appreciated the fact that he often bought supplies from their store and on more than one occasion, he had brought them a deer or antelope to butcher. He joked that Mary and Martin were the only young children he could tolerate. They were fascinated by the bigger-than-life scout who wore a buckskin shirt and rode the big buckskin horse. Little Mary was especially taken with him, so it was naturally she who asked, "What happened to the feather you always wear in your hat?"

"Oh, I reckon I musta lost it somewhere," he answered. "I'll find another one to take its place before long." Not wishing to discuss the circumstances that brought him to their door on this night, he abruptly changed the subject. "I declare, Lucy, you sure came up with a regular feast on such short notice. I feel right guilty to put you to so much trouble."

"Don't be silly," Lucy insisted. "I didn't go to any trouble at all. I was just getting ready to throw the rest of those potatoes to the hogs, and the biscuits, too. All I did was warm 'em up again."

After he finished his supper and the children went reluctantly off to bed, Hawk and Lem sat at the table and discussed the issue that brought him to their door. Lucy listened as she cleaned up her kitchen. "He was here, all right," Lem said. "Rode in here a little before noon three or four days ago. He wanted to know if I had any whiskey. I told him I didn't, so he didn't stay long. And I'm just as glad he didn't, 'cause I didn't like his looks." He paused when he thought about what Hawk had said Dubose had done to the girl Joanna. Shaking his head slowly, he said, "I knew that man was evil. He had a packhorse, but there wasn't much on it. I figured he'd be buyin' somethin'. That feller in Three Forks told you right, though. That horse he was ridin' is easy enough to spot. Looks like one the devil might be ridin'."

Making no comment until then, Lucy had to ask, "Why are you the only one trying to catch this man? Why doesn't the marshal send a deputy to find him?"

Hawk found it difficult to explain why he felt obligated to avenge Joanna, a childlike woman he had known only briefly before she was murdered so coldheartedly. So he didn't try. "I don't know," he said. "It just happened that I was the one who cut his trail, and I'm doin' my best to keep from losin' him."

They talked on until Hawk declared that he was going to leave at sunup, so it was time he turned in. In a small way to repay them for their hospitality, he bought some coffee beans and a small sack of flour. But he turned down Lucy's invitation to breakfast, saying he would be gone before then. "Mary's gonna be disappointed when she finds you're gone," Lucy said. "I think she's still planning to marry you when she grows up."

"Well, I sure hope so," Hawk said with a chuckle. "I know I'd really like to have Lem, here, as my father-in-law." He took his leave then, retiring to his blanket and his saddle as his pillow. As usual, he went to sleep right away, thinking that it was a welcome break from the grim business he found himself in. It made him remember that there were good people in this world.

CHAPTER 12

There was a decision to be made and Hawk kept rolling it over in his mind as he traveled the road to Bozeman. It was only a half-day's ride and Fort Ellis was only a few miles beyond it. He knew he should stop at the post to report the deaths of Bevo Brogan and Slim Perry, but he didn't want to be detained any more than necessary. So the temptation to bypass the fort was strong in his mind. He would check the town of Bozeman for any sign of Dubose, but then he would prefer to continue on to Big Timber. It was a day and a half's ride from Bozeman and any time he could save might mean the difference between catching up with Dubose before he started out in a new direction. There was also the question of whether or not he still had a job with the army. If it was left to Lieutenant Meade to decide, it could come down to an ultimatum—report to work right now, or be fired—if he hadn't been fired already. And Hawk would like to avoid that confrontation. The desire to bring

Zach Dubose to justice was so strong, he could not forgive himself if he simply broke off the chase. He was still trying to decide when the buildings of Bozeman came into view, so he turned his attention to the business at hand and left the decision until later.

Traveling the length of Bozeman's short street at a slow walk, he looked for the dappled gray horse, but there was no sign of it. So he turned around and headed back toward Grainger's Saloon in case Dubose might have stopped there, since he had tried to buy whiskey from Lem Wooten. When he passed the blacksmith shop again, he was hailed by Ernest Bloodworth, so he pulled Rascal over. "I thought that was you when you passed by a minute ago," Bloodworth said. "I was out back, splittin' some wood."

"I thought maybe you were over at Grainger's, gettin' your mornin' tonic," Hawk said.

"Too early for me to start in on any drinkin'," Bloodworth replied. "Ain't seen you around town lately. How are those shoes holdin' up on your horse? Have any more trouble since we put those new ones on?"

"Not a bit," Hawk replied, "and we've traveled some since then. If Rascal could talk, he'd say, *Much obliged.*"

Bloodworth smiled. "What brings you to town? You headed for Grainger's?"

"I'm tryin' to catch up with a fellow, thought he mighta rode into town a few days back. He's ridin' a dappled gray, dark as night."

"I saw that fellow," Bloodworth said right away.

"He tied his horse up in front of Grainger's. He didn't stay very long, maybe a half hour or so, and then the horse was gone. Just stopped to wet his whistle, I reckon. Whaddaya lookin' for him for?"

"He owes me somethin'," Hawk answered, preferring not to share the story. A little gurgle in his stomach suddenly reminded him that he had not taken the time to eat breakfast that morning, not even a cup of coffee. "I reckon I'll take time to visit Sadie up at the diner—give my horses a little rest before I get goin' again. I reckon that fellow on the gray rode on out toward the east."

"I can't say," Bloodworth said. "I didn't see him when he rode off."

It would have been helpful if he had confirmation on the direction Dubose rode off in, but it was safe to assume he continued in the same direction, since he didn't run smack into him going the other way when he rode into town. He was hungry, and his horses were ready for a rest, but he was also still laboring with the decision of visiting the fort or not. This would give him a little more time to make up his mind.

"Well, well," Sadie clucked when Hawk walked into her dining room. She walked over to the table where he had seated himself. "Haven't seen you in a while. I thought you musta found someplace where the cookin' was better'n mine."

He knew she was fishing for compliments, since he had told her that her stew was the best in the territory—like he did in every diner he patronized.

"Not hardly," he said. "I've just been out of town for a long time. Matter of fact, I planned my day just so I could get over here to eat some of your cookin'. I get to cravin' it when I've been out of town awhile."

Pleased, she nevertheless struggled to maintain her usual stern, no-nonsense demeanor, for which she had become famous. "I see you left your gun by the door this time," she said, remembering the first time he had eaten in her diner, and she had to inform him of her rules against guns in her dining room. "I might notta served you if you hadn't. I'll get you some coffee." She turned abruptly and went to the kitchen. "Keep your shirt on!" she growled at another customer, who was waving his cup in the air in an attempt to get her attention. Hawk couldn't help wondering how she did as well as she did, having such a sour disposition. It had to be the fact that hers was the best cooking in town. Of that, there was no question.

When she returned, she carried a plate piled high in one hand and a cup in the other. After placing them on the table, she went to get the coffeepot and returned to fill his cup. "You're lucky you got back this week," she said as she poured. "We killed a hog yesterday, so you're gettin' pork chops today, a little somethin' besides beef." She lingered a moment, waiting for him to sample the chops, ignoring the impatient patron waiting for more coffee.

"Mighty fine," Hawk expressed while chewing up the first bite of the fried pork chop. He shook his head for emphasis and said, "You've still got

every other cook in the territory whipped. No
doubt about it."

Pleased, she carried the coffeepot over to fill
her waiting customer's cup. "What the hell are you
in such a big hurry for, Henry? I know you ain't in
no hurry to get back to work." She went back to
the kitchen then, but she returned when Hawk was
finishing up his pork chops and sat down at the
table to talk. "You gonna be back in town awhile?"

"Reckon not," Hawk replied. "Gotta catch up with
a fellow that passed through here the other day."

She thought about that for a moment before
asking, "Ain't you still scoutin' for the soldiers?"

"Well, yeah," he answered, "but I need to see
this particular fellow for a reason that ain't got
nothin' to do with the soldiers."

"Has it got anything to do with the feather that
ain't in your hat no more?"

"What? No." He started, amazed that she even
noticed the absence of his hawk feather, then he
changed his mind. "Well, yeah, in a way I reckon it
does, at that. I just need to catch up with him."

"Dark, sorta mean-lookin' fellow, ridin' a horse
darker and meaner-lookin' than him?" she asked.

"Yeah," he replied, surprised. "How'd you guess
that?"

"'Cause he's the only stranger I've happened to
notice in town for the last few days," she declared.
"I saw him when he rode outta town."

She sparked Hawk's interest with that statement.
"Headed east, toward Big Timber?"

"Not the man I saw," she replied. "That fellow
on the dark gray horse didn't go out the east road.

That fellow took the trail straight up the valley, headed north."

"Are you sure?" Hawk exclaimed at once, taken totally by surprise. He was so sure that Dubose was heading for the Hog Ranch at Big Timber. "You sure he wasn't just ridin' around behind the general store?"

"Sure, I'm sure," Sadie replied. "Think I don't know what I'm lookin' at? I stopped and watched him ride up that trail between the hills, headed toward the Big Belt Mountains. At least the fellow I told you I saw rode up that way."

"Dark, heavyset fellow, riding a dappled gray horse?" Hawk pressed.

"Yes," she emphasized impatiently. "That's what I said."

There could be no doubt, it had to be Dubose! He hadn't given any thought toward the possibility that Dubose would head back north. It just made sense that he would want to put that territory far behind him and look for greener pastures up toward Billings or beyond, maybe Miles City. But the trail he took would lead him back to Helena unless he intended to turn and pass to the east of the Big Belts, possibly heading for his old haunts around Great Falls. He was stunned by the realization that he had been about to set out toward the Yellowstone, while Dubose was riding toward Helena. Then he became suddenly aware that Sadie was staring at him, puzzled by his sudden mental departure.

"What the hell's the matter with you? You look

like you swallowed a bone or a piece of gristle," she said. "You need some more coffee, or somethin'?"

"No, I reckon I'd best get on my way." He got to his feet and reached in his pocket for some money. The wheels in his brain were turning so fast, he could barely concentrate on how much he was putting on the table. The distinct possibility occurred to him that Dubose might be heading back to Helena to take his revenge on Bertie and Blossom. He thought about what Bertie had told him, that Zach Dubose was possessive to the point of brutality. Even though Hawk had spoiled his plan to kill Blossom that night at the Last Chance, she knew he would try again. The only thing that would stop him from trying was if he was dead. Thinking about that now, Hawk should have figured Dubose was on his way back to get to Blossom—especially when Dubose thought the one man after him had been sent off to chase shadows down in Mormon country. He would think he had free rein in Helena with no one to stop him.

Hawk turned to leave, but Sadie caught his sleeve. "Here," she said. "You don't owe me that much for one plate of food." She picked up a dollar and handed it back to him. "You sure you're all right?"

He quickly brought his mind back to focus on her. "Yeah, I'm all right," he said, then grinned. She had surely saved him from riding off on a fruitless chase. "Thanks," he blurted. "I'd give you a big kiss if I wasn't afraid you'd whop me over the head with that coffeepot."

She smiled, the first one he'd ever seen on that

no-nonsense face. "You'd do well to restrain yourself," she said. "Now, get on your way, so I can clean this table up." He gave her another big grin and headed for the door. *If I was about fifteen years younger*, she thought as she watched him leave.

He had planned to rest his horses a little longer, but he knew they were up to the task because it had not been a long ride from Lem Wooten's place that morning. Rascal seemed willing, as usual, and there was no balking on the part of the red roan packhorse that once belonged to the late Johnny Dent. Unfortunately, he had no distinct trail he could follow after leaving Bozeman, for he saw several sets of prints heading north, including a set of wagon tracks. When about a half mile out of the settlement, the tracks split off in two different directions, east or west, with only one pattern left by two horses continuing north on a trail very familiar to him. He had traveled that trail many times on his way to Helena. There was no question in his mind now as far as an obligation to report in to the army at Fort Ellis. The urgency caused by the thought of Dubose heading to Helena to harm Bertie and Blossom was foremost in his mind and all that mattered at this point. When he came to a wide, rolling plain of grass, the tracks he had followed disappeared, but he was not inclined to take the time to try to find them again. It was a good twenty-five miles to the southern foot of the Big Belt Mountains, so he held Rascal to a steady pace.

He remembered a good stream that came down out of the mountains on its way to empty into the Missouri. He had rested his horse there before. He would scout that area for any signs that could tell him if Dubose had veered more to the east, or headed more westerly on the eastern side of the Big Belts. That would depend, of course, on whether or not Dubose happened to stop at that particular spot. It was the obvious spot to camp, however, as witnessed by the traces of old campfires that he always found there.

It was late afternoon when he reached the stream and the popular campsite beside it. He immediately dismounted and looked around the short stretch of trees that framed the stream, but there was no evidence of a recent campfire. "Where the hell did he camp?" he asked his horses. It occurred to him then that Dubose might not have camped there, but merely stayed long enough to rest his horses before pushing on. He hadn't thought to ask Sadie if it was morning or afternoon when she saw Debose leave Bozeman. "That would make a helluva difference," he told Rascal, annoyed with himself for not asking the question. He relieved his horses of their packs and saddle and left them to graze on the plentiful grass. Only then did he begin a thorough search up and down the stream for any evidence of a camp, or save that, a trail leading more to the east.

His scout of the area around the stream bore no fruit. There was no recent sign of anyone ever having been there, only adding to his frustration and his sense of urgency. Maybe, he thought, he was chasing a ghost. He had lost Dubose's trail, if in fact he had ever found it in the first place. He saw no choice for him, however, except to assume Dubose was heading to Helena, so he determined to get there, himself, as quickly as he could. And that was at least fifty miles from where he now stood, a long day's ride. He kept reminding himself that if Blossom and Bertie were now in danger, it was his fault for being so gullible in buying Loafer Smith's tale about Dubose going to Salt Lake City.

It was out of the question to start out again before resting his horses. He decided to ride part of the way at night after they were rested to cut tomorrow's journey down to half a day to reach Helena. So he threw some sticks and branches together and built a fire. He didn't feel the desire for food, but a little coffee was desperately needed, so he filled his pot from the stream and waited for his fire to burn hot enough to make his coffee.

Zach Dubose sat beside a small fire on the bank of a wide stream two miles from Helena, eating a strip of sowbelly and drinking a cup of coffee. He was watching his horses drinking from the stream, but his mind was not focused on them at all. He was thinking of the last time he had seen Helena, and the thought of it caused a light pain in his shoulder, a reminder of the bullet that struck him as he, Red, and Hog had fled town. It had happened so suddenly that they didn't have time to see who was shooting at them and whether or not

they should try to stand and fight. All he knew for
sure was that he couldn't fight with a bullet in his
shoulder and Red and Hog were already running.
Even after Doc Sumner took the bullet out of his
shoulder and the three of them decided to leave
Great Falls, they weren't sure what they were running from, a single lawman or a posse. He didn't
know for sure until he caught up with him in
Nevada City. When he found out it was a single
lawman, it was too late to face him. Loafer had already sent him off toward Utah. Otherwise, he
would have chosen to deal with the man himself.
And the more he thought about it after the fact,
the more certain he was that he would have killed
him right there in Nevada City. It galled him now
to think that he had been on the run from one
single pursuer, even though it amused him to
think of a lawman wandering blindly in search of
him now in far-off Utah.

With his lone hunter off in the wilderness, it left
him free to return to Helena and the bitch who
had run out on him. All the time he had run since
then had caused his mind to dwell on the trouble
Blossom and her mother had caused him. He intended to make them pay for it. The thought of
Blossom's expression when he showed up again
brought a wicked smile to his face. Further thoughts
on the pleasure he was to have upon seeing his
wife again were interrupted momentarily by the
sound of the back door closing at the farmhouse
fifty yards away. "That'll be my biscuits," Dubose
mumbled. A few minutes later, a young boy named

Caleb appeared, carrying two biscuits wrapped in a cloth.

"Mama said you don't have to bother yourself with the rag," Caleb said. "Just hang it on a limb and I'll fetch it after you're gone."

"You tell your mama I 'preciate it," Dubose said. "I'll be ridin' on as soon as my horses are rested up a little. And thank you for bringin' the biscuits."

"Yes, sir," Caleb replied. "Weren't no trouble." He hesitated for a moment to watch Dubose take a bite out of one of the biscuits before turning to return to the house.

Dubose watched the boy until he got back to the kitchen door, and he snorted a derisive chuckle for the boy's parents' gullibility. When he came upon the simple farmhouse a couple of miles from town, he decided it was an opportunity to find out what was going on in Helena. Most important, he needed information regarding the law. Red Whitley had shot the sheriff when they fled the town before—put a slug right in his gut. Dubose needed to know if the sheriff died, or if not, was he recovered from the gunshot? If Red killed him, did they have a new sheriff? These were questions he wanted answers to before he rode in. He wanted no surprises. Thanks to his cleverness, he had been able to get all the answers to young Caleb's father—and a couple of biscuits to boot. He chuckled again when he thought about the story he had spun for them about his being a deputy U.S. marshal, chasing a fugitive. So now he was ready to ride into town and dare anyone to try to stop him. The sheriff was still laid up in bed and there was nobody in the sheriff's office. His horses didn't really need a rest, he was just biding his time until dark. There was no point in being careless and taking a chance on some do-gooder citizen taking a shot at him. He was counting on no one recognizing him, since he would be riding in on a horse drastically different from the Palouse he had ridden before.

When the light had faded away to the point where he felt it dark enough, he kicked his fire out and stepped up in the saddle. When he rode by the house, the boy and his father stepped out on the porch to watch him. "Good luck with findin' that outlaw," Caleb's father called out to Dubose.

"Much obliged," he returned.

The boy and his father remained on the porch to watch the ominous man on the dappled gray horse until he disappeared into the growing darkness. "That is one scary-looking man," the father commented to his son. "I almost feel sorry for that outlaw he's after. That can't be a very pleasant sight, to see him coming after you on that dark horse."

"He didn't rest his horses very long, did he?" Caleb asked. "Didn't even take the saddle off."

"I reckon he knows what he's doing. It looks like he mighta roped that horse outta the devil's herd. Maybe it doesn't need any rest."

Gladys Welch sat at a table alone in the half-empty saloon after the two miners she had been gabbing with finished their drinks and got up to leave. They didn't even offer to buy her a drink. In the old days, one or both of them might have wanted to go upstairs with her for a ride. But that was in the old days and she was undecided as to whether or not she was glad those times were past. For certain, she missed the money, and maybe the attention, but she could honestly say she didn't miss the rest of it. Nowadays, about all she was good for was conversation with old men, like the two leaving the saloon now, who were lacking the inclination or the ability, or both. She could lament about missing the good old days, save for the fact that there weren't any good old days in her memory. Times had always been hard ever since she left her father's home in Missouri to wake up one morning a week later to discover the lover she ran off with had left while she was still asleep.

Weary of such thoughts, she shifted her gaze to Bertie Brown, just coming from the storeroom carrying several bottles of whiskey in preparation for the busy nighttime customers. She wasn't sure how she felt about Bertie and her daughter. Sam Ingram had turned almost all the management of the saloon over to Bertie, and Gladys had to admit that Bertie knew how to run a saloon. She had worked with Bertie before, quite a few years back, and Bertie was capable back then, even while practicing the "oldest profession" herself. Like Gladys, Bertie was too old for anything more than management now, but at that, she was good. In the short time since Bertie had been here, Last Chance Saloon had already begun to recover some of the business it had lost to the Gold Nugget. Blossom was, of course, the main attraction, but business should improve even more since Bertie had persuaded Ginger Plover to leave the Gold Nugget and come to the Last Chance. Ginger should give Blossom some competition. Gladys had to give Bertie credit, and her thanks as well, for not kicking her out the door, even when Sam suggested it. Bertie convinced him that he needed someone who could serve as an available ear for the old ramblings of his older customers—ever encouraging them to buy more whiskey. So Gladys guessed that's what she was now. Bertie even had a name for it. She was a "persuader." She shook her head when she repeated it to herself.

When Bertie went back to the storeroom again, Gladys decided the "persuader" should get up and find another customer to visit with. Halfway up out of her chair, she was stopped by the sight of a man standing just outside the front doorway and looking in. Something about him looked familiar, but not like she would remember a regular customer. Then it struck her where she had seen him before and she sank back down in the chair, immediately alarmed. *Zach Dubose*, Blossom's husband! She looked around the room hurriedly, then remembered Blossom was upstairs entertaining a cowboy called Tex. Gladys didn't know what to do. Bertie was in the storeroom and might walk out at any minute, and Gladys was afraid that if she suddenly ran to warn her, Dubose would see her at once.

Thinking she couldn't just sit there and do nothing, she eased herself up out of the chair again, telling herself to appear casual. So far, he didn't seem to pay her any attention, standing just outside the doorway, scanning the room, searching for his prey. She forced herself to affect a casual stroll toward the storeroom door. When she opened it, she almost ran headlong into Bertie, who was carrying more bottles to the bar. Acting quickly then, Gladys pushed Bertie back into the storeroom and closed the door. "What the hell, Gladys?" Bertie exclaimed, almost dropping the bottles.

"It's him!" Gladys blurted. "He's come back!"

"Who?" Bertie demanded, getting a better grip on the bottles. "Who's come back?"

"That evil son of a bitch your daughter married," Gladys exclaimed. "He's standin' in the door and he's lookin' for Blossom."

Horrified, Bertie almost dropped the bottles again. She had never expected to see Zach Dubose again after he had been forced to run for his life. "Where's Blossom? Is she downstairs?"

"No, at least not when I came in here. She's still upstairs with that young fellow named Tex." She started wringing her hands, frightened. "If he finds her, he'll kill her. He said he was gonna kill her last time he was here."

Bertie tried to calm herself to gain control. "Not if I can help it," she declared, and placed the bottles down on a table while she tried to decide what to do. "I'd know what to do if I had my damn rifle in here." She looked around her, frantically searching for something to use as a weapon. "I owe that son of a bitch one," she declared as she reached up and felt the scar on the side of her forehead where he had knocked her senseless with the butt of his rifle. Unable to find anything to use for a weapon, she picked up one of the full bottles of whiskey and then opened the door just enough to peek out into the barroom. She felt a tremor of anger surge through her body when she saw his defiant swagger as he approached the bar. She saw Dewey suddenly freeze when he looked up and recognized Dubose. "Keep your mouth shut, Dewey," she mumbled to herself, afraid the bartender would tell Dubose where Blossom was.

Thinking of the double-barreled shotgun under the counter, she decided that if she could get to it, she'd shoot him down. She turned to Gladys as she opened the door. "Go upstairs and tell Blossom. Tell her to get my rifle and find herself a place to hide. Hurry!" She pushed her out the door when Gladys did not move at once. Gladys moved then, but not in time, for at that moment, Tex, with Blossom right behind him, appeared at the top of the stairs and started down. "Oh no, honey!" Bertie muttered in despair, and pushed by Gladys on her way to distract Dubose. Reacting at once, Gladys hurried across the room to the stairs.

"What the hell's wrong with you, showin' your face around here?" Bertie yelled as she hurried to the bar. "Didn't you learn your lesson last time? I've already sent somebody to get the sheriff!"

Dubose turned to face her, an evil sneer rapidly forming on his rough face. "Hello, Bertie," he drawled slowly, obviously enjoying her distress. "I've been missin' you and your lovely daughter. If you sent for the sheriff, I hope you sent a wagon to get him outta his bed. It'd pleasure me to put another bullet in him—finish the job Red started."

"I ain't talkin' about Porter Willis," Bertie retorted. "I'm talkin' about the new sheriff."

"Is that a fact?" Dubose responded, confident in the knowledge that there was no new sheriff. "Well, when he gets here, I'll buy him a drink." The few patrons in the saloon at this time suddenly became aware of the trouble brewing at the bar. So they began to draw away from the center of the room, creating a wide stage for the drama. In an effort to draw Dubose's gaze away from the stairs behind him, Bertie hastened to the bar. Dubose never took his eyes off her, so he was unaware of the frantic scene at the top of the stairs when Gladys intercepted Blossom and hustled her back down the hallway. Left standing on the stairs, confused by the obvious distress apparent in the two, the young cowhand descended the stairs, astonished to see the people scattering.

His confidence growing by the minute, Dubose got the feeling he could take over the whole town, if he chose. Watching Bertie carefully, aware that in all probability, there was a shotgun or handgun under the counter, he said, "I've come to fetch my wife. Where is she?"

"Halfway to Bozeman by now," Bertie lied. "She left here yesterday."

"Well, now, why don't I believe that?" Dubose smirked, still enjoying her efforts to bluff. "She don't go nowhere without you lately. I expect I'll have to go upstairs to make sure she ain't slipped back in without you knowin' it."

Aware now that her bluff wasn't working on the belligerent outlaw, Bertie dropped the pretense. "You low-down son of a bitch, Blossom don't want no part of you, so you'd just better get on your horse and leave this town before a deputy marshal shows up to arrest you." She moved around the end of the bar to stand beside Dewey, who was still struck motionless.

Dubose dropped his hand to rest on the handle of his .44. "You'd both best step back away from that counter," he warned. "'Cause I'm gonna figure the first one that reaches under there is comin' up with a shotgun and I ain't gonna wait to see it for sure." Dewey stepped back immediately, but Bertie hesitated, reluctant to move away from the shotgun she could see no more than three feet away from her. Dubose knew what she was thinking. "Go ahead, Bertie," he challenged. "Make a try for it." Still she hesitated, so he continued to dare her. "I thought I mighta knocked some sense into your head the last time I was here, but I reckon I was wrong. You gonna reach for that shotgun or not?"

"Don't you do it, Bertie." This came from Daisy, who had heard the confrontation from the kitchen. "He's just looking for an excuse to shoot you."

The one person in the saloon who had been mystified up to this point finally realized what was taking place. "Hold on there, mister," Tex called out from the foot of the stairs. "You got no call to talk to Bertie like that."

"Who the hell are you?" Dubose demanded. He shifted his eyes quickly toward the young cowhand, then back again to Bertie.

"I'm just sayin' there ain't no reason to threaten this lady," Tex said. "We'd do better to calm down and I'm sure whatever your complaint is, you and Bertie can talk it out."

Dubose almost laughed at the cowhand's naïveté. "You need to learn to mind your own business," he said. "And this ain't none of your business, so sit down over there and keep your mouth shut." He was about to return his full attention to Bertie, but Tex refused to back down to the bully.

"I asked you nice," Tex said. "Now I'm gonna tell you to walk on outta here and let these folks drink in peace."

Dubose couldn't believe the young man's innocence. With a shake of his head in wonder, he casually drew his .44 and shot him down. An instant murmur of shock was heard from the stunned witnesses before the room returned to total silence. Turning quickly in time to stop Bertie from reaching for the weapon under the counter, Dubose demanded, "Where's Blossom?"

"Where you can't find her," Bertie spat, hoping with all her heart that her daughter had fled down the back steps.

With his pistol trained on Bertie, Dubose looked at Dewey. "What about you? You wanna do somethin' about it?" Dewey didn't answer, but shook his head and backed away until stopped by the shelves underneath the giant mirror on the wall. Dubose

walked around the end of the bar then and shoved
Bertie aside. He reached under the counter and
pulled the shotgun out from under it, broke it
open, dropped the two shells on the floor, then
threw the shotgun toward the other end of the bar.
Then he stuck his face inches from Bertie's and
shouted, "Where's my wife?"

"Go to hell," Bertie retorted, only to receive a
sharp blow across her temple from the barrel of
Dubose's pistol. She slumped to the floor, unconscious.

Dubos pointed his .44 at her, but decided not to
kill her, thinking he might need to get information
out of her yet. He turned his attention to the
stunned witnesses of the murder. "Get the hell
outta here," he roared, and fired a shot into the far
wall to hurry them. A frantic rush for the door resulted immediately and he walked out from
behind the bar to fire another round over their
heads. Then, suddenly aware of someone at his
back, he whirled around to discover the cook
behind him.

"Come, Dewey," Daisy Smith said to her husband, showing no regard for the fearsome outlaw.
Dewey responded at once to her call, following
her dutifully toward the door, aware of Dubose at
his heels.

When they were out the door, Dubose closed it
and dropped the heavy bar to secure it. "Now, by
God," he swore, and headed for the stairs. Taking
the steps two at a time, he charged up to the
second floor to the rooms above the saloon. Kick-

ing open every door he came to, he stormed down the hall, finding no one in any of the rooms until the last one. When that door was slammed back against the inside wall, it revealed a terrified Gladys Welch seated on the bed, her knees drawn up under her chin protectively. Dubose glanced quickly around the room, expecting to find Blossom hiding somewhere. There being no place to hide except under the bed, he grabbed the side of it and turned it upside down, dumping the frightened woman on the floor. "Where is she?" he demanded.

"I don't know," Gladys answered between trembling lips. "She's not here. She's gone."

"Yeah, but you know where she went," he threatened, pointing his pistol at her face. "And if you don't tell me pretty damn quick, I'm gonna put another eye between them two on your ugly face."

"I swear, I don't know where she went," she cried. "She just ran down the back stairs. That's all I can tell you."

"Damn," he swore, but pulled the pistol away from her face while he thought about where Blossom could have run to. And the most important thing in his mind now was to catch her before she got too far, or found a good hiding place. So he ran for the door and headed toward the steps that led down to the backyard, leaving a limp and fearful Gladys to recover from her fright.

She sat there for only a moment, however, before scrambling on her hands and knees to the window before getting to her feet. She started to raise the window, but on second thought, ran to close the door before returning to the window. As fast as she could, she raised it then and stuck her head out. "Come quick, he's gone down the stairs!"

Blossom needed no encouragement. She wasn't sure how much longer she could hold on to the ends of the roof rafters that extended over the wall above her head. Already, her bare toes were threatening to fail her as she strained to press them into the rough wood siding to support her weight. Gladys reached out to help her, knowing that it would take no more than an upward glance from Dubose, once he was outside, to see the desperate woman clinging to the side of the building. When at last she was inside, Blossom almost collapsed, but Gladys told her there was no time for that now. She had to run. They would both be targets for Dubose's ire now. "It's a good thing he was too mad to notice that one pair of shoes lined up under the bed were smaller than the others," she said as she watched Blossom hurrying to put them on. "Where are you gonna run?"

"I don't know," Blossom answered. "There isn't anyplace in this town." She knew that there were very few people who would place themselves or their families in danger to protect a common whore.

While this was taking place, Bertie was struggling to regain consciousness downstairs behind the bar. When she managed to get on her hands and knees, she picked up the shotgun shells on the floor and crawled to the end of the bar to get the shotgun and load it. On her feet then, she hurried as much as she was able to get to the stairs, stepping around the young cowboy's body on the way. Unaware of what had just taken place upstairs, she held her shotgun ready to pull the trigger as soon as she saw Dubose. Blossom and Gladys were startled again when she suddenly opened the door. "Mama!" Blossom cried out when she saw her mother with a dried trickle of blood on the side of her face.

"Thank the Lord," Bertie exclaimed when finding her daughter safe. But that joy lasted just a second, before recalling the threat still in their midst.

At that moment, that threat was in the street after having checked the outhouse behind the saloon. Like a mad dog, he stalked his intended victim, going from shop to shop as he progressed up the street, daring anyone to stop him. Someone would surely try to kill this mad dog, and finally someone did. Chad Benton, who ran the general store, strapped his Colt .44 on and stood behind the corner of his building, watching Dubose's progress as he came up the street. When it became obvious that Dubose was not going to skip his store, Chad waited until he was closer before stepping out from the corner and firing at him. Due to frayed nerves, Chad's shot was wide, costing him his life. That incident discouraged everyone else from attempting to stop the fearsome-looking outlaw challenging the town unafraid.

When the three women over the saloon heard

the shot that killed Chad, it only increased the level of anxiety that was already intense. Bertie ran to the front room, which had a window facing the main street. From there, she could see Dubose in the street as he walked past the post office. There was a body lying in the street, but she couldn't tell who it was. A moment later, she saw Betty Benton run out of the store and fall on her knees beside her husband's body. "That mad dog is shootin' anybody that gets in his way," she said to Blossom. "He just killed Chad Benton. We've got to get away from here. He's gonna look in every crack and corner till he finds us." She turned to Gladys and said, "Or till he finds for sure that we ain't here." She looked back out the window to make sure Dubose was still walking toward the store at the far end of the street. "We gotta go," she repeated, certain now that it was their best chance. "Gather up whatever you need for a few days. I'll do the same. While he's still up at that end of town, we'll run to the stable and get our horse. Gladys, you'll have to tell Sam what happened when he gets back from Bozeman and tell him we'll be back when it's safe for Blossom. You and Dewey will have to run things till he's back."

Gladys nodded excitedly, then asked, "What if he comes after me?"

"He ain't got no reason to hurt you—or Daisy and Dewey, either. Just don't do nothin' to make him mad. When he finds out for sure that Blossom ain't here, he'll be comin' lookin' for her again."

She glanced at Blossom. "And he'll be our problem again. So let's get goin'."

They hurried to make their getaway, with some essential belongings in a cotton sack and Bertie's Henry rifle. Out the back of the saloon, they ran behind the few buildings between the saloon and the stable. When they ran in the door of the stable, they found the owner, Frank Bowen, talking to a young man wearing a buckskin shirt, who had a horse saddled and one he was planning to lead. "Thank goodness you're here!" Bertie exclaimed.

Startled, Bowen reacted in surprise. "Good gracious, Bertie, what are you women doin' runnin' around out there with that wild man tearin' up the town? He's done shot Chad Benton. You need to find you a hole somewhere till he's gone."

Bertie wasted little time telling him the cause of Dubose's behavior and the reason why she and her daughter had to run. "We need our horse. Will you saddle him for us?"

"Well, sure," Bowen said, hesitating. It was an opportunity for a man to come to the rescue of two women in danger. However, he was not inclined to go looking for trouble, so he had just as soon they didn't want to hide in his stable. That was the reason he was staying put in his stable with his rifle at hand. If Dubose showed up at his stable, he wouldn't put up any opposition unless it came down to saving his life. So he decided he would settle for helping them saddle that one horse they owned and speed them on their way. They were only whores, anyway, he thought.

The young man standing there said nothing, but listened with interest as Bertie told Bowen of the danger threatening her and her daughter. When Bowen hurried off to fetch the horse, he asked Bertie, "Where will you go?"

"I don't know," Bertie replied. "Just somewhere to hide in the mountains, I reckon. A woman don't usually prepare for something like this."

"Do you have food?" he asked. Bertie shook her head, all the while looking frantically for Bowen to return with her horse. "You have a rifle. Do you have anything to cook with?"

At this particular moment in her and her daughter's life, Bertie was distressed by the young man's pointless questions. Looking at him a little closer, she decided he was probably a half-breed. "No, we don't," she answered impatiently. "We just wanna get the hell away from here to keep from gettin' killed."

"Maybe you should come with me," the young man said. "My father has a trading post on the Clark Fork River, one day's ride from here. I am on my way there now. I think you would be safe there."

Bertie hesitated. His offer sounded like an answer to their problem, but she could not help but be suspicious of his real motives. Why would he want to risk his life to help someone like her and Blossom, who were complete strangers to him? Hearing the young man's suggestion as he was leading the horse out, Frank Bowen spoke up. "This here's Robert, Rubin Fagan's son. You don't have to worry, you can trust him. And what he said don't sound like a bad idea at that. Like he said, Rubin's place ain't but a day's ride from here, and I don't know anywhere else you two women can go, except up in the woods somewhere. And I don't think that's a good idea. You'd be a lot better off at Rubin's."

The offer sounded good again after Bowen's assurance that Robert could be trusted. "Well, we appreciate your offer," she said. "It's mighty kind of you, but I reckon I oughta tell you the man lookin' for us won't hesitate to kill you if he knows you helped us."

"I figured," Robert said.

"If you still wanna help us, then I say thank you very much, and let's get started," Bertie said. Blossom, who had been silent up to that point, stepped forward and thanked him as well. She tied the sack with their belongings on the saddle horn while Bowen helped her mother up into the saddle.

"You don't have to ride double," Robert said to Blossom. "You can ride my extra horse if you want, she's got a bridle on her—if you don't mind riding bareback. I can tie those two small packs behind my saddle. Or I can ride her and you can ride in my saddle."

"I can ride bareback," Blossom quickly informed him, and went to climb on. She hiked up her long skirt, and, holding it with one hand, hopped up to straddle the mare with Robert's helping hand.

"You want me to lead her, or you want the reins?" Robert asked.

"Give me the reins. Let's just get the hell outta here."

Robert jumped up into the saddle and led them out the back door of Bowen's stable, swinging around the back of the corral to keep the buildings of Helena between them and their stalker in the street. Once they were safely away from the town, he headed west toward MacDonald Pass to follow a winding trail that would lead them to the Clark Fork River.

CHAPTER 13

Even in the growing darkness, young Robert knew the trail he followed well enough to lead the women along at a reasonable pace. "It will be better when the moon rises," he told them, sensing their concern. He had been deciding whether to stay in Helena that night or head back home right away. The plight of the woman and her daughter made his decision for him. And it made no sense to be in Helena that night with a crazy white man roaming the streets looking for someone to shoot at, anyway. He would stop to rest the horses in MacDonald Pass and make some coffee and roast some deer jerky for the women. He knew for sure they had nothing to eat with them.

After a couple of hours following Robert along a dark passage between mountains on both sides, Bertie's feeling of anxiety began to give way to one of hunger. All of this chaos began just before suppertime and now she became aware of the fact she had made no provision for food. "About time to rest these horses, isn't it?" she called up ahead to their silent guide.

"Not yet," he called back. "Half a mile there's a stream, water for the horses, better place to stop."

Bertie looked back at Blossom on the mare, wondering if her bottom was as much in need of relief as hers. It had been some time since either of them had ridden a horse. The last time they had traveled any distance, they were sitting on a wagon seat and the horse she now rode had been on one side of the wagon tongue. They had both stopped looking behind them so frequently, fearing they might see Zach Dubose coming after them. There was a feeling of safety in the darkness between the mountains.

In a few minutes more, a large yellow full moon rose above the mountains, casting soft light along their way. It happened just at the moment Robert reined up at the stream. He turned to them and said, "We'll ride up the stream a little way. Good place to camp."

"Are we gonna camp the night?" Bertie asked. "Or just long enough to rest the horses?"

"Up to you," Robert said. "I don't think you came ready to camp. Maybe you'd rather go on to my home after the horses are rested." He saw no signs of blankets with them, and he guessed that the sack they brought held nothing but clothes. He was glad to see they had both brought coats, for the nights were already cold. "You decide after we eat."

Leaving the trail some thirty or forty yards, they came to a small clearing in the evergreen trees, wide enough to permit some grass to grow. In the moonlight that shone, though, there was evidence of old campfires. After taking care of the horses, Robert collected wood to start a fire on the ashes of one of the previous fires. When it was burning to his satisfaction, he went to one of his packs and removed a small coffeepot and a sack of roasted coffee beans. It was enough to lift the spirits of both women. Bertie leaned close to Blossom's ear and whispered, "I thought he was a Good Samaritan before, but now I believe he's a damn angel." She was still amazed that he would take the risk of harboring them. To Robert, then, she said, "Here, let me make that for you." He let her take the pot while he returned to his packs to get some jerky to roast over the flames that were already burning brightly.

"Did you bring cups in your sack?" he asked.

"No, we didn't," Blossom answered. "There were a lot of things we didn't think about. Eating was one of them."

"I have two cups. One of them is cracked, but it will hold coffee. You can use them. I will wait to drink coffee after you are finished."

"No," Bertie quickly replied, already feeling quite a bit inadequate in their preparation to flee. "Blossom and I can share a cup."

They finished the coffee and meat Robert provided almost in silence, for both women were still in a state of indecision and apprehension. The discussion that did take place between them was mostly centered on what they should do after that night. Robert, a young man of very few words, spoke only when asked a question, then answered in as few words as possible. Bertie decided that he must surely have more Indian blood than white. After their simple supper, they decided they would prefer to ride straight through the night rather than trying to fashion a bed out of the boughs from the fir trees, as Robert suggested. He was agreeable, having already told them it was an option. There was also the desire to put as much distance behind them as quickly as they could. So when the horses were ready, Robert led them back down the stream and continued on the trail to the Clark Fork.

Meanwhile, the town of Helena was still under siege from one man. With none of the shopkeepers or merchants willing to attempt to stop this fearsome intruder after seeing the fate of Chad Benton, Zach Dubose was free to search the length of the street unopposed. His search was thorough, with no doors remaining closed to him, and he left a trail of broken locks and damaged merchandise behind him, to no avail, however. So he returned to the Last Chance Saloon, thinking Blossom might have returned in hopes he would not search there again. When he got to the door, he found it barred, forgetting he had barred it himself. It served only to make him believe Blossom must have returned. He put his shoulder to the door, then tried to kick it open, but the door was stronger than he. In a furious rage, he began shouting that if the door was not opened from inside, he was going to smash out the window and kill everybody in the saloon. "I'll open it, I'll open it," came the voice of the frightened Dewey Smith. In a few seconds, the bar was lifted from the door. With his .44 ready to shoot, Dubose started to walk in, but paused for a few moments when he heard the sounds of some of the people leaving town, fleeing his wrath on the other end of the street. It brought a smile to his face, for it served to convince him of his power over the whole town and the fear they had of him.

Inside, he leveled his weapon at Dewey, who had hurried back from the door to stand behind the bar. "Reach under that counter and take that shotgun out and lay it on top of the bar," Dubose said. "Do it real easy-like."

"Ain't no shotgun under here," Dewey said. "Bertie took it with her." He held his hands up, both palms out. "I swear."

"Where's Blossom?"

"She's gone. Her and Bertie, too."

"Is that so? Who's that in the kitchen?" he asked when he heard a sound.

"That's just Daisy and Gladys," Dewey said. "Ain't nobody else in the whole place, upstairs or down."

Dubose cocked the hammer back on his Colt. "I'll take a look, myself, and if you're lyin' to me, I'm gonna put a bullet right through your head." He was disappointed to hear that he had not hit Bertie hard enough to crack her skull. "Get out from behind that bar. You're goin' in the kitchen with me." He walked Dewey through the door ahead of him. Inside, he found Gladys and Daisy standing by the table, Gladys staring wide-eyed in fear, Daisy with a heavy iron frying pan in her hand. Dubose took a quick look around the room before questioning Daisy. "Just what the hell are you thinkin' you're gonna do with that fryin' pan?" he demanded, thinking it was surely intended to be a weapon.

"I'm fixin' to fry some supper," she replied fearlessly. "With you runnin' around like a crazy man, ain't nobody in town had any time to eat supper." Both Dewey and Gladys cringed at her open disdain for the brutal killer.

Dubose pointed the cocked pistol at the stubborn woman, gesturing with it as he said, "You've got a real sassy mouth on you. It's liable to cause you to get a .44 slug in it for you to chew on." She made no reply, other than a defiant snort. "Now, just to be sure you ain't lyin' to me, the four of us are gonna go upstairs to make sure ain't nobody hidin' up there." He motioned with his pistol toward the door. When Daisy showed signs of balking, Dewey grabbed her by her elbow and guided her through the door.

The three of them went up the stairs before him and into each room on the second floor, knowing he was using them as a shield against Bertie waiting somewhere for him to walk in. When he had searched every room, he herded them back downstairs. "Dewey already told you Blossom and Bertie have gone," Daisy said. "You'da probably had a better chance to catch 'em if you hadn't wasted all your time scarin' the good folks in this town."

He considered it, glaring at the outspoken little

woman for a long moment, but he held back for no reason he could explain. Maybe it was because what she had just said was true. He had wasted a hell of a lot of time searching the town. If they had left town, they had to have horses and that meant he should have checked the stable before anywhere else. "Damn," he swore, thinking about it. Before leaving, however, he went behind the bar and opened the cash drawer, cleaning out the larger bills and the dollar coins.

"You ain't just a murderer, you're a thief, too," Daisy could not help saying.

"That's right, bitch," Dubose said with a twisted smile, then gave her a blow across her brow with the barrel of his pistol. She fell back to be caught in Gladys's arms. Dewey started toward Dubose, but stopped when Dubose smiled at him and encouraged him to come on.

"Stop, Dewey!" Daisy managed to command. "Don't give the son of a bitch a reason to shoot you."

"That's right, Dewey," Dubose mocked, "'cause I'd sure blow you straight to hell." He threw his head back and laughed as he went out the door.

"Right now is when I wish I had a gun," Daisy said as they watched from the window until the belligerent bully climbed on his dark dappled gray horse and loped off toward the stable. She stood still then while Gladys wiped the blood from her face with a clean bar towel. "I hope Bertie and Blossom ain't hidin' down at the stable." All they knew for sure was that the two women had fled to the stable with the intention of leaving town.

"There wasn't nothin' I could do," Dewey pleaded for his failure to act.

"I know there wasn't, hon," Daisy assured him. "I'da never forgave you if you'da tried to do somethin' stupid and got yourself killed."

"Oh Lord," Frank Bowen muttered when the dappled gray gelding pulled up at his stable door. He had been lucky so far, but it now appeared that he wasn't going to be spared the harassment his fellow citizens had suffered. Peering up the street from the door of his stable, he had seen Dubose come out of the Last Chance and climb on his horse. Much to his dismay, the brutal outlaw did not ride out of town, but started directly toward Bowen's stable. Bowen was faced with a decision that had to be made quickly. He had strapped on his gun belt with his .44 in the holster and was carrying his rifle in his hand in case he would be forced to defend himself. Now it occurred to him that he might be in more danger being so armed. *Maybe he'll just look around and leave me be when he doesn't find Blossom here,* he thought. *But if I'm carrying weapons, he might think I plan to fight.* He quickly made his decision, took the gun belt off, shoved it in a feed bin, and leaned his rifle in the corner behind the door. Stripped of all weapons, he hurried out to meet Dubose as he climbed down from his horse.

"You can save me a lot of time and maybe stay

alive if you just tell me right off where my wife is hidin'," Dubose blurted.

Hoping to appear innocent, Bowen answered. "Why, I surely don't know. They're not here. You can look around if you want to."

"Damn right I can," Dubose threatened, "and I will." He was smart enough to pick up on a slip Bowen had just made. He had asked where Blossom was, and Bowen said that *they* weren't here. He figured Bowen wouldn't know the two women had run off together unless they had come here, so they must have gotten horses here. "Now, me and you don't know each other very well," he said, "but I'm the kinda feller you don't wanna tell no lies. 'Cause, if you do, I'll shoot you down like the lyin' dog you are. Bertie and Blossom were here to get horses. Where were they goin'?" When Bowen didn't answer right away, Dubose drew his pistol and pulled the hammer back.

"I don't know where they went," Bowen answered, stumbling over his words.

"Wrong answer," Dubose said, and brought the .44 up to aim at Bowen's head. "You're goin' to your grave 'cause you tried to save two old whores."

"Wait!" Bowen pleaded. "I swear, I don't know where they were headin'. I asked them, but they said it was better if I didn't know. I swear."

"I'm tired of your damn lies," Dubose said. "I'm through foolin' with you." He aimed his pistol right at Bowen's eyes.

"They rode west!" Bowen exclaimed, "toward MacDonald Pass!"

"That's more like it," Dubose said, and lowered his pistol. "But if it turns out you're lyin', I'll be back to see you. You can count on that." Confident that Bowen had been too scared to lie, he didn't bother to search the stalls. He didn't want to waste any more time, so he turned and headed back to his horses. He was almost out the door when he heard the cocking of the rifle behind him. Without hesitating, he spun around and fired. Bowen doubled over in pain with a bullet in his gut. A second bullet finished him off when it struck his chest. "Ha!" Dubose exclaimed, impressed by his speed with a gun, even though his pistol had still been in his hand and not holstered. "He musta had that rifle hid behind the door."

He climbed up into the saddle and turned the gray toward the western trail, anxious to get started after the women. Even though he didn't know the trail well enough to follow it in the dark, he didn't want to take a chance on making camp for the night too close to Helena. He didn't want to be caught sleeping in the event there was a breakout of bravery on the part of the merchants. He figured he might not catch up with Blossom and Bertie before morning, but he would catch up with them eventually. He was determined to follow their trail until he did, no matter how long it took.

Hawk rode into Helena in the early afternoon, not sure how far behind he might be in his effort to overtake Zach Dubose. Off to his left, on the treeless hill that served as the graveyard, he saw a couple of wagons, a buckboard, and a small group of people gathered around what appeared to be two graves. He immediately knew they had something to do with Dubose, so he guided Rascal toward the hill. As he approached, he recognized the undertaker, Fred Carver, and a couple of the others standing in support of a woman dressed in black and openly sobbing. He was surprised that one of the mourners was Gladys Welch, a whore from the saloon. The gathering parted to look at him when they became aware of his presence. Getting a little closer, he realized there were three graves instead of two. Out of respect for the woman who had obviously lost someone dear to her, he reined his horses back until the ceremony was completed and some friends led the grieving woman back to the buckboard. When she had gone, he dismounted and walked over to talk with Grover Bramble, who was standing beside one of the graves, talking to Fred Carver.

"Hawk," Grover greeted him. "You're a little late for the funeral."

"Looks that way," Hawk returned. "Don't look like old age was the cause of death in all three cases."

"You can say that again," Fred commented. "We got visited by that damn monster looking for that new little whore at the Last Chance. He shot up the whole town and there wasn't anybody to stop him with Porter Willis still laid up in bed."

Having already assumed that the funeral was a

result of the outlaw's search for Blossom, Hawk was
not surprised. "Any chance one of those graves is
Dubose?"

"Afraid not," Grover answered, and pointed
them out. "That one is Chad Benton. That's his
wife drivin' off in the buckboard. The one in the
middle is Frank Bowen. We found him shot dead
in his stable. The other'un is a young cowboy
called Tex. Nobody knows his real name. He got
gunned down when he tried to face up to Dubose."
He nodded in Gladys's direction. "That's the
reason she's here, since he didn't have nobody to
mourn him."

"What about the women, Bertie and her daughter?" Hawk asked. "Are they all right?"

"Don't know," Grover replied. "They lit out, accordin' to what Gladys says, but she don't know
where. She said she helped 'em get away, but she
didn't know where they were goin'—just up in the
mountains somewhere to hide. All she knows is
they were goin' to the stable to get that sorrel
Bertie owns."

"What about Dubose? Is he still in town?"

"No, thank goodness, he's gone, so I reckon he
found out they took off and he's still chasin' after
'em." He shrugged. "Figure that's when he took
care of poor Frank."

"When did all this happen?" Hawk asked.

"Last night." When he saw that Hawk was seriously thinking that over, he asked, "How do you
happen to be back to town?"

"I've been tryin' to catch up with Dubose ever

since I realized he was headed back here," Hawk replied, "but I reckon I'm too late. I was hopin' I could keep something like this from happenin'."

"I reckon there's some folks lyin' in these graves that wish you'da got here, and especially Betty Benton." He shook his head as if apologizing. "I swear, Hawk, there ain't nobody in this town that was willin' to go up against that monster. Nobody even willin' to take a shot with a rifle at long distance. I'm ashamed to say I loaded my rifle and found me a place to protect myself behind my forge, but I didn't go out lookin' for him."

"I don't reckon it was your job to take on," Hawk said, fully understanding the reasoning of a man of Grover's age.

"It ain't your job, either. That's a damn dangerous man to mess with," Grover cautioned. "He's a case for the law to handle. We've already telegraphed the Marshals Service this mornin' about Dubose and they said the closest deputy marshal to us is three days away, but he's supposed to be headin' here as fast as he can."

That was something to think about, to let the law do their job, but the deputy was three days away from where he had to start looking for Dubose. During that length of time, anything could happen. Hawk had no choice but to keep on. Blossom did not deserve to die at the hands of that murderer, nor did Bertie. And he could not live with himself if he did not fulfill his solemn promise to JoJo. "Do you have any idea where they mighta gone?" Hawk asked.

"For a fact, I don't," Grover said, straining his brain to think of anything that might help. Then he remembered. "That young son of Rubin Fagan's was in the stable sometime before I heard the gunshot that killed poor Frank. He might be able to tell you somethin', if you can find him."

"Who's runnin' the stable now?"

"Nobody," Grover said. "I've been lookin' after the stock. Frank didn't have no family, just him."

"You gonna take it over?"

"I'm thinkin' about it. I've been talkin' to Sam Ingram about it and he said he'd help me get started if I needed it. It might work out pretty good with my blacksmithin'."

"Makes sense to me," Hawk said. "I'm gonna go down there and look around to see if I can find anything that might tell me which way they headed." He really didn't think there was much chance that he would, but he had nothing else, and his horses were due a rest, anyway.

"You might look around for a hoofprint with a toe clip on it—be kinda hard to find, but I had to make one for the right front foot of that sorrel of Bertie's."

"Much obliged," Hawk said, and returned to his horse. He didn't mention to Grover that he had to have Rascal reshod because of a hot nail Grover had driven in his shoe the last time he had done the job. He figured it wouldn't serve any purpose beyond making Grover feel bad.

* * *

Hawk took the opportunity to feed his two horses some oats after he relieved them of their packs and saddle, then he turned them out in Bowen's corral. He wanted them well rested when he decided which way he was going to go looking for Bertie and Blossom. Inside the stable, he could readily see where Grover had found Bowen's body. Grover had picked up the bloodiest patch of hay on the floor, but there were still specks of dried blood on some that was left. Hawk didn't spend much time looking around inside. There was not much chance he would find anything to help him, so he went outside and spent a good half hour examining the ground by the front door. There were plenty of tracks, but nothing that would indicate a toe clip on any of them. He decided to give up the search when Gladys Welch came in the stable to talk to him.

"Are you going after that man?" Gladys asked.

"I had that in mind," Hawk replied. "Right now, I don't have any idea where to start lookin'. Grover said you helped Bertie and Blossom escape. Did they tell you where they were goin'?"

She told him the same thing she had told Grover. "They were just going to try to find a place to hide and hope Dubose would give up and go away." She and Hawk exchanged hopeless glances, for they both knew Dubose would never give up. She went on to relate the entire happenings of that night as best she could remember. "I just wanted to come down here and tell you to be careful and I hope you find Blossom and Bertie safe," she said.

"I'm just glad they sneaked outta town without that bastard seeing them." Having said her peace, she returned to the saloon.

After she left, he started thinking about the circumstances she had described on the night of their escape. The two women were desperately trying to get away without being seen from the street where Dubose was prowling. *So most likely they went out the back door,* he thought. He went at once to that door, where he found about as many tracks as he had found by the front door, but none that might indicate a toe clip. About to give up again, he glanced toward the back corner of the corral where his horses were drinking from the horse trough. The ground outside the corral at that corner was soggy wet due to the water leaking out of the trough. He went at once to search the area affected. It was waiting for him there, one distinct hoofprint with a small, flat place in the toe where Grover had formed the clip and bent it back over the hoof to help hold the shoe on. It didn't tell him where they were going, but it did tell him they had left that way. He stood up and looked back toward town. If they were intent upon keeping the buildings of the town between them and their pursuer, they most likely had to keep going in that direction. He looked out toward the mountains beyond, and said, "That's gonna put you on the trail through MacDonald Pass." He would take that trail if he wanted to go to Rubin Fagan's trading post. *And Grover said he saw Rubin's boy, Robert, at the stable earlier,* he thought. It had to be more than

coincidence and he started building a possible
occurrence that could well have happened. They
might have gone to Rubin's place. At least it was
enough to get him started as soon as his horses
were ready, planning to ride straight to Rubin's
without wasting time to try to strike Dubose's trail.
*With a little more luck, maybe I'll catch up with Dubose
before he figures out they're headin' for Rubin's.* He knew
that was only possible if Dubose had not come to
the same conclusion he had and did not lose time
trying to track them.

His mind was heavily laden with thoughts of
anxiety for Blossom and Bertie, so much so, that
he tried to tell himself to give it some rest. So he
purposely thought about the attractive lady who
ran the dining room up at the other end of town.
He would think of Sophie Hicks from time to time
when his brain was idle. He liked to imagine that
she had special feelings for him, but he was modest
enough to know that she probably shined up to a
lot of men. It was good for business. He had even
considered walking up there to get some supper
on this night, since he had to wait for his horses to
rest. The only thing that kept him from doing so
was the fact that he would be in a hurry to leave.
The last time he was in town, he had to leave suddenly, telling her that he had intended to stay
longer. He was afraid if he did it again, she'd think
he was a jack-in-the-box, or a lunatic. So he stayed
with his horses and fixed supper for himself. When

he deemed Rascal and the packhorse were ready to go, he saddled up. Grover came in to look after things, so Hawk took a few more minutes to talk to him. Then he paid him for the oats he had given his horses and stepped up into the saddle.

Grover stepped back to let him ride past. He looked at the money in his hand and said, "I declare, Hawk, I reckon this makes you my first customer in the stable. Maybe I oughta put it in a jar to keep, so I'll always remember the first dollar I made in this business."

"Hell, if you're gonna do that, give it back and I'll write you a promissory note."

CHAPTER 14

"They eat like they're really hungry," Robert Fagan said to his father when he came into the store. "They didn't bring any food with 'em, they just ran."

Rubin had been giving the two women plenty of thought since they arrived with his son early that morning. At the moment, Blossom and Bertie were in the kitchen eating the food that his wife, Minnie, had prepared for them. He could not question his son's decision to bring them here. It would be wrong to deny help to a woman and her daughter in danger. At the same time, he was not sure he wanted to place his family in the path of the wanton killer the women had described. And it seemed almost certain that this man, Dubose, would continue to search for them until he tracked them here. "They're afeared for their lives," Rubin replied. "I reckon they didn't have much time to plan for their trip."

"I think it was lucky I was there to help them," Robert said.

"Yeah, I reckon it was," Rubin said, although without enthusiasm. He decided then that what was done was done, so he tried to be more receptive. "When they're done eatin', we'll let 'em put their possibles in your grandma's hut and they can stay there as long as they need to. And they won't be in the store if that feller shows up here lookin' for 'em. You'd best keep your rifle handy, just in case he does show up lookin' for trouble."

A few minutes later, Bertie came in from the kitchen, leaving Blossom to help Minnie clean up after their breakfast. "I wanna thank you again for takin' us in, Mr. Fagan. I know this musta been a big surprise to spring on you, but I'm sure your son, here, probably saved our lives. We didn't have much time to bring anything with us, but I want you to know that I did think to bring a little money with me. So I intend to pay you for the cost of takin' care of us and I hope we won't put you out too much."

Her declaration caused him to feel a little guilty about his reservations, thinking maybe he should have a more compassionate nature, like his wife, and welcome the women openly. "Well," he forced, "we're happy to help you any way we can." He glanced at his son in time to see his satisfied smile. "I think we've got just the place for you. I built that hut out behind the store for Minnie's mama. It was either that or set up a tipi for her." He paused to exchange chuckles with Robert. "She wanted her own place, so I built her one and she liked it just fine, but she passed on a little over a year ago and ain't nobody been in it since."

"That sounds like the perfect place," Bertie said. At that point, she would have settled for a tipi or a tent, herself. From what she had seen of the rooms behind the store, there would be little privacy for Blossom and her, had that been the only option.

"Good," Rubin said. "Come on and we'll go look at it." He opened a drawer and retrieved a key to the padlock on the door of the hut. He led them outside then, past the corner of the corral to a small log cabin sitting beside a trickle of water that ran down to empty into the river.

Bertie was pleasantly surprised when Rubin opened the door for her. Expecting a dingy little room covered with over a year's layer of dust, she instead found a neat, orderly little cabin that had obviously been continually maintained by Minnie Red Shirt, Rubin's Blackfoot wife. There was a stone fireplace at one end of the cabin and a window on each side wall. It looked ideal for Blossom and her. They could even cook in the fireplace if they so chose, even though Minnie insisted she would do the cooking while they were there. Evidently the grandmother had chosen to do some cooking, because there was a heavy iron skillet sitting on the side of the hearth. Blossom once again thought of how grateful she was that Robert Fagan was put in their path.

Zach Dubose was not much of a tracker, but he could see that there were recent tracks on the winding trail he had been following since sunup that morning. He had no way of knowing how far behind he was and if the tracks belonged to the two women he chased. But considering the terrain he rode, the trail he followed was the only sensible way to go. His progress was slow, however, since he sometimes veered off the trail to check out a cut or ravine that looked to be a good hiding place. He lost considerable time when he saw some tracks leave the trail and he followed them up a stream into the hills. He found a frequently used campsite, but no indication that anyone had camped there recently. Had he felt the ashes of one of the campsites, he might have discovered that deep down there were a few still warm. Maybe, he thought, he could have passed the point where they might have ridden up into the hills to hide. That only made him more frustrated and angry to think they might have gotten the best of him, maybe even riding back to Helena now while he continued on through these mountains. They might be playing him the fool like he had with that lawman when Loafer Smith sent him off into Utah Territory. To further frustrate him, the dark horse he rode was in need of rest. He wanted to drive the weary horse on, but knew he had to stop for a while. He was hungry, so he built a small fire on top of one of the old campfires and made a small pot of coffee. As he sat there drinking his coffee, he wondered where this trail he followed eventually wound up, if anywhere. He cursed the woman who had led him off into the wilderness, unaware that he was sitting in the same spot as she had the night before.

When he first started out to look for Blossom,

he had thought he would force her to come with him and if he had to kill Bertie to do it, all the better. Now as his frustration continued to mount, he decided Blossom would only continue to be a problem. As much as he would enjoy abusing her, he now desired to see her dead, her pretty face smashed by a .44 slug. That's what she deserved.

When the dappled gray had been rested, he rode back to join the trail again, thinking that surely he would come to a point where the women had to stop. He smiled when he thought of the two of them, most likely on foot now, after having foundered their horses in their fright. He pushed on, carefully approaching every hidden bend where the ornery bitch that was her mother might be in ambush with that Henry rifle of hers. He would take great delight in bending the barrel of it around her neck.

Just when he decided he was going to have to call it quits for the day, after another half a day's ride from his last stop, he came to a wide curve that led down to a river. If he had to guess, he would have said it was most likely the Clark Fork. A few dozen yards off the trail, he discovered what appeared to be a trading post. He pulled the gray up at once. Could this be where they were heading all along? It damn sure had possibilities! He had to check his emotions then to remind himself to play the part of innocence until he had a chance to look the place over. There was a corral behind the building with eight or ten horses inside, a small cabin beyond, an outhouse, and what looked to be a smokehouse. It would have been his intention to see if their horses were among those in the corral, but he had no idea what horses they rode. Only thing to do, he decided, was to go in the front door like any other traveler.

Rubin Fagan looked up when the door opened, expecting to see his son walk in. He had heard a horse approaching and figured it was Robert back from hunting. He almost started when he encountered the dark image of the man standing with his hand still on the handle of the door as he surveyed the room before entering. He knew at once who he was and had to rapidly pull himself together to manage a greeting. "Well, howdy, stranger, you're ridin' late tonight."

"Yeah," Dubose sneered while trying to affect a friendly smile. "I reckon I am. I musta got off on the wrong trail. I'm a deputy U.S. marshal on the trail of two women who've been robbin' and killin' storekeepers like you that are too far from any town where there's some law. Don't reckon they passed by your place, did they?"

Rubin knew he was bluffing, so he bluffed as well. "No, sir, Deputy, I ain't seen nobody like that. Two women, you say? No, I doubt they'd be ridin' up this way without any protection. But I'll keep an eye out for 'em. I appreciate the warnin'."

Dubose had a gut feeling they were both bluffing, but he decided not to call him on it until he had a better idea what he might be faced with. There might be more than this proprietor to deal with, including Bertie and her Henry. As if to confirm that precaution, Robert walked in at that moment, his rifle propped on his shoulder. His first impression of the stranger was the same as his father had and he immediately pulled the rifle off his shoulder. Rubin, with a tight shake of his head, quickly warned him to wait. He had seen Dubose's hand drop to the handle of his pistol as soon as Robert walked in. "Have any luck, son? This is a deputy marshal lookin' for two women outlaws. I told him we ain't seen nobody like that around here. You see any sign of 'em where you was huntin'?"

Robert caught on to the charade. "Nope, no sign of 'em. I got me a deer, though. I'm fixing to hang him up and skin him."

"Good, we can use some fresh meat." Rubin looked at Dubose. "Was there somethin' else you'd be needin'?"

"No, reckon not," Dubose answered. "I reckon I got sent on the wrong trail. I'll just turn around and head back to Helena while there's a little light left. Those two women show up at your door, you be careful. Don't turn your back on 'em."

"Thanks for the warnin'. Stop in again when you've got time to visit," Rubin invited as Dubose walked out the door. *You lying son of a bitch*, he thought to himself.

Robert stepped to the door and listened to hear him ride away. When he did, he walked out on the porch to make sure Dubose was gone. He was joined a second later by Rubin. "He rode back up the trail toward the pass," Robert said, and turned

to face his father. "That was him, wasn't it?" Rubin
nodded. "I shoulda just shot him down."

"I know," Rubin said, "but I saw him gettin'
ready to whip that .44 out as soon as you came in
the door. He'da got one of us for sure and I didn't
want no gun battle in the store. One of the women
mighta got hit. They're right there in the kitchen."

All three women were in the kitchen and all
three quiet as mice, pressed up against the wall between them and the store. Minnie and Blossom
each held a butcher knife and since there were
only two, Bertie held the large iron frying pan
from the hearth to use as a weapon. "He found
us!" Blossom whispered, even though she knew he
was gone. "He knows we're here!"

Seeing her daughter about to panic, Bertie tried
to calm her. "Maybe, maybe not. Ain't no way he
can know for sure, 'cause he didn't see us. He
couldn't." She looked to Minnie for confirmation.

"He no see," Minnie assured her.

Blossom shook her head slowly, still frightened.
"I don't know," she said. "That man's a devil."

The door opened then and Rubin walked into
the kitchen to tell them that Dubose had ridden
back the way he had come. "He's gone. I don't
know if he swallowed my story or not, but he left.
Just so you'll feel safe, Robert and I will stay awake
tonight to keep an eye on the place in case he de-
cides to show up again." This seemed to add some
comfort to the terrified woman holding on to her
mother's arm, so he gave her a smile and said, "So
you ladies go ahead and finish fixin' supper. If you
wanna wait for a few minutes, you can cook some

fresh venison. Robert's fixin' to skin a deer he just killed."

Outside, Robert was in the process of hauling the carcass of a young doe up to hang on a heavy porch beam extending out over the ground for just that purpose. His rifle was propped against the front wall of the store, in case it was needed in a hurry. He knew he was going to be out there butchering his deer for quite some time and he knew he would see anybody coming back down the trail to the river. His father was going to take his post by the outside kitchen door. They figured to be ready in the event Dubose decided to make a later visit.

Darkness descended upon the river valley of the Clark Fork, and the night creatures that dwelled along the riverbanks came out of their holes to serenade the rising moon. A colony of crickets endeavored to fill the empty air with their calls on this peaceful night, the ardent males doing their best to attract the ladies. Oblivious to this chorus of nature's night world, Zach Dubose sat uninspired. He watched the trading post patiently, knowing in his heart that this would be the night he found restitution. The women were there. He knew that for sure. From his position in a laurel thicket above the store, he saw the young man butchering the deer out front. He saw his father lingering near the back stoop outside the kitchen door. He saw the Indian woman come out the door to bring him a cup of coffee. He would wait. They would soon tire of their watching and decide he was not coming back, so he waited. His horses were tied well back in the trees where they would not send signals to the horses in the corral. For this business tonight, he left his rifle in his saddle sling. His Colt .44 would be handier in close quarters. He checked it again to make sure all six cylinders were loaded. He waited.

Finally, he saw what he had waited to see. The kitchen door opened and two huddled figures paused only a moment to speak to the man on the back stoop before scurrying across the yard to the small cabin by the corral. His whole body tensed, almost causing him to shout out to proclaim his victory, unaware of his tightly clenched fists until he finally felt his fingernails cutting into his palms. Eager to seek his vengeance, he nevertheless cautioned himself to remain patient and wait for his opportunity. At long last in a position to strike, he was determined not to make the mistake of striking too soon. He was pretty sure now what opposition he would be facing, an old man and a young boy, hardly anything to concern him, but still no reason to be careless. There was always Bertie to consider, but he planned to strike before she knew what was happening. He counseled himself to bide his time and continue to watch the store until the early morning hours. By that time, he felt sure that everyone there would believe there was no danger of his return.

It might be less risky if he got his rifle and waited for Blossom to come out of the cabin in the morning and simply shoot her down. There was a good chance he would get a shot at Bertie, too, if she ran to help her daughter. Then he could wait in ambush on the trail up from the river in case the young man decided to come after him. That would be the easy way to do it, but he wanted Blossom to know for sure who killed her, and he craved the satisfaction of witnessing her pain and horror. There would be a reaction from one or both of the men there, but he was willing to bet that neither had come up against a man as fast with a gun as he was. And he would be working in close quarters, where his speed would offer an advantage. He could not really see that his risk was that great. It was to be their misfortune if they tried to interfere.

Unknown to the malicious hunter in position on the ridge above the river, awaiting the hour to kill, another hunter rode through the night in desperate determination. Fearing that every moment it took him to reach Rubin Fagan's store was a moment too late for Bertie and Blossom, he drove his horses as hard and long as he dared. Rascal's hooves pounded against the firm ground of the passage, causing Hawk to think of the ticking of a clock that could be counting out the life seconds left to the two women. He was going to be forced to rest his hardworking horses one more time before he reached Rubin's, otherwise, he would find himself on foot. It was going to be hard to do, but he could not bring himself to run them to death. Finally, he pulled Rascal up when he came to a stream and dismounted. Both horses went immediately to the edge of the stream to drink. It would not be many hours before daylight, but he would wait for them to rest.

At about an hour before dawn, Rubin roused himself from the step he had been sitting on all night. He stood up and tried to stretch his tired muscles that had begun to cramp up from his uncomfortable position. Just as a precaution, he took a look around the cabin and the back of the store before going around to check on Robert. Taking extra caution, lest he be shot by accident, he peeked around the front corner of the store, ready to let Robert know it was him. He soon saw that his concern was unnecessary, for Robert looked to have gone to sleep where he sat on the porch floor, his back against the wall.

Rubin quietly stepped up on the porch and walked over to his son. He took hold of the barrel of Robert's rifle and gently removed it from his hand in case he suddenly awoke and pulled the trigger, scaring all the women half to death. Robert slowly opened his eyes to find his father standing over him. His first reaction was to jump, startled. "Pa!" he blurted.

"Wake up, boy," Rubin said. "It's almost sunrise. That bastard ain't comin' back here tonight. He'da already been here if he was of a mind to. Come on, let's go start up a fire in the kitchen and get some coffee goin'. I swear I need some. I ain't used to settin' on the back step all night."

"I musta just fell asleep," Robert said, feeling

ashamed for having been caught napping. "I was wide awake all night."

"Sure you were," Rubin said. "I'm sure you woulda woke up if that feller had come back, anyway." Robert got up and followed his father inside to make the coffee.

Watching their every move, Dubose couldn't have asked for any better circumstances, both men inside and it still dark outside. He was satisfied to see Robert's rifle still leaning against the wall on the front porch. *A good place for it*, he thought, smiling to himself. It told him that they were no longer concerned about his coming back. He got to his feet and quickly made his way down the ridge toward the cabin. With little concern for the would-be guardians inside the house, he strode up to the front of the cabin, taking only a moment to consider the door. It was as he had hoped, built to keep people out, but not to withstand the force he was about to apply. Walking forcefully up to it, he kicked it open with one mighty blow with his boot. The two women in the bed, exhausted from their ordeal of the night before, sat bolt upright. Far too startled to know what was happening for a second, their shock was immediately replaced with terror when they saw the outline of Zach Dubose in the dark doorway.

"Hello, darlin'," he smirked. "Are you glad to see me?" He went immediately to the rifle he knew would be propped up close beside Bertie's head and when she reached for it, he slammed her with his fist to her face, driving her back down on the bed. "You won't be needin' this, you old bitch."

Horrified, Blossom screamed. Dubose turned to her and threatened, "I'm gonna get to you, darlin', soon as I take care of your friends." He quickly emptied the cartridges from Bertie's rifle and threw it aside. "That's in case I get busy in a minute or two."

As he expected, the kitchen door in the store swung open and Robert came running out, charging toward the cabin. Dubose stood back inside the darkness of the cabin and fired one shot from his pistol through the open door. The shot spun Robert around and dropped him. Rubin yelled for his son and started out the door to go to him, only to be chased back by another shot from Dubose. "Come on!" Dubose yelled. "Send me another one!"

Rubin pulled back away from the door, ran past a frightened Minnie Red Shirt, and out the front door. With his shotgun in one hand, he ran around the side of the store in order to get to Robert without passing in front of the cabin door. "Son," he pleaded, "can you get up if I help you?" Robert nodded and struggled to help himself, not sure how badly he was hurt. With his father's help, he was able to walk back around to the front door. Unaware of what was happening outside the cabin until too late, Dubose stuck his head out the door and took a shot at them that just knocked a chunk of wood from the corner of the store before they disappeared behind it.

He stepped back from the door again. "I missed a good opportunity there," he told Blossom, who was still sitting up, frozen with terror. "I coulda got both of 'em right then, if I'd been a little bit quicker." He reached over and took her chin in his hand. "You're real glad to see me, ain't you, sweetheart?" Finding humor in that, he threw his head back and laughed. "Yes, ma'am, we're gonna have us a grand ol' time. You see, your two heroes out there can't come in that door to save you without gettin' shot. And they can't shoot in here 'cause they might hit one of you fair ladies. That's how smart your husband is." To emphasize his point, he suddenly backhanded her. "You made a mistake when you ran off from me."

"Let us go, Zach," Blossom pleaded, his slap having brought her out of her shock. "Let me help Mama. You damn near killed her." She rolled Bertie over and tried to wipe the blood from her face, only to have Dubose grab her by her hair and pull her back. "Let her be!"

She was still trying to hang on to her wits, thinking there may be a chance to talk her way out of this horror. He had always been mean, but now he was acting insane. Seeking some way to reason with him, she said, "You can still get away, if you leave right now. You're trapped in here and they can wait for you to come out the door to shoot you. But you still have time now."

He chuckled in response. "You don't understand, do you? As long as I've got you two nice ladies, they can't do a damn thing. And when I'm ready, I'm gonna tell 'em I'm gonna kill both of you if they don't back away. And you know what? That ain't just a bluff, 'cause when I leave here, you'll both be dead." He was distracted then by a shout from the store.

"You in the cabin!" It was Rubin who called out. "Why don't you let those women go? You've already put a bullet in my son. Ain't that enough to satisfy you? Come on out and won't nobody shoot at you. Just get on your horse and go."

Seeming delighted, Dubose looked at Blossom and said, "See, he don't know the real story, either." Turning his head back toward the door, he shouted back, "I got a better idea. You and your boy, if he ain't dead, throw your guns out and walk out in the yard where I can see you, and I'll walk out then."

"I don't think I can trust you to keep your word," Rubin yelled back.

"Well, that's the only way it's gonna work, 'cause if you don't, I'm gonna start killin' women."

"Hold on!" Rubin shouted. "Let me see if Robert can make it back to the yard." He quickly checked with his son and Robert said he could make it. "All right," Rubin called. "We'll walk back around the house to where we were. Then we'll drop our guns."

"Now you're makin' sense," Dubose yelled back. "Come on out." He edged up to the side of the doorframe where he could just peek out, but still be protected by the solid log wall. In a few minutes, both father and son appeared, the son barely able to make it, leaning on Rubin for support. Rubin held a handgun, which he kept pointed at the cabin doorway.

When they reached the spot angled away from

the cabin door, Rubin said, "All right, I'm dropping my gun. You can come on out and get goin'."

Dubose smirked. They were making it too easy. With his pistol ready, he stepped outside the cabin. As soon as he did, the kitchen door swung open and he was knocked backward from the blast of the shotgun in Minnie Red Shirt's hands. She quickly closed the door again to reload. Rubin picked up his pistol and he and Robert took refuge behind the corner of the cabin, not sure how bad Dubose was hurt, and not sure what the fate of the two women would now be. But Minnie's blast was low and while wounding Dubose seriously, only served to enrage him. He got to his feet, his clothes from his waist down in tatters and already bloody, and still roaring his defiance, he came out the door again, shooting at the kitchen door as he staggered drunkenly. Looking wildly for Rubin and Robert, he was met instead with the image of what he thought at first a ghost, advancing toward him. *The lawman!* How could he be here? He raised his .44 again and aimed a shot at him that missed, and reeled when a slug from Hawk's rifle backed him up to the cabin door. Desperate now and terrified at the sight of the relentless hunter, he stumbled back inside, only to be met with the butt of Bertie's rifle across the back of his head, knocking him to his knees. He struggled to retrieve the pistol that had dropped to the floor, but was knocked over on his side by a blow from the iron skillet wielded by Blossom. Fueled by a rage long suffered at the hands of the evil predator, the two women struck the fallen brute repeatedly until Dubose finally rolled over face-first on the cabin floor.

"Bertie," Hawk calmly announced, "he's finished. He's dead." Both mother and daughter looked up as if not really seeing him, still lost in their desperate attempt to remove this evil from their lives. Finally, first Blossom, then Bertie, dropped their weapons and backed away from the battered corpse. Drained of emotion, Blossom began to cry and went to her mother's embrace. "Come on," Hawk said, "let's get you outta here." He led them outside the cabin, where Minnie was now waiting to take them inside the kitchen. "We've got wounds to take care of," he said to Rubin, who was already helping his son back inside. "I'll drag that piece of dung outta your cabin."

CHAPTER 15

In spite of the aftermath left by the visit from Zach Dubose, there was a sense of relief and optimism at the trading post as the morning progressed. Robert's wound was in his shoulder and Minnie was able to remove the bullet. Bertie and Blossom had some facial cuts and bruises that were of no real concern to them compared to what had been promised by Dubose. At Minnie's insistence, cleanup of the cabin was put off until after a big breakfast was prepared. They had fresh venison that needed to be roasted before it went bad, so there was plenty of food.

While the women were cooking breakfast, Hawk returned to the ridge where he had come upon Dubose's horses that morning and he led them back to the corral. After dragging Dubose's body out of the cabin, he loaded it across the saddle on the dappled gray and carried it away from the store to be buried after he ate breakfast. When he returned to the kitchen, the others were already eating, even Robert, who was seated at the table with his right arm in a sling fashioned by his mother. Hawk helped himself to a cup of coffee and sat down to join them. He placed a roll of money on the table in front of Blossom. "Seein' as how you're the widow, I reckon this is your inheritance from your late husband." It was enough to bring gasps of surprise from everyone there. Hawk had heard from Loafer Smith and Rufus Tubbs that Dubose had plenty of money. They had not exaggerated. The day seemed to be getting better as each hour passed. Soon the matter of returning to Helena came up for discussion. Rubin and Minnie said the women were welcome to stay over and rest up before starting back, but there was a distinct urgency on the part of the two women to start back as soon as possible. "We've already put you folks out enough," Bertie insisted. "I think it's time to return the peace to your home, like it was before we showed up, bringing our troubles with us. If we start back this afternoon after we clean up your cabin, we should get back to Helena tomorrow noon." She glanced at Hawk for confirmation. He nodded and she continued. "We can't thank you enough for takin' us in and we want to repay you for your kindness. Especially you, Robert," she said, glancing his way. "Now that my daughter can afford it," she added.

After breakfast, the women went back to clean the floor of the cabin in an effort to remove all traces of the late Mr. Dubose and to pack up once again to ride. Hawk went to the spot where he had dumped the body and dug a hole for it. He paused to take a long look at the battered corpse, thinking how many miles he had traveled to finally reach this moment. Maybe now he could free his mind of the pledge to JoJo he had carried since that night in Helena. He would see Blossom and Bertie back to Helena safely and then it was high time he returned to his life—what there was left of it after being absent from his job for so long.

When all were ready to travel, Hawk asked Blossom if she was sure she hadn't rather wait to start back in the morning. "I want to start right now," she said. "I don't wanna stay in that place where he came after Mama and me. I'd have nightmares for sure." He glanced at Bertie and saw from her expression that she was of like mind. So they settled up with Rubin, partially with cash, but mostly in a trade for Dubose's satanic-looking gelding, which Robert had taken quite a fancy to. Rubin had some negative concerns about the trade, but went along with it, even though he was not sure he could ever look at the horse without reliving the morning just past. They exchanged good-byes then and Hawk and the two women started back on the trail to Helena.

As predicted, they arrived in Helena around noon, when Hawk delivered Blossom and Bertie to the Last Chance Saloon safe and sound. He waited long enough to enjoy one drink in the celebration Sam Ingram provided before he excused himself to take their horses to Grover Bramble's stable. "Just these horses?" Grover asked, indicating the extra horse that returned with Bertie's. "Ain't you gonna stable yours?"

"Reckon not," Hawk replied. "I'd best get started back toward Bozeman to see if I've still got a job." He had no intention of returning to the celebration going on at the Last Chance. Bertie and Blossom would both want to thank him for coming after them and he knew he would find that uncomfortable. It was best to say good-bye to this day and see what tomorrow brought. He had one farewell to say before he left town, however, so after he finished talking to Grover, he turned Rascal toward the graveyard on the hill outside of town.

Fred Carver had honored his promise to Hawk and buried her under the only tree on the hill. He had fashioned a nice headstone, too, with the name Joanna Feeley on it, as Hawk had instructed. "I'm sorry it took so long to settle the score for you, JoJo, and I'm sorry I wasn't there to keep you safe when you needed me. I hope you're restin' easy somewhere safe now." His thoughts were interrupted then by a screeching noise in the oak overhead and he looked up to see two red-tailed hawks fighting. They flew away when he looked up at them, leaving behind one solitary feather to float down and land softly on his leg. Struck motionless for a long moment, he stared at the feather, dumbfounded. Then he smiled, accepting it as a message, removed his hat, and carefully fixed the feather back inside his hatband.

He wheeled the big buckskin around and started down the hill to strike the trail to Bozeman. When he reached it, he pulled Rascal up for a moment while he made a decision—to turn to the right and head for Bozeman or turn to the left toward Sophie's Diner? Rascal snorted, as if ready to get started. "Yep," Hawk said. "I reckon so, but I'll be back." He nudged the big horse and wheeled to the right.

Connect with Us

Visit us online at
KensingtonBooks.com
to read more from your favorite authors, see books
by series, view reading group guides, and more.

 Join us on social media

for sneak peeks, chances to win books and prize packs,
and to share your thoughts with other readers.

facebook.com/kensingtonpublishing
twitter.com/kensingtonbooks

Tell us what you think!

To share your thoughts, submit a review,
or sign up for our eNewsletters, please visit:
KensingtonBooks.com/TellUs.